THE CON ARTIST

KITTY THOMAS

THE Con ARTIST

Kitty Thomas

Burlesque Press

1

It was the fund raising event of the year at a hip up-and-coming gallery. Saskia wasn't officially invited. She was a *plus one* to tech tycoon and art collector, Lachlan Niche.

It was twenty thousand a head just to get in to the night's festivities. That didn't include the VIP tour or the silent auction of the pieces on display. Even if she'd been invited, she wouldn't have been able to afford it with only thirty-two dollars and eighty-eight cents in her bank account. If she didn't get a cash infusion soon she'd be eating a lot of ramen to make that stretch.

The event was white tie—the theme demanding guests wear only black and white. The invitations had been engraved on fine linen stationery. Simple black lettering on the most subtle shade of eggshell.

The art was modern—bright splashes of reds and purples and blues and yellows and greens with the occasional smattering of orange, making statements the assembled could only guess about. The great thing about abstract art was how smart people could feel about themselves while saying ludicrous things about shapeless objects. *Feeling* smart was the important part.

If more care had gone into the event, perhaps guests could have worn all white. They would have moved in and out of the art pieces, looking like blank walls and canvases themselves—becoming a part of the paintings and installations.

Lachlan waved from across the room. Mr. Tall, dark, and handsome. He looked too dangerous to be at home surrounded by art. He was Saskia's benefactor for the evening, allowing her to rub shoulders with the people who gave to charity primarily so they wouldn't have to feel guilty about the frivolous things they did with the other ninety-eight percent of their money.

No, that wasn't fair. A good portion of it was reinvested and making them more money to feel guilty about while they clinked their champagne glasses and had another toast point with caviar.

He grew insistent, calling her over now. There was that glint in his eyes that reminded her he always got whatever he wanted.

How nice for him.

What he wanted right now was to use Saskia as his conversation piece. Apparently there weren't enough of those scattered about the gallery.

She squeezed past huddled insular groups talking bullshit about art they would never understand because they didn't have the heart for it. Money didn't buy comprehension or depth, but they were all good enough at faking it. My, aren't the emperor's new clothes stunning? Look at those golden threads!

Saskia knew more about art than most of these people could search on the Internet—or have their assistants search. Wouldn't want them to have to put themselves out in the quest for knowledge.

"Saskia," Lachlan said in that congenial patronizing tone one hears when they know they've just been the subject of a conversation. His arm stretched outward, pulling her into his claw-like embrace. On the surface, she was lucky to have his attention tonight. He was good-looking, wealthy, and at least seemed cultured to the untrained eye. Odds were good he wouldn't belch out the National Anthem, at least.

"I was just telling them you're an art forger."

Of course he was.

There was polite, uncomfortable laughter as they waited for offense or denial. Saskia smiled mildly and took another sip of her champagne as the group pressed in closer.

"So it's true, then?" one of the older ladies asked, her eyes wide.

"Don't get too excited. I don't pass them off as real. I sell them as reproductions. All long-dead artists. Nothing illegal about it."

Except maybe this one she was about to do. The artist in question was still somewhat recently deceased. That made things tricky from a legal standpoint. But Lachlan assured her he'd gained permission from the artist's estate to have the reproduction made. And as if by magic, he'd produced the official-looking paperwork to prove it. Saskia wasn't sure if the papers were legit, but she was too hungry to grill him about it in any meaningful way.

One of the men seemed intrigued. He offered his hand as if at a business meeting. "Nolan," he said. His grip was firm. He dropped Saskia's hand a split second before she could pull away. "What's the market for something like that?" he asked.

The night might not be a total waste after all. Lots of alcohol flowing and shallow people with money in their pockets to burn. Perhaps she could pick up some small potatoes. You could make potatoes stretch almost as far as ramen if you knew what you were doing.

She blushed, feeling somewhat pinned down by the intensity of his stare, the way he pulled her into him with such focus. There was something hawk-like in his features—which seemed fitting, given how much she felt like prey.

"More than you'd think. They make good conversation starters—novelties mostly. But there are dry spells as with any business," she said.

Lachlan's hand drifted down her back in a proprietary way, coming to stop just shy of public scandal. She shrugged out of his grasp and sent him a tight smile. He returned it with that same dark look she'd received from across the room only moments before.

"I'm trying to talk her into doing a piece for me," Lachlan said as if it weren't already a done deal between them.

"Oh, yeah, which one?" Nolan asked.

"The Joseph Quill piece."

"Ah. So the owner won't sell?"

Lachlan shook his head. "I offered more than it was worth. They still refused. So I've resigned myself to a fake that will look more real than the real deal. Or so I'm told by Miss Roth here."

"If you'll excuse me, I need to touch up my makeup," Saskia said. The older woman in the group looked as if she might try to come along, but Saskia managed to extricate herself without an entourage.

She wandered down the dimly lit halls of the gallery, away from the buzzing din of voices and heels clicking on tile—away from the area the guests had been corralled into. It hadn't been stated explicitly that they weren't allowed in other parts of the gallery. Wouldn't want to offend the generous donors. But it had been made to look as unwelcoming as a dirty alley strewn with used heroin needles, and the guests had taken the hint.

Saskia could barely stand to hear Joseph Quill's name. She'd idolized him and had the pleasure of meeting him at one of his gallery showings when he was just beginning to become famous. Living artists rarely got so famous or claimed so high a price for their work.

She was sure she'd made a blubbering fool of herself that night and couldn't even remember what idiotic things she'd said. She'd been shaking just from proximity to him.

Three months later, Quill was dead—a plane crash while traveling abroad. He'd been far too brilliant to die so young, leaving all the work that could have been... unfinished, languishing in the universal creative void just waiting for an artist far less talented to take up the mantle of a body of work far outside their range.

Saskia had mourned him as if he'd been a dear

friend—even though she'd spoken all of four sentences to the man when she'd met him the one time. Sentences she wasn't even sure had been coherent.

But she'd admired him so much. He'd inspired her. He'd painted the most haunting nudes she'd ever seen, some of them in far-too-compromising—even kinky— poses. But that wasn't why people were drawn to the work.

It was the eyes.

Each woman he'd painted in his too-brief lifetime had a look about her as if Quill had taken and broken her apart, carved away all the pieces of her soul that didn't appeal to him, and made her into something new that lit up the canvas like sunrise. Saskia was sure he'd slept with all of them—perhaps just before painting them. She'd spent nights fantasizing about being one of his subjects with all the dark eroticism she imagined such a position might entail.

Sometimes collectors were so captivated by the eyes of Quill's women, they forgot to look at anything else, no matter how lurid the pose.

Saskia ducked into a bathroom at the end of the hallway and leaned against the counter. She'd convinced Lachlan that not only was she an excellent art forger, but a competent art thief as well. She'd regaled him with a few bullshit stories about a couple of low profile art heists that had never been solved, and he'd bought the story. Tonight was all about planting a seed so that when the real Quill nude hung in Lachlan's home, all of his friends would think it was merely a clever forgery.

Or at least that's how *he* thought it would play. Saskia could never steal the work of an artist she admired for a foul creature like Lachlan, but he couldn't know he was her real mark.

She reapplied her lipstick and straightened the straps of the black dress. A strand of long dark hair had escaped her updo. She carefully pinned it back into place.

"You look lovely as you are."

She spun, working to wipe any trace of startled guilt from her face.

"Lachlan, get out of here! This is the ladies room." As if that needed stating.

He must have followed directly behind her. He'd been quiet as a panther stalking prey.

He looked ridiculous in such a rigid black tuxedo, standing in the midst of pale pink lace and cushions. His hand trailed down her cheek. "Saskia..." It was more a breath, a sigh, than speech.

She batted his hand away. "No, Lachlan. I told you, business only. If you're smart, you'll reserve your fucking for women who don't have other skills you need."

He wasn't used to hearing the word 'no', or at least he wasn't used to it being anything more than a prelude to 'yes'. All part of a coy tease—a game a man like Lachlan was obligated to play to get to the warm, wet, excited prize.

He moved closer. "I understand. A woman doesn't want to feel like a slut, so she pretends she never does this. She says no a few times and pushes you away. You slip your fingers underneath her panties, and you find the lie. And then it changes to yes. This isn't a new game for me."

Lachlan pressed her against the wall, his hand skimming down the side of her dress as if looking for an entrance to prove his point.

Saskia put her hands on his shoulders and tried to shove him, but he wouldn't budge. He was a solid block of muscle. He may as well have been a solid block of stone. "I said, No!"

He shrugged and stepped away from her. "As you wish. We can leave if you're ready to go. We've done what we needed to do."

Saskia straightened her dress again in an attempt to hide her shaking and just how threatening she found him. "You didn't bid on the silent auction?" she asked, trying to shift the topic to something safe.

"You know I don't like abstract art."

It was his sole redeeming quality.

She'd only been inside Lachlan's home once. His preferences seemed to trend toward older, more classic work, but she couldn't be sure if it was because of the difficulty and expense of acquiring the pieces he most coveted or because he actually had taste.

They slipped out a side door and didn't speak again until they were ensconced in the privacy of his Bentley. Warning buzzers sounded in her head over being alone in such a restrictive space with him after what just happened in the bathroom. But he was her ride and ultimately her continued survival.

The engine purred to life, and Lachlan put the car into drive.

"Do you think they bought it?" Saskia asked as they pulled away from the gallery.

"I know they did. They'll believe it's a reproduction once it's hanging in my house."

"I never said I'd steal the real one. I only promised the fake," she said. It was important for Lachlan to believe this was all his idea. The more he thought he had to convince her, the more committed he'd be to the version of events she wanted him to see.

"We both know you're going to cave and give me what I want." His hand moved to her knee. The double-entendre was probably sleazier hovering in the air between them than when it had been safely cocooned inside the privacy of his own head. At least that was what she'd decided to tell herself.

He was fifteen years her senior, but that wasn't why she didn't want to sleep with him. Or maybe it was. Maybe it was that despite his wealth and fitness, he was skating dangerously into age-inappropriate. And she didn't want to be any man's amusing piece on the side to make him feel like he still had it. What could the two of them possibly have in common? None of their cultural reference points overlapped. There was nothing to discuss.

Except maybe art.

But he didn't understand it in the way an artist did. He was a sideline spectator at best. And owning a Quill piece wasn't going to give him the soul of the man who'd envisioned it.

Saskia sighed. "Okay, let me be clear. If you want even a chance that I'll steal the piece for you, you'll keep your hands to yourself. I'm about ready to walk as it is. I get plenty of work from people less grabby and more respectful of my personal boundaries."

"That must be why you stuffed your purse with left-overs. Because you're living so large."

Saskia ignored the bait and remained silent for the rest of the drive. The last thing she ever planned to discuss with him were her meager finances. Up next to *Niche Industries*, her net worth was a joke. And they both knew it.

She was surprised when he pulled up in front of her building instead of his own sprawling estate. The way he'd been going tonight, she'd expected to have to escape his home like a refugee, barely clinging to whatever virtue she might have left, pressing her ripped dress tight against her body.

But her dress wasn't even creased, and Lachlan had *magnanimously* allowed her to remain unmolested.

He turned off the ignition. "What is it about me that you find so repulsive, Miss Roth?"

Besides everything?

She wasn't sure she could articulate it, at least not without pissing him off to the point she might have to dig through dumpsters to eat.

On the surface, all the columns of Lachlan Niche lined up right. He was a man who was beautiful in just the right lighting and angle, but the slightest shift changed the picture to something hideous—at least on the psychic level. To Saskia, Lachlan was like a holographic trading card—a suave, handsome businessman if you turned him to the right, monster skulking through dark alleys if caught by light on the left.

Either way, she didn't want to be part of his collection —just another possession he kept in a case and bragged about to all his friends. But because he clearly seemed to think such a fate for her was an honor, it was pointless to try to explain it. It would sail too far over his entitled head.

She opened the car door before he could do the fake-gallantry and come around and open it for her. "Good-night, Lachlan."

He reached out, stopping her exit. "Saskia, wait. What about the job?"

Thirty-two dollars and eight-eight cents. Four packages of ramen. Three cans of beans. Crab puffs in her purse. Business wasn't just on a downswing. It had cratered entirely. Honest reproductions weren't the big business she'd been letting on. People only liked forgery if it was passed off as the real thing. And then they only liked what they believed was real.

"How much?" she asked.

"Seven million."

"Sorry, no. If I get caught, I'm looking at prison time. You're offering me just what the painting is worth. And I know you offered the owner more than that. You have to pay for the crime, not just the result. Seventeen." She was outrageously overreaching, but he was arrogant and foolish.

"Twelve."

Saskia smiled. "Sold, to the gentleman in the Bentley."

The grip on her arm loosened, and his hand fell away. "I'll call you in a couple of weeks. We can meet and finalize the plan."

Right when she'd be in a gutter emaciated from lack of food. Possibly dead.

"I need an advance."

Lachlan chuckled. She watched the devious glint come into his eyes again. She could practically see the sex-for-food offer coming. Would that be so horrible just until the job was done?

Yes.

And she didn't work well with someone lurking over her shoulder. What she was attempting this time was big. She'd never do the work justice no matter how clean the copy she produced.

Before Lachlan could voice a lewd suggestion, she said, "In two weeks I could be nearly done with the reproduction. But I can't buy supplies without money."

He withdrew a checkbook from the inner pocket of his coat along with a pen. He really was a relic. Who wrote checks anymore?

"Five thousand. And I want the reproduction *complete* in two weeks. This is your full time job until that time. You eat it; you breathe it; you sleep it. You'll get more money when you deliver."

Saskia snatched the check from his hand. "I hope you know, all future payments will be in the form of a wire transfer. I'll give you the account number the next time we meet."

"Of course."

She got out of the car and slammed the door.

The window eased down. "Saskia?"

"What?"

"Forgot your lunch." He tossed the purse at her. She almost toppled in the heels as she reached out and grabbed it mid-air. That really *was* her lunch.

She'd failed as an original artist and as a reproduction artist. So why not attempt con artist?

Stealing from Lachlan Niche would be the most satisfying thing she'd ever done. She couldn't imagine a more deserving mark.

2

Saskia stepped out of the car that had been sent for her and gawked at Lachlan's exquisite, imposing home as if seeing it for the first time. If only Lachlan didn't live in it, this could be a pleasant experience. The driver took the wrapped painting out of the trunk.

"Careful with that!" she snapped.

He gave her an annoyed look as if he felt somehow offended he'd been sent to pick her up to begin with, and now that she dared speak to him as if he were the help, it was too much for him to bear. In truth, he looked more like a bodyguard than a driver. Tall, broad, bald on purpose. Maybe he was filling in for someone.

She had to stay focused and remember why she was doing this. The payoff would be worth it. One big score, and then it was a tropical island for her far away from Lachlan Niche.

The gold bangles at her wrists jangled as she straightened the vermillion skirt and pulled it down a couple of inches. The skirt was a bit too short, the white top dipped a touch too low. Her legs were bare because the nude heels on her feet were sling-backs with a cut-out toe and never looked quite right with pantyhose. Ordinarily an outfit like this made her feel like a civilized person—as if she weren't barely scraping by. But today, it made her feel vulnerable. If she hadn't been running late, she would have changed.

Lachlan waited in the entryway just inside the house as if it had taken all his self-control not to run out to meet her at the car. "Marcus, take the painting to my study."

Marcus nodded and disappeared down the hall. She'd had to work from a bad photograph of the piece, but it was the only thing that might save her from having to do the real heist. She could possibly pull it off, but that wasn't part of the plan. Lachlan didn't deserve to own the real piece.

Running a tech company as well as being an art collector, he'd be well aware of all the art authenticating software available. She'd studied Quill's work with an almost religious fervor, but the software made it nearly impossible to perfectly duplicate another's already-existing work without getting caught. Brushstrokes were analyzed. A scanned image of the original work could be broken down into small geometric cubes and compared frame by frame with the questioned piece.

It was easier these days to commit forgery by pawning off "lost or undiscovered works" as authentic. Though with enough samples of other work by the same artist, the software could still detect less-skilled forgeries. The bar just kept rising higher.

With this particular piece in private hands well before Quill had gotten famous, there had been no good scan of the image available to analyze. Lucky for her.

Lachlan held out both his hands to Saskia as if welcoming the Prodigal Son home. She pasted on a fake smile and allowed him to draw her in. If both of his hands were in hers, they couldn't be drifting over other parts of her body. Being conned was exactly what he'd earned for all the times he'd pawed at her.

It took great effort to keep her breakfast down at that thought. Saskia couldn't understand how women fell repeatedly into Lachlan's arms. He was ridiculously wealthy and conventionally attractive. And he gave off that dominant alpha-male vibe that so many women seemed to swoon over. But could those same women not feel the ick? The sleaze that dripped off him like motor oil? This was a man who would use, abuse, and then laugh at you for trusting him.

No, thanks.

Could a semi-intelligent, lucid woman actually tolerate his touch? Even with him only holding Saskia's hands, she couldn't pull out of his embrace fast enough.

When the driver returned, Lachlan said, "Shall we?"

Saskia nodded with a tight smile and followed him to the study where they'd have some privacy. She was sure the staff couldn't be trusted to be in on this, but the idea of being alone in a small dark-paneled room with him made her skin crawl.

When he closed and locked the study door, Saskia had to steel herself against the temptation to run out the French doors and vault off the balcony, even though it was on the second story, and she'd break her ankle at the very least from this height—particularly since he had high ceilings. Sixteen feet at least.

As if sensing her strong desire to flee, Lachlan closed the French doors and slid the deadbolt into place.

He moved to the side bar and poured an amber liquid into a glass. "Drink?"

"No, thank you. Let's just talk business."

"You don't trust me?"

"No farther than I could drop-kick you."

He smiled—a smile he probably thought was charming—and he hadn't met a woman with enough sense to disabuse him of the notion yet. The evolutionary urge not to starve was pretty strong in women. If it weren't, Saskia wouldn't be here. Men like Lachlan seemed like the easy road. The path of least resistance—if you could snag them.

It must be killing him that Saskia didn't want to.

"Judging from your petite stature, that wouldn't be very far."

She sat in an overstuffed chair at the far corner of the study to avoid taking a seat he might try to share.

Undeterred, Lachlan pulled a rolling leather chair up to her, his knee mere inches from her own. He pushed a button on a remote, and jazz piped in through the sound system. She tensed.

"I'm not making a move on you. Relax. Don't flatter yourself. I've just got some nosy help, and I want to ensure they don't overhear."

"On second thought, I *will* have that drink."

He smiled and rose. When he returned, the drink was barely out of his hand and into hers before she'd slammed it back and put the glass on the table.

He arched a brow. "Another?"

"No. Thank you."

"Once I sit again, I'm not getting up to fetch you a second drink, so if you—"

"I said no."

Lachlan held up his hands in surrender. "To business then. Do you have a finalized plan?"

"I do. Aren't you going to look at the reproduction?"

Lachlan sighed and crossed to the painting still wrapped in brown paper. "You're right. If you aren't as good as you say you are, the rest of your skills won't matter."

He ripped the protective paper away and let out a low whistle. "You weren't overstating your talent. I'm impressed. Why aren't you doing original work? If money's the problem... I could help you."

He seemed genuine, as if he'd put her up in an isolated cottage somewhere and allow her to paint all day without a care in the world. But of course, that wasn't what he was offering. He wanted a live-in whore with a side talent he could be amused by.

And anyway, she hadn't done original work in a long time. Not since the apartment before her current one had burned down. She'd lost all her original work in the fire—some of it going back over a decade. She'd lost the heart for it after that. Saskia couldn't stand the idea of putting all she had on canvas or paper only for it to go up in flame.

Lachlan continued to stare at the painting as if he could scarcely believe what he was looking at. "How can I be sure you're as good a thief as you are a forger?"

"The proof will be when you have the real thing in your hands."

"With a forgery this good, how will I know I have the real thing? Perhaps I should just keep this and be done with it. I'd save a lot of money."

Saskia held her breath. He was just fucking with her. He'd already bragged about how he liked to get away with things under other people's noses. He would get an endless kick out of having a famous stolen painting hanging in his parlor for all the world to see with no one ever the wiser.

He enjoyed manipulation and lies. How he thought divulging this information would make her want to form any sort of personal relationship with him, she had no idea.

"I assume you have someone you trust?" Saskia said. "Someone discreet who can authenticate the work? Just let him analyze this one and then compare to the one I bring you after I finish the job. I'm sure the differences will be clear to a skilled professional."

"I have someone."

Saskia knew Lachlan's guy. Eli. She wasn't friends with him, but she knew who he was. He wasn't the best, but he was passable, and he was probably the only option available that Lachlan trusted to handle things discreetly. She'd put just enough small errors in this one so that the new forgery could pass for the real piece, and Eli would feel smart for having seen the subtle differences.

"So then you're just having second thoughts about spending all that money?" Saskia said, trying to steer Lachlan back on track.

He laughed. "It's nothing to me."

It was everything to Saskia. And he knew it. After the fire, she'd gotten a few clients and reproduced some of the classic works. It wasn't as if her original work had been selling anyway. The reproductions had been enough to keep her going, but all of that had run dry. Lachlan was her big score. His obsession with Quill's work could rescue her financially. And maybe, with real financial freedom, she could find the heart to create again.

Lachlan had appeared from out of the mist at just the right time like a fairy godmother. This payoff would ensure she could stop pandering endlessly to bored rich people where both she and her work existed as a mere novelty to tamp down their boredom for half an hour.

She tried not to entertain the idea of being supported while doing original work. The not-quite-starving artist living in modest but comfortable surroundings paid for by a mysterious benefactor fantasy had its appeal. But if this went well, she could pay for her own comfortable surroundings and paint her own work for once and not care whether it could feed her.

"How will we do this?" he asked, moving to sit uncomfortably close again.

Saskia uncrossed and recrossed her legs away from his line of sight, giving herself another few inches of breathing room. "I think you meant to ask how *I* will do this. You're just meant to sit and look pretty."

She smiled when he blanched. *Some of your own gross medicine too much to take there, champ?*

She didn't wait for an invitation to continue. "You will hang the reproduction and talk it up a bit more with your friends. You'll let it hang for a good six months before I take the real one. I'll need living expenses during that time, of course."

"Why so long?"

"In the event that anything goes wrong—but it doesn't go completely wrong—you don't want to have just gotten the reproduction, do you?" Nothing would look more suspicious to law enforcement than that. Lachlan only lived a couple of hours from the estate that housed the painting he wanted stolen. That proximity made everything trickier.

"So, something could go wrong? Maybe I should find someone else for this job."

"Something can always go wrong."

He wouldn't find someone else for the job. He'd only let his guard down enough to consider this scam with Saskia because he wanted to sleep with her. Little Lachlan was doing most of his thinking for him.

"So, is there a reason for six months? Why not three or twelve or twenty-four? Why don't I just give you living expenses for a few years? Suspicion would be damn-near nonexistent by that point, wouldn't you say?"

If not for the irritated edge in his voice, it might have been teasing. He didn't like stretching this out so long. Neither did she. Ideally, she'd get in and out and be done with him that much sooner. There were too many opportunities between this moment and the moment she could escape him forever for him to try something sleazy. And the way his gaze panned over her only emphasized that point. The timeline on his self-control was finite.

Why didn't I wear jeans and a sloppy T-shirt?

Saskia pulled the skirt down again and recrossed her legs—this time at her ankles. It wasn't a skirt for sitting. Maybe she should have remained on her feet. Sitting only made it appear as if she was willing for this visit to drag on. She should have dropped the painting off, spoken quickly about her plan, and left. She should have appeared busy instead of like she had all day to do this.

Flustered, Saskia said, "There will be a big twenty-first birthday party for Eric Raine at the Raine Estate in six months. I've managed to swing an invite."

Lachlan raised a brow. "And how exactly did you *swing* such an invite? I'm intrigued."

She blushed. "I didn't do anything wrong. I bumped into the guest of honor accidentally on purpose and..."

"You wore the outfit you're wearing now?" he completed.

"N-no. B-but, you get the idea. I didn't... we didn't..." God, why was she explaining herself to him? She could fuck who she wanted.

"Continue, Miss Roth."

He always seemed to address her more formally when he wanted to emphasize their age difference—how much older and more sophisticated he was than her. He was just forty-five. And thirty wasn't exactly a child. But when he spoke to her this way he made her feel as if he was her professor and had just caught her cheating on an exam.

She pulled the skirt down again, almost ready to give up on it. "You said the painting hangs in the guest room on the third floor. I'll slip away from the party when everyone has had a few drinks and make the switch then."

"And what if someone recognizes you? What about the gala we just attended?"

That shit had been his idea. He must have expected some sort of smash-and-grab, something which would be a lot more difficult for her to fake. It was true some of Lachlan's and the Raine family's associates could very well overlap, but the crowd at Eric's party would be younger and not so much into the art world as the people Lachlan knew. It was doubtful anyone who had ever seen them together would be at this party.

"Are you kidding?" she said. "Your friends have their heads so far up their pampered asses, I could have been topless and they wouldn't have recounted a single detail about me the next day. I'll get a haircut and highlights before the party. I'll wear a very different dress and a completely different make-up look, and some glasses. If any of your friends from the gallery somehow happen to be there, I'll avoid them. They're not going to remember one five-minute meeting that happened months before."

Lachlan seemed satisfied. "And how will you get the fake *into* the house?"

"Okay, well there's more to the plan."

Lachlan leaned forward as if hanging on her every word, but she was sure it was more to get a better view of her cleavage.

Her chair made a grating sound on the hardwood as she scooted out of his reach. She stood, crossing to the French doors just to get away from him and his fierce gaze.

He swiveled his chair to face her. "Well? I'm breathless here."

"Okay, so I thought about trying to get a job with the

catering company and getting into the party that way, but I already had the invite from Eric, and getting hired on for the party would be more difficult than it seems. They'd have way too much personal information about me, and those places are intense with background checks. Plus, it's not as if I can work at the party and be a guest at the same time."

"Does this side trail have a point?"

"I'm getting there. So... my friend Beth works at the company that makes their uniforms. I'm sure she can get me one to match. I thought I'd smuggle the forgery onto the catering truck and slip in a few hours before the party dressed as one of the employees. It would allow me to get the fake in for the switch later that night."

"And how is the real painting getting *out*? Surely not on the catering truck."

"I thought I could drop it out the window."

Lachlan stood at that. The force of the movement sent his chair rolling back several feet. "You want to drop a Joseph Quill nude out a third story window?"

"Relax. Jesus. It'll be properly protected and inserted into a tube. If someone is down there to catch it, it won't be a problem."

"And who's going to catch it? I can't be seen anywhere near the Raine Estate. They already know how much I covet that painting. I can't be lurking around outside like a cat burglar. That's why I have you."

And if he could be there, her scam wouldn't work. She knew he couldn't be there. He'd simply have to trust her, and implying she needed him on site as part of the plan would lower his guard that much more.

"Beth can—"

"Absolutely not." Lachlan moved closer, indifferent to how he might be intimidating her. His eyes narrowed. "Does she know why she's getting you the uniform?"

"No... I haven't even said anything about it yet, but..."

"No. Get the uniform well ahead of the event so she won't make any connections, but otherwise do not involve her. What's your alternate plan?"

"Well, I mean... I've seen the estate. I went to Eric's house and..." Off Lachlan's renewed lascivious interest she said, "Not that! I didn't sleep with him. I'm not a whore."

"Of course not, Miss Roth. I never suggested such a thing. You seem awfully sensitive about it, though."

But he had suggested it with the way he kept inching closer, and the way his gaze scanned her body as if with enough concentration he'd be able to see through the fabric entirely. Or perhaps the material might shift just the slightest amount to show him the expanse of skin he wanted to ogle.

Saskia sidestepped him and moved behind his desk. She knew it looked like she was running. She didn't care.

He chuckled in response.

"There's a giant rhododendron on the south side of the house. It's not under the guest room, but a few doors down from it. I could drop it out that window, let the foliage catch it, and pick it up on my way out."

Lachlan cringed as if he could see each of the million ways that could go wrong. And if she were doing the heist for real, she'd feel pretty anxious about it as well. As it was, she planned to dance and sip some champagne with Eric and wait until she had to meet Lachlan for the hand off.

He moved swiftly behind her before she could make another maneuver to get around the heavy oak desk. Saskia tensed when he touched her back. He pressed her forward until her cheek rested against the smooth wood surface. She was intently aware of how the skirt she'd chosen exposed her to his gaze.

Inches from her face—at eye level now—was what appeared to be a heavy, long, yellow glass paperweight. But it wasn't a paperweight even though it *was* holding down stray papers. She realized this close to it, that it was a dildo. Dear God. Really? Did he intend to...?

Lachlan leaned forward, his fine linen suit pressing against her mid-priced, on-sale skirt "If you get caught... if anything goes wrong..." he hissed against her ear, "... you will not implicate me. Do you understand?" His hand slipped under the skirt and between her thighs.

"S-stop."

"Do. You. Understand?"

"Y-yes, sir." Where had *that* come from?

"Sir. I like that." He eased off her, pulled the skirt back into place, and patted her ass.

Saskia straightened and stumbled away to put some distance between them. She looked out the window, unable to meet his gaze. She just wanted him out of her life. She'd never felt less guilty about the plan than she did right now. She only wished she could find a way to steal more from him.

Lachlan didn't pursue her across the room. Instead, he sat at the desk. "Do you have the account number for the transfer?"

"Y-yes." Saskia retrieved a folded piece of paper from

the pocket in her skirt and inched toward him, holding it out.

When she was close enough, he snatched it from her hand. Lachlan unfolded the paper and smoothed it out in front of him. He pointedly lifted the glass sex toy from the desk and slid the paper underneath it, his eyes never leaving hers.

"I'll wire twenty-five thousand to your account tomorrow to last you the next six months. The forgery will be returned to you for the switch after Eli analyzes it. You may go now. It would be best if we didn't see each other again until after the party. You'll meet me here at one o'clock in the morning as soon as you've completed the job."

Saskia nodded, still trembling from the way he'd touched her only moments before. She practically ran from his house. Not having to see him again for months was the best thing he could have suggested.

3

Saskia checked her hair and makeup in a bathroom on the second floor of the Raine Estate. She straightened the strap on her plum-colored evening gown for the third time of the night, wishing she had the kind of shoulders that didn't inspire clothing mutiny.

With weeks of radio silence from Eric, Saskia had thought she might not even be able to get into the party. Maybe he'd forgotten her altogether. But when she'd arrived, the alias she'd given him was on the list.

In the grand scheme, it wouldn't have mattered if she couldn't get in. She didn't need to be there at all. She'd just wanted one good night before she had to steel herself to see Lachlan again and deal with whatever smarmy bullshit he'd try with her during their next—and hopefully last—encounter.

Saskia didn't have a friend named Beth. She couldn't get a uniform to match those worn by the caterers—partly because she had no idea where the uniforms came from. Nothing had been smuggled on a truck. And she sure as shit wasn't about to switch out the authentic Joseph Quill for her fake—convincing though it was.

When she left the bathroom she went up to the third floor to sneak a look at the original painting. She'd itched to see it in person, knowing it would be her only chance. As she slipped down the quiet hallway, she was grateful she wasn't really stealing anything. She felt like a loosely connected bundle of nerves just being alone on this floor. What would she say if someone found her snooping around up here?

The door she sought creaked when she pushed it open. A spotlight shone on the painting, taking all the attention in the cavernous room. It called to her, luring her closer. Her breath caught in her throat being this close to the real thing. She had to stop herself from reaching out to touch it. It was clearly earlier work. But it was breathtaking and haunting like all the other Quill nudes she'd studied. And Lachlan didn't deserve to have it hanging in his parlor.

She took one last lingering look, then moved quietly back down the stairs. At the end of the second floor hallway, she looked down over the balcony into the sea of party guests mingling in the grand foyer. She spotted Eric at the foot of the stairs gazing up at her. Waiting.

He was a tan, blond Adonis with cheerful eyes the color of blue topaz. He raised a glass of champagne, a question in his gaze. She nodded and carefully descended the staircase and took the glass of *demi-sec* from him. It was tart and sweet, the lush flavor blooming over her tongue in sharp bursts. The only thing that would make it better was a strawberry—the strawberry that seemed to have just mysteriously appeared in Eric's gorgeous hand. He held the sweet fruit to her lips, and she bit into it, a trickle of juice running down her chin. He caught it with his finger and sucked the juice off.

Saskia watched him, transfixed.

There was nothing she'd like more than to stay until the festivities died down and wake in Eric's bed in the morning, but the clock ticked toward the dreaded meeting. Lachlan was the last human she ever wanted to see again—and *human* was being generous. True to his word, he'd stayed away from her the full six months, with only a brief, cryptic phone call the day before asking if everything was in place for the switch.

Not seeing him for so long had only heightened her fear of the inevitable meeting. She almost wished she *was* stealing the Quill piece. What if Lachlan suspected? She'd worked extra hard on the new forgery, taking a full three months reviewing all of Quill's work even more obsessively than she had before. She'd studied the bad photograph of the piece as well as the slightly inferior forgery she'd done at the start for comparison.

It was the best work Saskia had ever done because she was pretty sure her life depended on it in more ways than one. She was certain even the artist himself could have been fooled by it, but it didn't stop her jangled nerves over the scam and the man she was pulling it on. Still, her odds of getting away with this were way better than an actual heist during the middle of a birthday party. So there was that.

Eric flashed her a warm smile. "I'm sorry I've been so busy the past few months, Alice. Please don't think it was anything personal. My father is in poor health. He's been grooming me to take over his company. It's a lot to take in. And a lot to deal with."

Saskia winced at the alias. She couldn't even tell him her real name.

He was kind enough that his existence alone almost forced her to rewrite all her nasty assumptions about the wealthy. He didn't seem spoiled or entitled, or as if he didn't care about anyone else. Despite the ostentatious nature of the party, Eric Raine didn't appear to be trying to impress anyone or rub their faces in anything.

He was so nice looking—not just handsome, but like a *nice*, caring guy. And funny and charming. And he didn't scare her like Lachlan did. Of course there was no future with Eric, even if he'd found a momentary interest in her. He could have anyone he wanted, and she was nine years older than him. If he wasn't aware of that now, he'd pick up on it in a few years when she stopped passing for twenty-four.

Eric navigated her through the crowd in the entryway, underneath the stairs, and into the ballroom. He swept her onto the dance floor as a love song that still topped the charts played. It wasn't canned music pumped in through a sound system. It was live. She couldn't begin to imagine how much it had cost to get a chart topping band to a private party.

As they moved across the dance floor, Saskia felt the panic beginning to bubble inside her. She could pretend it was the jealous looks from women who had their sights set on Eric, but it wasn't that. It was this whole situation.

Couldn't she find some way to get out of meeting with Lachlan? He'd want the money he'd already given her returned—money she had no way of getting, aside from throwing herself on Eric's mercy. Which would only make her look like a gold digger. As if he'd rescue her anyway. She wasn't still young and naïve enough to believe in fairy tales.

She couldn't explain to Eric why she owed this money. Even if he somehow understood her circumstances, Lachlan had been clear about not being implicated in anything. She couldn't imagine she'd ever be safe from the man she feared if she opened her mouth now with anything approaching the truth.

Even in some enchanted world where Eric could shield and protect her, they weren't in love. They weren't even a couple. It was so casual they may as well be poker buddies.

"Alice? Alice?"

Saskia startled and looked up, still not used to the name she'd chosen. "Yes?"

Every time he called her *Alice*, she felt as though she were digging the knife into him a little deeper.

"Is something wrong?"

God, he was so genuine and sweet. He deserved all the good the world had to offer him, and Saskia wanted nothing more than to inhabit that world with him. But there were too many lies and too little true attachment between them. He was just having some fun. And why shouldn't he? It was his birthday.

The music stopped, and the woman who'd been singing spoke into the microphone to wish Eric a happy birthday. Her words blended into the background as Saskia realized she was going to be late to the meeting. She wanted to be late for her meeting with Lachlan even less than she wanted to see him again in the first place.

"Eric, I'm so sorry, but I have to go." She'd never see him again. *Don't cry, Saskia. Just don't be an idiot and cry.*

"What's the rush?" He winked at her. "Is your car going to turn into a pumpkin? If you're secretly poor as a church mouse, I won't judge you. We can skip the whole shoe drama and just move ahead to the happy ending."

He didn't realize how close he was to the truth—or how much his light-hearted joking hurt.

"I'm sorry, I have an early day." Saskia pulled away from him.

Another slow romantic song began to play and he tried to draw her back in for another dance.

"Alice, stay."

God, please stop calling me that. At least she was stealing from someone who deserved it and not Eric or his family.

"I really can't."

"I'll call you, tomorrow?" he said. It was a question, not a statement.

The number will be changed, and I'll be long gone.

"I'd like that," Saskia said, just to get him to release her. "Happy Birthday."

"Hey, thanks."

Unexpectedly, he pulled her in for a kiss. Warm, soft, gentle—the promise of all the things that life didn't seem to want to give her. But it was already too late to escape the path she'd set in motion.

A few whistles and catcalls rose from around the ballroom. Eric *was* kissing her in front of nearly sixty people, after all.

"By the way, you look so hot in those glasses," he whispered. "Kind of a nerdy sexy librarian."

She blushed. "Thanks. I had a great time tonight, but I really have to go." Saskia turned and left the party without looking back. In another life, maybe. But unfortunately, not in this one.

"You're late," Lachlan said.

Saskia stood tense in the darkened study, the tube with the painting slung over her shoulder like luggage. The only light in the room came from the flickering fire and the illuminated laptop screen Lachlan sat behind. The fire made shadows on the wall that seemed to jump, startled each time his deep voice pierced the silence.

He closed the laptop and rose from behind the desk. He'd dressed more casually tonight. Dark jeans and a lemon yellow polo shirt. His feet were bare. Lemon yellow and bare feet—only Lachlan could make that intimidating.

"Well?" His hand extended impatiently, greedy for the painting.

All at once, she began having second thoughts. What the fuck would he do if he caught her trying to con him like this? Was she sure her new forgery was that convincing?

Lachlan raised a brow, and she handed it over, trying to mask the tremble surging down her arm. She expected him to turn some lights on so he could inspect the painting, but the two of them remained shrouded in semi-darkness.

"Marcus will sit with you while I scan and compare this to the known forgery."

So he *was* using the authenticating software. Of course. He had two things to compare and had no doubt already scanned the first one she'd brought.

Saskia wondered if she imagined the threat—as if Marcus might restrain her should anything suspicious be found.

"I thought Eli..."

"Eli was only needed for the forgery. I wanted his opinion on how good you were. I'll be able to see the differences between that and the original you've brought me. Something wrong, Miss Roth?"

Saskia shrank back, trying to wipe her face of all expression. "N-no."

"This *is* the original Quill nude isn't it?"

"Y-yes."

"Good. You will wait." Lachlan opened the door and called for Marcus, then disappeared down the hallway with the new forgery.

Marcus looked unhappy with the babysitting assignment, just as he'd looked unhappy fetching her the last time she'd been here.

"You really don't have to stay," she said.

Marcus just glared and slouched into the chair opposite her. Saskia straightened the strap on her dress again. At least this time she didn't have to keep pulling her skirt down. The fabric of the evening gown reached the floor.

The only sounds brave enough to intrude upon the room were the flickering fire spitting in the grate and the rhythmic tick of the clock on the mantel. Marcus didn't engage. He simply watched her in the way a sociopath might watch a small animal drawing its last breath.

An agonizing hour passed as Saskia's fear reached a fever pitch. She was sure Lachlan would burst through the door at any moment, shouting and threatening her.

Finally, he returned. "Marcus, you can go."

Lachlan sat behind the desk. Saskia's eyes darted again to the glass sex toy between them, as if it acting as a paperweight were completely normal. Maybe he didn't know what it... no of course he knew what it was. He was a grown man. Just the shape and size of it...

Marcus slipped out the door.

When they were alone, Quill said, "I'm satisfied. I've already wired the money to your account. Tomorrow, you can log on and see that everything is in order. Goodnight, Miss Roth. It was a pleasure working with you. I hope we meet again."

That was it? He wasn't going to make another creepy pass at her? Not that she wanted that. It was just that the fear of what he might try to do the next time she saw him had sat as a background horror track for the past several months as the days lurched on moving closer and closer to this moment. This moment where he'd gone back to studying something on his computer screen as if he'd lost all interest in her.

Well, so much the better. For her part, she hoped there was never a reason for their paths to cross again.

4

F our months, three weeks, and two glorious days had passed since Saskia had run off with twelve million dollars of Lachlan's money while Joseph Quill's nude remained unmolested at the Raine Estate. Even with sunglasses, she had to shield her eyes against the blazing sun at Venice's *Piazza San Marco*, or as the locals called it, *la Piazza.*

She never tired of coming here. On first arriving, she'd bought up every tourist-y book she could get her hands on and learned everything she could. The *Piazza San Marco* had supposedly once been called the drawing room of Europe by Napoleon. Whether he'd truly said it or not could never be proven, but it felt true nonetheless. This place kept drawing her back to it.

After a couple months of traveling and seeing everything she could think to cram into that time—every famous art museum and gallery dotted across the world —she'd finally settled back in Venice. The tropical island idea had gotten boring after two weeks. Italy was where she belonged. It was an artist's paradise.

Sometimes she liked to sit inside St. Mark's Basilica, staring up at the awe-inspiring gold mosaics so long it made her neck hurt. Even with tourists fluttering about, the space felt sacred. But even inside a church as grand as St. Mark's Saskia had barely a flutter of guilt about her crime. Why should she? Lachlan had billions. Twelve million was so laughable he wouldn't have missed it if she'd taken it right out of his bank account while he looked the other way.

"Having fun, Miss Roth?"

That voice.

Saskia considered running, screaming, anything but turning around to confirm who she knew stood just behind her, his hot breath mixing with the warm breeze against her neck.

She exhaled.

People ran into people—even in Venice. There was no reason to think he knew...

"If you run, I'll have you arrested."

Okay, so he knew.

When she finally turned, he looked far more smug and self-satisfied than a man who's learned he's been robbed should look. He wore a crisp, dark suit and appeared as if he were on his way to a funeral. Hers, maybe?

"How did you find me?"

"Why don't we have this discussion at that lovely expensive villa you bought with my money? It's not far from here, is it?"

She'd just bought it a month ago.

"No, Mr. Niche."

"Oh, it's Mr. Niche, now. So formal. You think the formality will do you any good?"

His hand slid into hers, and for the first time in their association, she didn't pull away from his touch. Maybe he could be reasoned with. He might make good on his arrest threat. But then again he might kill her if he got her somewhere private. Maybe she should take her chances with the police. Which option would be worse? Which might save her?

"Just relax," he whispered. "I'm not going to hurt you. Much."

It was close enough to walk, though each step dragged so that it seemed impossible one could span the distance by foot—even though she'd done it easily just that morning.

Her hand trembled when she tried to put the key in the door.

Lachlan's fingers closed over hers. "Relax," he said again as if simply repeating the word would have any effect on the way everything inside her convulsed over what he might do with her now that he'd isolated her from possible witnesses. He unlocked the door with a steady hand and walked in like he owned it.

And really, he kind of did.

"Not bad," he said. "But I can tell you with this kind of money management you'd be a starving artist again inside of three years. Why don't we sit out beside the pool?"

"So you can drown me more easily?"

He laughed, and the tightly bound breath that had been stuck inside Saskia's chest came rushing out. Surely he wouldn't laugh like that if he planned to kill her. It wasn't an evil laugh; it wasn't even a sleazy laugh. It was... musical somehow.

And all at once the guilt appeared.

Have I been dehumanizing him this whole time just so I could steal from him? It wasn't a pretty thought. It didn't match the trees and clouds and sky and all the beautiful old buildings that seemed like art installations on their own. There was no denying how uncomfortable he made her. And that one day in his study when he'd touched her inappropriately—she hadn't imagined that. But beyond that one moment, had she created the image of a monster for her own convenience?

"Did you paint the *trompe l'oeil* on the walls yourself?"

"I did."

"It's good."

Saskia tried not to let the compliment affect her. Who cared what Lachlan thought about it? She remained unconvinced he'd know real art on his own if it bit him on the dick.

She followed him to the terrace and sat in the chair he indicated. He reclined next to her and watched her for several minutes—so long she couldn't stand the scrutiny and silence any longer.

"Lachlan, I'm sorry, I..."

He held up a hand. "No. You're not sorry. You're sorry you got caught. You'd rob me blind again if you thought you'd get away with it."

A fair point.

"Holding back and giving me a lower quality forgery the first time was a nice touch. Lesser men might have been fooled. How much of my money have you spent?"

"Six million," she mumbled.

"I'm sorry, what was that?"

"Six million. H-half of what you gave me."

"A three-year countdown to your renewed destitution was generous. I give it two, tops. Were you planning to invest any of it? Even millions run dry if you just keep spending."

"I wanted to travel and get settled first."

He nodded as if any of this mattered now. It was all just trivia of a life that could have been. She wondered how many *lives that could have been* would be dangled in front of her and then ripped away before her true fate unfolded. The fantasy of the fairy tale with Eric, the illusion of this independent life in a villa in Venice... both lovely ideas, both impossible dreams.

"So, you owe me six million dollars."

"I'll sell the villa, and..."

He twisted his chair to face her. "No. That's not the deal. You stole from me; I decide the terms. I want a wire transfer by the end of the day in the full amount."

"But you know I can't..." It was ridiculous for him to demand she return the money on such short notice. It took time to sell a villa. And the furniture. And the Ferrari—which had already depreciated. She didn't want to think about the amount she wouldn't be able to get back—the small things that added up. Clothes. Jewelry. And the intangibles: spa appointments, all the travel.

"So we'll handle it the old-fashioned way. You will indenture yourself in servitude to me to pay off your debt—likely for the rest of your life given the amount of money anyone would reasonably pay you for anything you're actually qualified to do."

Just what he'd wanted all along: her at his mercy in a compromising position where she'd have to warm his bed to survive. It was no doubt like winning the lottery for him. He knew everything could be bought, even her —given the right circumstances. And here the circumstances were, wrapped up and gleaming.

Saskia wasn't unattractive, but she knew there were other women more beautiful than her. The appeal to him was acquiring something that was difficult to acquire—just like all the art he collected. If she'd been eager to jump in bed with him, he wouldn't want her. Was that worse or better?

"And if I don't agree to your terms, you'll what? Kidnap me? Exactly how would your felony cross out my felony?"

He laughed. It was decidedly less endearing this time around. "I'll turn you over to the authorities. You can go to prison, or you can give yourself to me. The accommodations with me will be better."

"But not the company."

Lachlan's eyes narrowed. "I'm going to do something about that smart mouth of yours the moment we get home."

"I haven't agreed. You said you wouldn't kidnap me. So you don't think you'd go to prison right along with me? Didn't you conspire to steal a multi-million dollar painting?"

"I've got fantastic lawyers and connections in high places. Most likely I'll know the judge that gets my case. I won't go to prison, and if I play it right, I'll be able to keep the whole nasty mess out of trial and out of the media. But *you'll* go to prison. And I'll make sure they throw the book at you to make an example. Our justice system is far too lenient on art crimes if you ask me."

Maybe he was bluffing, but somehow Saskia was sure this man didn't know the meaning of the word. And even if the judge was lenient, even if he had mercy on her, she was still looking at a few years behind bars. Best case scenario.

No amount of prison was a small matter that one easily moved on from. She'd known a guy who'd been to prison once. The system seemed to revel in making it absolutely impossible for a criminal to mend their ways. It seemed like they didn't *want* people to change and be better. They wanted you to pay and pay and pay for your crime and never stop paying even if you were free.

On release, they'd maybe give you a twenty dollar gift card. And that was it. And no one would hire you. How would someone fresh out of prison get a job to pay for things if nobody would hire them? The only choice left was to steal more things until you got caught and thrown in prison again. The only hope of breaking the cycle was if you were fortunate enough to actually know somebody with some standing in life who could help you back on your feet. Otherwise, it was almost impossible.

Saskia might have been able to imagine and cope with some of this if the threat of prison came on the heels of living with less than a hundred dollars in her bank account most of the time. But instead, cruelly, the threat came after four months of the kind of luxury she'd never before known. And here, Lachlan Niche was giving her the choice between a worse fate than where she'd started—one she was unlikely to ever fully recover from

—or continuing on in this luxury... as some sort of concubine.

The tears started to fall. Finally. Saskia flinched as his thumb reached out to wipe those tears away.

"I'm not so bad. You'll see. Whatever ideas you have in your head about me are wrong. I'm prepared to provide for you. You have an immense talent which you've squandered. I can help that talent flourish. I'll mold you into the kind of artist you've only dreamed of being."

This time it was Saskia who laughed. "You can't afford it. It's not something you can buy. You know nothing that would benefit me as an artist."

"Really? I knew the second you gave it to me that the painting you supposedly stole wasn't authentic."

"I thought you used the software. You knew that night? You just wanted to entrap me in deeper debt. You'd already given me thirty thousand. Wasn't that enough?" Though maybe he wouldn't count the five for the known forgery against her.

"No. It wasn't. And I didn't use the software. I didn't need it. I just wanted to make you sweat a while before I gave you some money to squander because it makes the moment of acquiring you that much sweeter and your debt to me that much larger."

She'd thought she'd been running a long con on him, but it was clearly just the opposite. If he'd known he didn't have the real painting the night of the party, he'd simply been following and watching and waiting for the right moment to spring the trap on her.

"Saskia, I knew the game you were pulling the moment I didn't see the mistake in the painting."

"The mistake?" He was speaking in riddles she couldn't unravel.

"It was one of my earlier works and had sentimental value. I only sold it because I was hungry, and my start-up was still stumbling and trying to get funding. There is a small defect, a few brushstrokes that aren't quite right —not quite what I wanted them to be. Nobody else ever sees it, but I know it's there. But it wasn't there on the painting you gave me."

Everyone knew Quill had been a perfectionist to an obsessive degree that, had it not come wrapped in such talent, surely would have gained him entrance to a mental institution. Niche knowing this fact about the artist wasn't nearly enough for her to accept something so impossible.

"If you expect me to believe you're Joseph Quill... He died. What's more, I met him in person, and you're nothing like him."

"No, Saskia, you met my assistant, Derick. I was trying to run a family-friendly tech business that had a real shot at financial success. Initially, the art didn't seem like a wise bet. The subject matter alone would have killed Niche Industries before it was off the ground. Joseph Quill was an alias I created, and my loner assistant agreed to pose as him in public. He signed non-disclosure agreements. He had no one in his life who would miss him."

"You mean..."

His eyes widened a fraction, mirroring the horror she was sure her own face held.

"My God, Saskia, don't be so dramatic. I didn't have him killed. Why would I? For God's sake. I was able to manage the business and paint. It was an ideal set-up, especially once I could afford to offload most of the day-to-day operations of the tech firm to someone else. I just meant there was no one who could say with authority that my assistant *wasn't* Joseph Quill."

"But the subjects of the paintings..."

"...All signed non-disclosure agreements and were each paid handsomely for their silence. And it isn't as if I've been a media hound under this name, either. You didn't recognize me as Lachlan Niche when we met. There are benefits to keeping my face out of the media and letting representatives speak on my behalf."

All of that was true, but she'd also been so drunk it was amazing she'd been able to stand under her own steam. She wouldn't have recognized the pope under those conditions.

"By the way," he said, "I was there, blending into the crowd as a guest the night you met Derick. He was going to use who you thought he was to fuck you under false pretenses. I stopped him. You're welcome."

Had he recognized her when he'd bumped into her the night she'd been so drunk? Had the seeds of all this already been planted all the way back when she'd met his assistant posing as him? A lot of time had passed between those moments. No, that was crazy. He couldn't have lain in wait that long. Could he? What was *wrong* with this man? Even the idea that he could be so calculating on such an impossibly long timeline made him that much more of a threat to her.

Saskia couldn't find a sarcastic retort. He could be lying. He probably *was* lying. But somehow, when she thought back to her encounter with the man she'd thought was Quill, something hadn't been right about any of it. She'd been starstruck and nervous because of how she'd admired his talent. He'd been quiet and shy and seemed more like an accountant than the commanding artist she'd envisioned him as—like he'd be far more comfortable locked in a closet with numbers than pigments.

She'd imagined Joseph Quill would be frightening in person. Much as Lachlan was. And she believed without any doubt Lachlan could strip a woman bare and paint her in such a way that you couldn't look away from her eyes. The idea of Quill was far less dangerous than the reality. She would have gone to bed with Derick—lying to herself the whole way—because he wasn't a threat to any piece of her.

Not like the real thing.

"I *will* paint you, of course."

Her breath hitched, and all the foolish fantasies of Joseph Quill came rushing back. Except this time, there was a face and body to go with them. She'd never questioned why, even after meeting who she'd thought was the artist, the fantasy had remained vague—a faceless, nameless stranger. It was as if her subconscious had known all along and refused to participate in the ruse of that man being Quill.

"How can you let the world think you dead and never share your art again?" On balance, that might be the biggest crime here. She was no less terrified of him than she'd been before, but she also felt the pull of the artist she'd so deeply worshiped.

"Something you must learn now, Saskia, before your heart is broken... People prefer their artists dead. They don't want a real flesh and blood human interrupting their hedonistic consumption of the work. Nor do they want someone who can talk back. Though talking back won't be your problem when I'm finished with you. So you may just have a shot out there after all."

Saskia shivered.

She stared at the gentle ripple of the pool water. The birds chirped in the distance while the Mediterranean sun beat down, interrupted only by the warm, soothing breeze. There should be thunder and lightning and a sky so grim and black that the only relief would be the cool rain of a torrential downpour.

The day outside didn't match the storms churning within her. It didn't fit with what Lachlan or Quill or... "What am I supposed to call you?"

"You will call me Master."

Oh, hell no.

This was her fantasy—the exact thing wrapped with a bow. And despite all her protests, the actual living in-the-flesh Joseph Quill exceeded all expectations. But up close... no, she couldn't. She'd actually mourned this asshole back when she'd thought the artist dead. To resurrect him and play out this sordid... no. Just... no.

She knew it wouldn't matter what she called him. Now that she knew the truth, she couldn't think of him as anyone other than Quill. It didn't matter that Lachlan was his real name. That name meant nothing to her.

What came after denial? Bargaining? "W-what if I stole the painting for you? Really, this time? Couldn't we call it even and forget this?"

As if she could bring herself to steal anything out of Eric's family home. Even for Quill.

He leaned back in the chair and regarded her as if considering it, but she knew from the way the side of his mouth quirked in pleasure that the offer was no longer on the table—if it ever had been at all.

"Miss Roth."

Her name hung there on the air, open, exposed... naked. He was her judge, jury, and executioner. Everything paused as she awaited her sentencing.

Her breath.

Her heartbeat.

When he spoke again, her heart and lungs came back online. "The woman in that painting was very dear to me. She was a muse of sorts, and without her, I never would have painted the things I've painted. But our relationship grew too... intense for her. She scampered off to the east coast, and all I had left were the paintings. I never forgave myself for selling the one I sold. I promised myself I'd never sell any in that series. I thought I wanted the painting, but the more time passed, and once I saw how much talent you were wasting... the short answer is no. I've moved on. The price is you, Saskia. Just you."

He'd planned this for months while she'd believed she'd gotten away with it.

Quill stood and looked down at her. She felt herself shrink under that dark gaze.

"Collect whatever things you've accumulated that you want to keep and can carry. The jet is leaving to return to the states in three hours. You're being watched, so don't think about running. At least step onto the plane with some dignity. It'll be the last you get for a good long time."

5

O f course she thought about running—despite the warning. Maybe he was bluffing about having her so closely watched. Or maybe she could escape through a crowd. How many eyes could he really have on her?

And if he were just Lachlan Niche of Niche Industries—smug arrogant tech tycoon, casually collecting art to look more cultured than he was—she would have attempted it. It might have been worth the risk.

But he was Quill. He was everything. She'd gone to art school solely because of exposure to his work. It wasn't until after she'd been there a while that she'd started to develop an appreciation for anything else— even the famous classic art.

He seemed to her now like a god—a resurrected miracle that hymns should be written to. Even without the ability to investigate his story, she knew on an instinctual level it was the truth. And despite his scary intensity and all the warning buzzers his presence had caused to go off inside her, she couldn't help being pulled under the wave of his charisma.

Marcus and some other men loaded her things into the cargo hold while Saskia stood awkwardly out of their way. There was so much open space around her and no credible way to slip off unnoticed. She wondered how long Quill's goon had known about this plan to bring her back in chains. Had he been the one sent to watch and follow her? Given his undisguised distaste for her, that had probably gone over well.

The plane was larger than she'd anticipated when a jet had first been mentioned, but then a tiny metal bird like what she'd imagined could hardly make an intercontinental flight. And it would be great if the plane didn't sputter out and die in the middle of the ocean.

Quill stepped onto the platform of the stairs still in the same dark suit from earlier. He motioned for her. Saskia's heart dropped into her stomach, and for a moment, she didn't think she could propel herself forward. This was a thousand times worse and more intimidating than meeting the fake Joseph Quill had been. And she'd barely been able to stay standing under her own power that night. It wasn't meeting Derick that had that effect, it was simply the *idea* of Quill.

There was no doubt in her mind he would expect sex on demand—in whatever way he wanted it. And from his paintings, she knew exactly how he wanted it. If she were being honest, she wasn't sure she was going with him over fear of prison. Oh, she believed his threat. She knew she would absolutely go to prison if she didn't agree to be his willing concubine instead, but even without that threat... he was Quill.

Which was really the only fact her brain was willing to process at the moment. She'd lost this game before she'd even started. They both knew it.

What had happened to her repulsion? Was the draw of the artist so compelling that just knowing his true identity could change how she saw him so completely? He was still terrifying. That hadn't changed. But she could no longer say the idea of him touching her was revolting. In the hours since he'd left her to pack her things, everything had sunk in. She wasn't sure she wanted to escape him now.

But what if he was too intense—just like he'd been with the subject of the painting she'd forged? At least that girl had the option of leaving.

Saskia thought back to that moment leaned over his desk with Quill's hand under her skirt. He'd been intentionally intimidating her, violating her personal boundaries. If she'd known who he was, would she have wanted his hand there? She didn't know. She wanted the answer to be *yes*, because then she'd be able to make herself go to him. But she didn't know.

She couldn't believe she'd stolen twelve million dollars from Joseph Quill. Fuck. And the joke of thinking she could replicate his work and pass it off as the real thing... He must have had a good laugh over that when she'd left his study after the party that night.

Quill's face darkened, signaling his growing impatience as she stood there like some idiot stuck in hardening cement.

"Saskia!" he barked over the engines. "Now!"

The men loading the cargo hold jumped at his voice. Even grown men were jumping. How could she be expected to fare better? She wanted to melt into the pavement when they stared at her like, "Better you than me, honey." Or maybe they were watching to see if she'd walk up those stairs and get on the plane with him.

Maybe they'd jerk off later to thoughts of what he might be doing to her as the jet cruised over the Atlantic.

Quill's eyes narrowed, and he took another step—a step that promised if he took just one more, he'd go down there and drag her onto the plane. And if he did that, there went that last moment of dignity he'd offered.

Saskia somehow found the strength of will to walk to the plane. He watched as she took each step but didn't move aside to give her space when she reached him at the top of the stairs.

"Good girl," he whispered when she brushed past.

A chill slipped down her spine as she crossed the threshold.

Inside, she was greeted with an interior that looked nothing like a plane. Curves had been built into the walls so that it looked like a swank living room. She sank onto one of the plush sofas and started to cry, her head dropping into her hands.

Quill entered moments later, said a few words to someone outside the plane, and then pulled the door closed, sealing them in.

Saskia looked up. "W-what about Marcus and those other guys?"

"They were hired to help load the plane. They aren't with us. Marcus is taking a commercial flight. I wanted some time alone with you."

Was he trying to help her acclimate? Was that the smallest hint of kindness?

The plane began coasting down the runway.

"I'm really very sorry I stole from you," Saskia said.

"I'm not swayed by tearful apologies. And we already established you weren't sorry."

"I-I wasn't sorry until I knew who..."

"I see."

At least he didn't make her say the whole pathetic sentence. She hadn't given a shit about stealing from Lachlan, but the idea of stealing from Quill was almost too mortifying to ever get past.

"It's just... you have no idea what your work has meant to me. I'm so ashamed that I..." Even with the extreme dichotomy of their financial means, the idea of taking something from Quill made a hard knot form in her stomach.

He sat beside her, and this time she didn't try to put distance between them. He put a hand over hers. "Shhh, Saskia. You're paying me back. Everything is all right between us. Believe me when I say I'll extract every penny from you."

She looked out the window as the plane began its climb into the sky. More tears, this time for a different reason. "I'll miss Venice." She'd only been really settled there for a few weeks and had started to believe somehow that this could really be her life.

"We'll be back to visit someday. I've got that great Villa," he said.

She was surprised by his answer—as well as the gentle teasing in his tone. Maybe there was something inside this man that she could relate to after all. Something besides just art.

"You're keeping it?"

"Of course I'm keeping it. It's a great property. The paperwork will obviously be transferred into my name. And you will wire all the money you didn't spend back to me."

She nodded quickly. A second later, Quill grasped her chin and forced her to meet his eyes. "Answer."

"O-okay. Yes. O-of course." As if it were a question he'd get the rest of his money back. Or at least what could be retrieved.

"Don't play dumb, Saskia. It doesn't suit you. If you're wondering, no, I was not kidding about what you are to call me. And if you're shy about it now, you'll have much more trouble when we get home, and you have to say it in front of the servants."

She should have run. She should have found an opening and slipped off into a crowd and used the rest of his money to find a way outside his reach. But even the idea of running from Quill seemed insane to her. What aspiring artist would ever run from the painter who most inspired them? However foolish this may be, it was a way to be inside his orbit. Maybe she'd absorb some genius by osmosis.

"Y-yes, Master."

"Good. In a fully public setting, you may call me *sir*. People will think you're an assistant."

"Since you're keeping the villa, will you take that off my debt?" Saskia shifted as if she could slip outside his scrutiny.

"Just because I like the property and have chosen to keep it does not mean you didn't essentially steal that money from me. Why should I knock anything off what you owe?"

She shrugged. So keeping her as a slave was justice? But she didn't dare voice the thought.

"How much did you pay for it?" he asked.

"Four million."

"I'll knock two off the debt. Now you're down to owing me four total. Does that make you feel better?"

What did it matter? Short of full forgiveness, he could hold her captive forever. It wasn't as if even four million was something she could ever pay back. If she could make that kind of money on her own, she wouldn't have conned him in the first place.

And by what method would he keep track of everything? Did he have a special ledger? Did he plan to put a price on each sexual service she completed to his satisfaction? Because it seemed clear that was primarily what he wanted her for. Would there be interest, making it impossible for her to ever climb out of servitude? He'd invented his own system of accounting for his own questionable purposes. It wasn't as if he'd be held to any lending laws.

It was all a ruse—just blackmail to make her submit to what he'd wanted from her from the beginning. He always got what he wanted. She'd been mad to think she'd be an exception to that rule.

"It's a fourteen hour flight. We'll have dinner, but you will let me know anytime you are hungry. All basic needs, you will let me know immediately, and I will provide them."

"Will that be added to my tab as well?"

"Careful, Saskia."

"Yes, Master."

Each time she addressed him this way, the whole scenario felt more surreal.

Minutes passed. Except for the noise of the plane, they were surrounded by a silence so intense she felt forced to stare at her hands, which were folded on her lap. This time she'd worn jeans and a T-shirt. Quill hadn't commented on her underwhelming attire. It was her last stand of defiance before he began to impose his own tastes.

"Saskia," His voice was low and smooth—a seduction. "I want you to go into the bathroom and remove your clothing. Fold it neatly and place it on the counter. Then return to me. Don't be longer than five minutes, or there will be consequences."

And so it began.

He must have seen the abject terror in her eyes. She wasn't ready for any of this. A few months ago, if someone had told her Joseph Quill was alive and well and he wanted a long-term sexual relationship with her —even one where she was his slave—she would have jumped at the idea.

The idea.

In the idea alone, she was safe. In the fantasy, he couldn't humiliate or hurt her. He couldn't discard her when he was finished. She would simply discard him— or his phantom—once she reached orgasm. Until the next time.

Saskia flushed at that thought. All the sordid things she'd fantasized about him... Now they might happen, and all she felt was panic at the possibilities.

"Don't worry, Miss Roth. I'm not going to fuck you for quite some time. And when I do, it will only be because you begged so hard and cried so long that I took pity on you. Now, go."

She didn't dare offer a retort. She didn't want to remind him that he had plans to deal with her smart mouth when they reached his estate. She didn't even believe he was being all that arrogant. In reality, she could absolutely envision almost any woman being driven by Quill to beg for it.

The bathroom was bigger than she expected. But then, it was a large jet just for him and whoever he wanted to travel with. It wasn't going to be some cramped box like on a commercial plane.

Even so, this was as nice as her bathroom in the villa had been and far more luxurious than the one she'd suffered through in her pre-fake-heist apartment.

Small marble tiles covered the floor and walls. The shower had blue glass doors. Both doors slid open and closed back to meet in the middle. She couldn't believe there was a shower.

A fat vase of lilies sat on the counter. Saskia tried to pick up the vase. Nope, that sucker was glued down with something industrial. No danger it would get knocked around in turbulence. Her finger trailed over one of the velvety petals. The flowers were real.

All at once she remembered he'd put a clock on her. She must have stood in the bathroom gawking at her surroundings for three minutes at least. If not for anxiety over what her future with Quill would hold, she might have paused to appreciate just how far she was from ever having to worry about ramen noodles again. Or electricity. Or any of the other basic annoying things that meant the difference between comfort and hanging to the edge of survival by her fingernails. No, she was well outside the range of those worries. And fate had happily supplied her with a new set to keep her occupied.

Saskia slipped off her shoes, then removed the clothes and folded them as he'd asked. She tried to avoid looking too hard at her reflection. She didn't want to see all the imperfections which would be bared to his gaze in mere moments. She took a deep breath and went back to the living area.

She stood in the doorway, unsure. She'd never seen herself as a person who was unsure, but Quill unmade her somehow just by his nearness. Maybe it wasn't repulsion that had made her avoid succumbing to his earlier seductions. Maybe it was fear of the total obliteration of her identity. She didn't know how to be anything when sharing oxygen with this man. She didn't know how to make her voice heard next to his or her presence felt or seen. As an artist, he'd inspired her, but as a person, she felt he made her disappear.

He motioned her forward.

"Turn, slowly," he said, when she reached him. "I'd like to assess my latest piece of art properly."

She turned, but it wasn't slow enough for him. His hand on her back stopped her. She had a brief flash to the last time his hand had been on her like this. Back in that moment in his study, she never would have believed this one could exist. Or that she could feel how she felt now.

Any previous fleeting thought she'd had of being naked in his presence had included running, crying, trying to push his hands off her while she desperately sought to wriggle away or hoped for a savior to rip him off her. It was the fear that had played in her mind on repeat nearly every time she'd been near him before today.

But now...

His hands pressed gently into her hips, pulling her closer. He kissed an achingly slow trail down her back. A whimper escaped her mouth as his hands moved, sliding up over her belly to end cupping her breasts.

"Exquisite," he whispered. "I can't wait to put you on canvas."

Saskia felt him stand behind her and heard a box open. She tensed.

He kissed her cheek. "I'm not going to hurt you." There was a tiny click, and then cold metal locked around her throat.

A collar. Only one of his subjects had ever worn a collar like this—the one in the painting at the Raine Estate. It had been a white metal with rows of diamonds going around the band. None of his other women had been painted in anything like it. Some of them had worn collars and various restraints, of course, but they were black leather with rings—standard fetish wear only. Nothing worth noting. From the moment she'd seen that painting with the jeweled collar, she'd imagined that woman must have been special to him. That she'd belonged to him.

"Is this the same collar...?" Despite her fear and ambivalence, she hated the idea of being nothing more than a placeholder for someone else—an inferior copy. She didn't want to be his forgery.

"No. I sold that when she left."

Quill held up the open box. There was a mirror

inside. Saskia ducked to get a good look. No, it wasn't the same. It was a white metal like the collar in the painting, but instead of several rows of small glittering diamonds, these were black stones.

"They're black diamonds. They don't sparkle much, but it's understated and elegant. You can wear it anywhere and with anything. And you will." He closed the empty box and set it back on the sofa.

Saskia gasped when his hand moved between her legs, a finger pressing inside her. Without conscious thought, her hips began to move, seeking deeper penetration.

"I knew you'd be wet when I finally touched you."

She was sure he was about to bend her over one of the sofas and fuck her. She didn't believe he'd put aside that urge even for a day—despite his speech on the subject. Unless, of course, he thought she'd be begging for his cock within the next few hours. What an ego.

Before she could learn whether Quill meant any of the words he spoke, they were interrupted by a woman much closer to his age than Saskia. She was attractive and polished. Saskia had the sinking fear he was married—or at least romantically entangled with someone else.

It wasn't as if she were in the position to bargain over the nature of his interactions with other women, but still.

Wouldn't Saskia have taken any piece of Joseph Quill on offer? When she'd met the assistant, she hadn't cared who else he might be fucking—only that she might get to be among that number. It was embarrassing now to realize what a groupie she'd been. And still was.

Quill's hand remained buried between Saskia's legs,

leaving no question as to what was going on. He didn't attempt to hide his behavior. She tried to twist out of his grasp, as if fleeing the room or hiding would cause the stranger to unsee what she'd just seen. But Quill held her tight and whispered a firm, "No," in her ear.

She stilled.

"Sir, I apologize for interrupting. I'll come back." The woman barely spared a glance to Saskia.

"It's all right, Lacy. What was it you needed?"

"I know it's earlier than anticipated, but dinner is ready if you'd like it."

"That'll be fine. We'll eat at the table."

The woman nodded and disappeared back to another part of the plane.

When they were alone again, Quill spun Saskia to face him. "You will *never* try to pull away from me again. I don't care where we are or who is watching. You will never deny me."

Her gaze lowered. In spite of everything, she couldn't stand the idea of disappointing him now. "I'm sorry, Master. I... I thought you said it was just us."

"Obviously, it's not *just* us. We've got the pilot, the co-pilot, and my cook. But we're down to a skeleton crew. Lacy will stay out of sight and out of the way. She's got something going on with the pilot, so she'll be preoccupied. Marcus would have been on top of us the whole flight, which is why I sent him back commercial."

"Oh."

He might want Marcus out of the way, but no doubt the man would see her many times in compromising positions. Marcus was good-looking. Not as good-looking as Quill, but he was rocking the bald-security-guy look. Even the idea of him seeing her like this or hearing her address Quill in such a degrading way made her face flame.

Clearly everyone in Quill's employ knew about his kinks.

He raised the finger that had been inside her and pressed it to her lips. "Taste yourself."

Saskia opened her mouth and sucked her juices off the offered finger.

Quill crossed to a small closet and removed a long sheer purple robe and helped her into it. "Let's eat."

AFTER DINNER, Quill returned to the living area. He ordered her out of the robe, and once again the fear surfaced over what was next, if she could handle it, and if they might be interrupted again. No matter what he said, Saskia didn't think she could cope with sex—or whatever things he intended to do with her—in public. It was scary enough thinking about what might happen between them in private.

She waited.

But nothing happened. Instead, he ordered her to kneel beside him and took out his laptop and started working. He spent hours engrossed in whatever work had gotten his attention. Every now and then, he reached down to pet her hair as if she were a domesticated pet curled at his feet.

Saskia leaned her head against his thigh and tried to process everything that had happened that day. She hadn't had the opportunity to think since she'd bumped into him in the *Piazza*. Everything had happened so fast. The revelation of his identity alone had taken up nearly all the space in her brain as she'd dutifully packed her things.

Because no matter how much the possibility of escape and freedom had screamed at her, and no matter how much her previous feelings for Lachlan bumped against the new revelation of Quill, all she wanted was to learn from him and to be painted by him. And all the rest... it wasn't as if these were new thoughts. It wasn't as if she hadn't masturbated to a scenario not unlike this one countless times already.

What difference was the reality going to make?

He finally closed the laptop and looked down at her. Saskia held her breath, both scared and excited over what might be next. He took her hand and stood, leading her to a door on the opposite end from where they'd had dinner. Behind this door was a bedroom.

The bed was probably a queen. Not a giant bed, but large enough for two people to comfortably toss and turn on. The bedding was all white, stark against a black steel frame. The headboard had sturdy, steel bars—something Saskia could easily imagine being tied to.

Her attention shifted a few degrees to the right. A large black metal cage sat beside the bed with fluffy white bedding inside that matched what was on the bed. It was plenty large enough for a person to stretch out and lie down, even to sit in, but not large enough to stand.

Quill withdrew a key from his pocket and unlocked the cage. "Inside."

Saskia crawled in through the door and stretched out on the bedding. He locked the cage behind her. She watched as he undressed down to boxer briefs and hung his suit in the closet. He disappeared down the hall, and she heard water running. It went on for a while.

He returned wrapped in a dark blue towel. Stray drops of water slid from his hair and rolled down his tan, muscular back. Saskia couldn't stop staring. He dropped the towel, revealing an ass and thighs as muscled as the rest of him. No tan-lines.

She'd never paused to consider whether he tanned or if this was his natural complexion, and she was no closer to knowing. Nevertheless, an image of him lying naked on a beach somewhere jumped into her head unbidden.

When he turned, she gasped at his erection. But why should she be surprised? It was just as intimidating as everything else about him. Had she expected anything less?

Quill moved to stand beside the cage and looked down at her. Saskia reached through the bars, her fingers barely skimming over his cock. He smacked her hand, and she jerked it back into the cage.

"No. I don't recall saying you could touch me."

But he'd taken her for this, right? He was hard. Didn't he want...? Didn't he want her to please him?

He gripped the top of the cage with one hand and his erection with the other and began to stroke himself. "Spread your legs. I want to look at you."

But not fuck her? Not be touched by her? Not get a blow job even?

Somehow this felt more objectifying than if he'd just fucked her or ordered her to suck him off. And from the hard look in his eyes, he knew it, too.

He took in the full picture of her splayed naked beneath him, then he stared into her eyes, jerking himself off. Minutes later, he came on her.

"Don't wipe it off," he said, his voice little more than a growl.

She lay still as his spendings slid off her hip, making a wet spot on the bedding.

Quill shut the light off so that only a thin strip of illumination spilled in under the door. Then he got in his own bed. Saskia tried to keep her tears quiet, but it wasn't working.

After a few minutes of this, he sighed. "Why are you crying?" As if he didn't know how much this hurt her, how much he was humiliating her. It wasn't even what he'd just done. In some artist-worshiping part of her brain, the whole sordid thing aroused her.

"You're making me sleep in a cage?"

"You have to earn a spot in my bed. And I told you, you'll beg for my cock like a good little slut."

More tears.

Quill moved to the edge of the bed and slipped his hand inside the cage. "Come here."

Saskia went to him. He stroked the back of her neck. "I can't do all the things I want to do with you until we get home. It's better if we wait. Just try to appreciate this space I'm offering you to process your situation. It's a gift."

It didn't feel like a gift. It felt like he was punishing her already.

6

The jet landed at six o'clock in the morning. It was still dark out. They ate a large breakfast on the plane and then Quill finally allowed Saskia to put some clothes on before disembarking. To her further surprise, he let her wear jeans and a black, thin-strapped tank-top. She suspected it would be the last bit of comfort and modesty she'd get except for when they were in public.

She still couldn't believe he planned to let her go out in public. Didn't he consider it a risk? In the strictest sense—despite the way he'd presented it—if not kidnapping, it was at least blackmail and false imprisonment. She wasn't an idiot. They both knew what he was doing was criminal—no less criminal than what she'd done. Maybe more. After all, all she'd stolen was money. He'd stolen a human being's freedom. They weren't even in the same category of offense. Yet, somehow she was sure she felt more guilt for what she'd taken than Quill did for taking her.

She'd slept so much and so well on the plane that she didn't even feel jet-lagged. If anything, it might be hard for her to fall asleep tonight when it was time.

She looked in the bathroom mirror one last time, her fingers trailing over the black diamonds of the collar. Maybe it was the lighting he'd chosen in this room, but she thought the stones sparkled plenty. He was right, though. It was understated. It looked just as good with jeans as it would look paired with an evening gown. Did he plan to take her to more art events? Gallery openings?

Would she actually be mingling in the art world at the side of Joseph Quill, being one of only a select few who knew his secret? Either he was exactly the smug, arrogant bastard she'd always thought Lachlan to be, or he was trusting her. She felt honored by even the idea he'd include her in his private world.

Saskia shook herself. She was well aware that her school-girl crush on this man would be her undoing. She could imagine herself forgiving him so many things she'd never forgive another man for. As Lachlan, barely touching her cheek had elicited outrage and restraining order fantasies. As Quill, he could lock her in a cage and come on her. It was horrifying that neither scenario was theoretical. She looked away from the mirror before she could catch the red she was sure burst into her cheeks at those thoughts.

When she emerged, Quill led her to the Bentley, his hand resting possessively on her lower back. The last time she'd been alone in this car with him, he'd been throwing a purse filled with crab puffs at her. He opened the passenger door with a sweeping flourish, ever the gentleman.

The drive was silent for the most part, except for the sound of windshield wipers when a light rain began to fall. Saskia watched the passing landscape out the window, her stomach tightening in greater apprehension with each mile they drove closer to his home.

When his hand strayed to her knee, she didn't pull away. Instead of hoping he'd stop touching her, she hoped his hand would inch up the inside of her thigh. She wished now that she hadn't worn jeans.

The rain had let up by the time they reached the estate, the sun peering out from behind now-fluffy clouds. At least Marcus wouldn't be home yet. Going commercial, there would have been a layover some-where. If she was lucky, it would be a few hours before she had to deal with his snide distaste.

"Let me show you where you'll be staying," Quill said. Somehow, despite the wording, the phrase came out as a command.

Her things would be delayed. When the jet landed they'd been loaded onto a small white van that was waiting for them on the tarmac. Marcus would drive it home when he arrived at the airport later.

She followed Quill through the main part of the house and out a glass door at the back. There was a large pool, hot tub, and terrace—and then a partially covered and partially open outdoor living space with a bar and an impressive set-up for grilling.

Saskia had never seen the back side of the estate before. The first few times she'd been there, her mission had been to get in and get out before he got any ideas— or at least before he tried to act on them. And the last time, it had been the middle of the night.

Beyond this outdoor living space, lay a few acres of open land, the center of which had been transformed into a rose garden filled with large bushes of white blooms and paths that carefully wound in and around them. She half-expected to catch someone painting the roses red or for a white rabbit to race past.

But nothing out of the ordinary happened, and Quill led her through the fragrant rose garden without incident. On the other side of the garden stood a broad stone building with skylights and ivy crawling all over it. The structure was enclosed on one side by the rose bushes and on the other by well-packed, tall evergreens. Saskia caught glimpses of a high fence beyond the trees. The extreme privacy of this space, made her wonder if he was hiding some sort of contraband.

"Saskia? This way."

The main part of the building was an enormous gallery, with a single large circular skylight in the center. There was a cage on the marble floor beneath the skylight, much like the one she'd slept in on the plane. Saskia didn't want to think about that, but she couldn't hide her disappointment that he might isolate her out here alone at night.

As if reading her mind, Quill said, "I told you, you must earn a spot in my bed. This is your room and where you will sleep until that time."

Saskia looked away from the cage, determined to think about it later. Not now.

The room seemed propped up and held together by white Greek columns, many of which had chains attached to them. Scattered about the gallery were several pieces of kinky sex furniture and equipment—as if they were art installations, statement pieces.

The walls were covered in his work—each piece behind protective glass. Paintings she'd never seen. Paintings which had never hung in a museum or gallery. His private collection—the things he created only for himself.

"You will hang in this gallery soon," Quill said.

Given the chains on the columns, she wasn't sure which way he meant that. Given what she knew about him, probably both.

"This way," he said.

She followed him through the gallery to a door hidden at one end. On the other side was a glassed-in room. It looked like a greenhouse, except that there were no plants. Instead, the room was filled with easels, canvas, brushes, paints, drawing paper, and charcoal. Like the gallery, this room also contained fetish furniture as well as a few elegant chaise lounges for the more subtle series of nudes he painted. All the furniture was covered in protective plastic, on top of which lay a thin layer of dust.

The room seemed dead, as if it had fallen into hibernation one winter and never awakened when the spring came.

"This will be your studio. You will work here. I work here occasionally, but I like to paint in the gallery as well. Or... I did."

"Why did you stop?"

Quill looked pained. "Saskia, you know why."

She thought she did, but she wasn't sure.

"It's not as if any of my work could be hung in a

gallery with Derick dead. The risk of exposure is too great, and Niche Industries' stock would plummet if this came out."

"Or it could soar. You don't know how people would react."

He sighed. "Trust me, I know. You underestimate the pearl-clutching disdain of the American public. They're all a bunch of perverts in private, but bring anything out into the open, and it's nothing but self-righteous denial and hand-wringing. As if the existence of a woman's cunt was a brand new discovery threatening to end the world in flames if its power were to be unleashed."

"But what about all those paintings in the gallery I've never seen before?"

"They were all completed when Derick was alive. I've done nothing since."

She wondered if it was depression or grief over the loss of his friend rather than fear of exposure that had stalled him. After all, couldn't someone mysteriously discover work created before the artist had died? At some point such a ruse had to end of course, but a gallery full of work no one else had seen seemed to suggest the credibility of the idea.

"So why now? If you can't sell them or display them out in the larger world..."

It was a long time for an artist not to work with or without a payoff. Saskia could feel the creative impulse inside him itching to be free. With that much down time, she imagined once he started painting again, it would consume him and everyone in his orbit.

Quill's eyes narrowed. "I notice you are speaking to me as if we are equals. Don't think I'm not keeping a mental tally of the number of lashes you're getting for each instance of casual speech. You're forgetting your place with me. I can assure you that won't be a problem much longer."

"Master, I'm sorry," she whispered.

"Not yet. But you will be. Sit, and do not move a muscle until I return."

She looked around the gallery. "Sit... where?"

"On the ground. Anywhere. I don't care. Just sit. And wait."

He hadn't answered her question, and she didn't have the bravery to ask it again. There was a strange new intensity to him which Saskia wasn't sure she liked. She sat on the marble and crossed her legs like some seasoned yogi. She only wished she felt that calm on the inside.

The door clanged shut behind him. There was a place deep within that screamed for her to run—make an escape while she still could. She doubted he'd locked her in. What if she just... left?

And go where? He'd confiscated all her bank cards on the plane. She no longer had access to the money he'd given her. And even if she did, if she started using it, he'd find her again. Even if she could take cash out of machines, with the withdrawal limits, there would still be a neat trail outlining her path. She may as well draw him a map.

Without his money, she had nothing. Her few semi-close friends were married and currently on the part of the life path that included small children with sticky hands. They were too wrapped up in their cozy families to pay much mind to her needs or even her existence. It wasn't as if she could crash on just anybody's couch at the moment.

Little Kaylee had ballet. And little Justin had a cold. And on and on. She didn't blame them—really. They'd remember her as the kids got a bit older and more independent. She didn't begrudge them their lives, but she'd picked differently. And the lack of a partner at this point in her life made for a lonely stretch of highway.

The people whose couches she *could* possibly crash on were all men—men who would want to take and use her body just like Quill did. Maybe it wouldn't be as kinky or scary, but it would be just as wrong. Probably more so in its way.

There was a small comfort and peace in knowing that at least Quill was willing to acknowledge the power he had over her—what she was to him. The lack of pretense was refreshing. She at least respected his honesty and thought that honesty somehow respected her in return.

By the time she could work up the nerve to slip out a side door and head for homelessness or blowing a casual acquaintance for a bed to sleep in, Quill was back.

She hadn't moved an inch. He seemed impressed with what he must perceive as striking obedience, not knowing it had simply been the result of a verbose mental monologue she couldn't manage to tunnel all the way through before his return. Let him think what he wanted—especially if it might offer her a stay of execution.

He'd changed into jeans and a black T-shirt. The two of them made a matching set. He wore casual shoes that slipped on without trouble so he could kick them off and out of the way as he did now. He carried a cardboard box like what one might use for packing belongings for a move.

Quill set the box next to the cage and walked the few feet to where Saskia sat like a sculpture on the ground. He pulled her up and, without a word, began to undress her. She didn't dare speak.

He unbuttoned her jeans and slid them off her hips, his hands running carefully over each inch of skin as he exposed it to the cool air. She braced her hands against his shoulders as she stepped out of the jeans, kicking her own shoes off in the process.

She'd worn a thong under the pants—subconsciously seducing him, knowing he'd discover it because of course this was coming. Quill ran an appreciative hand over the bared flesh, then removed the thong as well. She was left in the black cami top and collar. She hadn't bothered with a bra on the plane. She'd tried not to think too much about that choice.

It took almost nothing, not even the hint of a breeze, for her nipples to stand at attention. Typically, she wore bras with padding, not to look larger, but to avoid looking sexually excited even when she wasn't. It attracted the wrong kind of attention. And she couldn't be bothered to constantly explain to men with a frat-boy mentality that they just *did that*.

Quill cupped her breasts over the thin fabric and tweaked her nipples into even harder points as he stared into her eyes in the most unnerving way. She tried to look down. Some demure submissive instinct? She wasn't sure, but when her gaze dropped, he slipped a hand under her chin and forced her gaze back to his.

Minutes passed in this aching silence. It was a challenge. A game. Who would speak first? As in any negotiation, whoever spoke first, lost. She knew that at least. She'd already lost once with this man, and she wasn't willing to keep doing it.

Finally, he peeled her top off, and she stood on the cold marble floor, the sun from the skylight warming her back... waiting.

She didn't wait long. He led her quietly to one of the Greek columns on the south end of the gallery and extracted a key from his pocket to unlock the chains. He turned her to face the column and locked each wrist in place so that her arms were stretched high over her head in a *V*. Then he did the same with her ankles. She felt as if she'd been left for a lion to rip apart in some huge amphitheater while the bored elite looked on.

Quill dragged the mystery box over to the column. She wouldn't let herself look inside, too afraid if she saw what all he'd brought out here to torture her with, she'd start screaming and begging for mercy. She closed her eyes as large, strong hands skimmed over her back. Despite her fear, her body arched into his caress. He pressed a soft kiss against her shoulder, then he rooted around in the box until he found what he was looking for.

Saskia wished there was a clock on the wall, something to mark this length of silence. Some tiny clicking tick tick tick so she could feel and know that time was still a thing that moved even as she stood frozen in this space.

She waited for him to say something. Anything. But

now that it had begun, he seemed devoted to this eerie peace.

She jumped as something thudded against the skylight. There was a flapping of wings, and she looked up in time to see a disoriented raven fly off. A beat later, the whip came down across her back, and she winced against its bite.

She hadn't had time to register the sound as it sliced through the air, the noise competing with the bird outside. But she heard it the second time, so sharp and loud it seemed it could rip time and space apart. The leather licked across her flesh like a serpent made of flame, and all she could do in response was tremble in his chains.

Screaming, crying, begging, all of these things would have been appropriate, but Saskia couldn't do it. She couldn't break this vow of silence she'd committed to, and it seemed neither could he. Neither of them spoke, too locked into this trance to interrupt its flow now.

The only sounds that spilled forth into the gallery were the snap and crack of the whip and the tiny gasps as it stole her breath. The tears finally came, sliding down her cheeks in that same respectful silence. And she knew, even without words between them, that he was pleased.

She counted each lash in her mind. She felt his strength, not in how hard he waled on her, but in how he restrained himself and held each strike in check.

Finally, he returned the whip to the box. She tensed, waiting for something else—not sure she could take more when no comfort was offered. While he hadn't put her in physical peril, the lashes were much harder and more intense than the light play she'd experienced at the few kinky parties she'd been to on a lark.

And here there was no magic word she could say to make it all stop. All she could do if it became too much was beg and hope he'd have mercy on her.

Saskia startled when his hand wrapped around her throat, pulling her back, turning her tear-streaked face toward him. He left a long, lingering kiss on her mouth that took her breath away.

When he pulled back, he said, "I'm going to paint you now. Just like this."

SEVERAL HOURS LATER, a door slammed. Saskia jerked in the chains, straining to see who'd come in. She groaned from moving too fast when everything hurt so much. Her back felt raw, the sting still vibrating along her nerve endings.

True to his word, Quill had painted her, but whenever she'd started to lose the desperately relieved expression he wanted on her face, he'd taken breaks to whip her more to bring her back to the mental zone he wanted her in. Then he'd return to the canvas and his work as if nothing had happened.

"Marcus," Quill said when the man entered with Saskia's things. She'd begun to think of Marcus as Quill's henchman.

Marcus made several trips, not sparing her a glance, and left everything in an open space at the far end of the gallery. It was the pieces of her life—so much promise and possibility contained in those bags and crates. All of that gone now except for trinkets—mere shadows.

Saskia closed her eyes, waiting for him to leave, mortified that this man she'd once snapped at could now watch her degradation at his leisure.

More silence followed. There was no sound of a door shutting to grant her the hope of privacy. Instead, a large hand—less smooth than Quill's—trailed down her side and over her hip. Lips pressed against her throat. Not Quill's lips. She trembled against him.

"Marcus will guard you at night in case you need something. With me so far away in the main house, leaving you in the cage alone would be unsafe."

He really was just going to abandon her at night, wasn't he? More tears began to fall. Marcus wiped them away. "Shhhh." The attempt at comfort startled her. The last thing she'd expected from this cold, indifferent man, was kindness. She'd been certain he was annoyed by her very existence.

Quill continued. "Since he'll be moving to the night shift, I'm giving him a bonus. He will be allowed to do whatever he wants with you short of fucking you or drawing blood. I have cameras around the gallery to ensure those rules are followed." She hadn't noticed the small black monitoring devices near the ceiling. She'd been too taken in by the breathtaking art on the walls that so few eyes had seen. "No objection to this, right, Saskia?"

"N-no, Master." As if she'd object to anything he ordered. Not only had the clear consequences of his displeasure now been demonstrated to her, but she still couldn't kill off her adoration of the artist in spite of it. She was in so much trouble here.

"Good girl." Quill left the painting he'd created of her to dry, packed up his other art supplies, and took them back to the studio. She knew he worked in the wet-on-wet technique from various things she'd read about him. She also knew he did a nude portrait in a single session. But actually being here while he created something from nothing like that in such a short period of time, she could hardly believe it.

In art school she'd learned the traditional method for oils of painting in layers and letting each layer dry in between. A painting could take weeks or months to complete that way. The wet-on-wet technique could create a finished painting in a matter of hours, but even though she'd been taught that technique in art school as well, she'd been far too intimidated by it and felt she'd never acquire the necessary skill to create something brilliant on the first try. Not like Quill could. So she'd reverted back to waiting for each layer to dry before adding a new one.

When Quill returned, he said, "I'm going to let you and Marcus get better acquainted. Bring her to lunch in an hour."

"Yes, sir."

"Let's get you cleaned up." Marcus said when Quill left the gallery. His tone remained gentle.

Had she misread him the times they'd met before? Had he known what Quill had planned for her from the beginning? Maybe he didn't like it. But if he didn't like it, why would he accept partial sexual access to her in exchange for guarding her at night?

Guarding her. Like a museum piece. Was that all she was to Quill? She wanted to be more. She couldn't believe she actually wanted to be in his bed. He'd built it up like some coveted sign of status. And she'd already bitten into that bait.

Marcus picked the keys up off the ground and unlocked the cuffs holding her to the column. She fell into his arms when the metal sprang open, unable to support her own weight anymore. He unlocked her ankles and scooped her up, extracting a hiss of pain from her as his arms pressed into the whip marks on her back. He didn't comment on her discomfort as he carried her out a side door. Behind this door was a short hallway with another door at the end.

It was a bathroom. Though that was a mild way to describe a room containing a large dressing area and bench, a glassed-in shower, toilet, hot tub big enough for multiple people, and a counter that ran the full length of one wall and contained dual sinks. Quill didn't know how to do anything moderately.

Marcus helped her into a terrycloth robe and guided her to the bench to sit while he filled the tub. He poured fragrant oils into the bath. The scent she recognized immediately was lavender. Then he added a few large scoops of bath salts—no doubt of the therapeutic variety —to the bubbling water.

When the tub was full, he guided her to sit on the edge. "Tell me if you think this is too hot."

Saskia's hand sank beneath the water. She shook her head. "I think it's okay."

"Sir," he said, firmly.

When her eyes met his, they were intense like Quill's had been—just intense in a different way.

"Y-yes, sir."

He nodded and helped her into the tub. Saskia whimpered when the hot water touched her back.

"You okay?"

"Yes, sir."

The therapeutic salts made her back tingle, but it only took a moment for the feeling to become soothing. Saskia looked down to find the water had turned the palest shade of pink.

"H-he made me bleed?"

She should have run from him. She never should have let his identity trip her up. What was different from before when he'd been Lachlan to her? Nothing. In fact, it was worse than she imagined it would be if Lachlan ever got her into his bed. Because at least in those paranoid daydreams, it had been horrifying, but vanilla and violence-free.

"It's not bad," Marcus said. "He barely broke the skin. Was it a punishment?"

Saskia nodded. But she wasn't sure anymore. It had started that way. She wasn't sure what it had become in the end. It had become a frenetic creative feeding frenzy, while she'd been offered up to appease some unseen god of artistic inspiration. In return for this sacrifice, a painting had been born. Judging from Quill's satisfied expression as he'd studied the finished piece, the gods must have been pleased with the offering.

"Then that's why. If you obey him, it won't be like this. It will be intense, but not like this."

How could he know that?

How many women had Marcus watched Quill do this to? How could he keep getting away with it? If they were all like her with insipid art crushes, it couldn't have been too difficult. But Quill was demented if he thought she'd beg for him to fuck her after what he'd done in there. The arrogance of thinking she'd actually grovel and plead for him to be inside her was unbelievable.

Yet even the idea of doing that already made a dull throbbing start between her legs.

Marcus sat on the bench and let her soak until the water grew cool. He remained silent and distant, neither touching her, nor leering. She found she was grateful for the space, even if he wouldn't give her any real privacy. When the water turned cool, he pulled the drain and helped her stand, then wrapped her in the terrycloth and took her back out through the gallery to the studio.

He ripped away the plastic covering one of the chaise lounges.

"Take the robe off and lie on your stomach," he said. When she hesitated, he added, "I'm just going to put something on your back. Something to soothe it. Don't be afraid."

The late afternoon sun streamed in through the glass. If not for the trees and fence, she might have felt more exposed. Saskia glanced up to find more cameras hovering above. They were attached along the metal strips in between the panes of glass, with wires that ran the full length and down to the ground, disappearing behind some art supplies.

Was Quill watching? He no doubt had the entire building wired for his voyeuristic pleasure.

Marcus was patient while she worked through the

anxieties in her head. It seemed as if he would wait forever—however long it took—for her compliance. Meanwhile, Quill's savage intensity would have meant obey now or pay the price. Was Marcus meant to warm her up for Quill?

After a long mental back and forth, she took the robe off and lay across the chaise—convincing herself this was somehow a free choice. Marcus sat next to her and began to rub a salve on her back. It was cooling and almost immediately drained the rest of the sting away.

"Stay here." He rose and left her alone in the bright, sunlit studio.

She could hear him a few yards away in the gallery as he sorted through her things. When he returned, he held a short, white cotton nightgown. One of her favorites. When she'd bought it, she'd felt silly without a man to share it with. But it hadn't been over-the-top sexy and was comfortable on humid Venice nights. Still, it was a bit sheer. It was sexy in that *playing at innocence* way. But once the gown was draped over a female form, it was impossible to keep believing the virginal ruse.

His eyes didn't leave hers as he slid the fabric over her curves. "You're wearing this to lunch. I'm sure your master will like it as much as I do." He guided her down to the floor and pressed her gently back. The cool marble kissed her skin through the cotton.

"Spread your legs."

She hesitated. "I..."

Marcus shoved the gown up over her hips and pressed her legs open. He stared at her smooth, bare mound.

"I always wondered how you kept it."

She hadn't kept it before she'd started traveling on Quill's endless dimes. But on a lark she'd gotten a Brazilian two stops before Venice and had maintained it. She liked the way it felt to slip her fingers underneath her panties and find nothing but sensitive flesh, ready for pleasure with no obstructions. And she'd known if she were to meet a man in Italy, he might also enjoy it. She just hadn't expected it to be Quill. Or Marcus.

He pressed his palm flat against the smooth skin and dragged his finger across her opening. She could already feel herself growing wet, unable to resist the gentle way he stroked her. He bent between her legs, and then it was his tongue doing the stroking. At first, she was tense, ever aware of the cameras that watched her, afraid Quill might be angry even though he'd practically given her to Marcus on a platter.

But Marcus's insistent expert tongue pressing inside her soon made her forget someone else might be observing. She twisted, unsure if she was trying to escape him or move closer. He gripped her wrists and held her down as if she could otherwise get away. Within minutes, she came, writhing against his mouth and moaning his name.

"Sir," he corrected, when she finished.

Any normal man might have been pleased to have her body on display for him as his name dripped off her lips. And so soon after being left alone together. But Marcus was cut from part of the same cloth as Quill. She wondered if the two men were perhaps closer friends than their employer/employee status suggested.

Saskia averted her gaze.

"What do you say to me?"

Off Saskia's confused look he said, "Politeness... gratitude for the pleasure?"

"Oh. Thank you, sir."

He nodded and helped her up off the cold floor.

Back in the gallery, she was drawn immediately to the painting Quill had created while she'd hung in chains. He'd captured her at just the right angle. He'd gotten the stripes on her back, but he'd also gotten the hint of her waxed pussy as her lower half twisted toward him.

His voice reverberated in her mind, *Yes, let me see that lovely cunt. Arch toward me.*

Saskia saw the collar painted around her throat, the heavy chains at her wrists, the pained expression on her face. But if she were a casual viewer walking by this painting in a gallery, she would have skipped all that and seen only the eyes.

Somehow he'd painted her in such a way that all of her longing for him clashed against all her fear and the almost-dead tinge of resentment and masked defiance. It was all so stark and naked in oil. If he could get it on the canvas, he had to know. If he knew he could do anything to her, and she'd still look at him in that starved, desperate way... what was stopping him?

7

Saskia shielded her eyes from the glaring late afternoon sun. She was famished. Quill had lunch set up outside on the terrace, but there was only one plate of sandwiches and one goblet of tea, along with a pitcher to refill it. Next to the plate was one bowl of strawberries. Nothing had been set aside for her.

Quill extended a hand. Would one of the servants bring something for her? Was he going to eat all of this by himself? Marcus was suddenly nowhere to be found, and she felt self-conscious in the semi-sheer gown he'd dressed her in.

She went to Quill. His arm encircled her waist, slipping underneath the lightweight fabric.

One of the servants stepped outside then, carrying a large cushion. She placed it next to his chair and left without a word.

"On your knees," Quill said, nudging her.

Saskia knelt beside him, and he started to eat.

"Did you wear that for me?"

"Yes, Master." There was no sense in bringing Marcus's tastes into it. She wasn't sure the information would be appreciated.

He nodded. "I like it, but I want you to take it off and kneel with your legs spread for me."

He watched as she took the gown off and positioned herself on the cushion like he'd asked.

"Back straight. Don't slouch. It breaks up the lovely lines of your body."

She straightened and fought to stay still as he fondled her breast. She felt so exposed out here. Not like the studio. This space was more open, as if anyone could just wander by. Feeling watched, Saskia turned her gaze toward the house. A curtain covering a first floor window closed abruptly. Was Marcus watching her? Or one of the other servants?

"Do you like cucumber sandwiches?"

"Yes, Master."

He broke off a piece of one of them and offered it to her. She reached out to take it, but he snatched the food away. "No. You'll eat it from my hand like a good pet."

All at once, any lingering bad feeling toward him evaporated. It was so hard to hold how much she'd thought she hated him in her mind when his very nearness made her feel weak and flushed. He alternated between feeding himself and feeding her. His hand lingered at her mouth after each bite he offered, so she could lick and kiss the stray bits of cream cheese from his fingers.

The outline of an erection pushed against his pants, and she had the sudden urge... to beg him.

"Drink?"

Oh yes, please.

But that wasn't what he meant.

"Yes, Master."

He held the goblet for her and tipped it back so she could drink. Then he offered her strawberries. It reminded her of Eric feeding her that strawberry that had seemed to materialize out of nowhere after the champagne at his party. But this... even if she hadn't been kneeling naked at Quill's feet under the open sky, the way he pressed food into her mouth, the way his fingers lingered, slipping between her lips... it was practically sex all by itself.

She found herself disappointed when they ran out of food but not because she was hungry. Her eyes strayed to his hard on.

Quill noticed. "Something you want?"

She nodded, suddenly feeling herself go shy under his gaze. She shouldn't want it. She shouldn't want him. She knew she was falling like a row of dominoes at his feet—exactly in the pattern he'd designed. Every part of her, except for the part between her legs, wanted to resist and fight him.

"Beg me." He scooted the chair back and angled it toward her, opening his legs. It would only require crawling a mere few inches to be between his thighs.

She looked back down at the cushion. "I can't."

He cupped her chin and raised it so their eyes met. "I didn't expect you to be so shy, particularly not after the captivating way you came for Marcus in the studio." So he'd watched the video feed.

There was a softness to the way he touched and

spoke to her. She'd do nearly anything to get more of that from him.

Saskia felt her face burn.

The curtain on the first floor was pulled back again. Saskia could barely make out an outline of a person standing in the shadows.

"Crawl behind me into the house." When she hesitated, he said, "Don't worry, I'll bandage up your scrapes."

Quill rose from the chair and disappeared into the house. Saskia stared after him as if her brain had finally re-engaged to question what the hell she was doing. But after a split second of contemplation, she crawled over the terrace behind him and in through the French doors.

He led her to the study. Of course. The room she'd tried so hard to get away from him in. The room where her skirt riding a bit too high had once been scandalous, and him slipping his hand between her legs was the most lewd act imaginable. If only.

That room and this room were worlds apart.

Quill sat in the leather swivel chair and undid his pants.

"Now, you can have it, but you will worship it like it's fucking God, do you understand little slut?"

"Yes, Master." The nastier he spoke to her, the more aroused she became, and from the glint in his eyes, he knew it.

He was fully erect and seemed larger somehow than she remembered when she'd knelt in front of him. But the last time, she'd only tried to touch him from inside a cage. She could barely imagine how she would take him between her legs, let alone how she'd manage between her lips.

He stroked her hair. "I know it's rather frightening, but you'll find a way."

Tentatively, she caressed him and began to lick his shaft in long, slow strokes, but when it came to the actual deed, she couldn't go very far.

"Relax your throat," he said, as he continued to stroke her hair. She tensed and tried to pull away, afraid he'd grab the back of her head and force himself down her throat.

"Saskia. Stop it. I'm not hurting you. I'm not going to skull fuck you. I would never do that."

It was hard to know what Quill would do, given the course of events so far. One could hardly blame her for any fears she might maintain.

After a few minutes of failed attempts, he sighed. "We'll work on it. Make me come, however you have to accomplish it."

"I'm sorry, Master."

"It's all right. You're a work in progress."

She felt like a fumbling teenager, as if she'd never done this before. She had to use her hand and mouth together to get him off.

"You will swallow," he said. There were limits to his compromises.

Saskia sucked the tip into her mouth as he came down her throat and swallowed as he'd demanded.

When she'd finished, Quill pushed an intercom button on his desk. "Lacy, please bring Miss Roth an ice pop." He glanced down at Saskia. "Do you have a flavor preference?"

"No, Master."

"Whatever's in the freezer, Lacy."

"Yes, sir," came the reply.

Saskia slid to the floor as he zipped up and rose from the chair.

Her face flamed when the cook came into the study several minutes later with a grape ice pop. She handed Quill the frozen treat and left the room without a word of comment.

He unwrapped it and passed it to Saskia. "I'm sure you know what I want you to do with this."

"Practice?" she asked. It was far smaller than Quill's cock so she didn't know what they could possibly accomplish this way beyond a pornified version of eating.

He nodded. "I want you to practice deep throating it. The cold will numb the back of your throat so you can learn to relax it without gagging or choking. You're going to practice at some point every day. My freezer is your freezer for this exercise. When you can take me fully, I'll knock $100,000 off your debt. Say thank you."

"Thank you, Master."

As if her debt were anything more than a game to him. She was sure he tossed it in her face because, in a perverse way, the idea of her owing him money made him hard.

"You can start any time." He towered above her, his arms crossed over his chest, as she sat on the ground sliding the phallic sweet slowly in and out of her mouth, going a little deeper each time.

Quill sat back down and watched her until there wasn't enough left to practice with.

"You can eat the rest," he said, his attention shifting

back to the desk. He shuffled some papers around. "Do you remember the day we discussed the plan to steal the painting, when you wore that short red skirt and I leaned you over the desk?"

As if she'd ever forget that moment and how conflicted she felt now over it, given how mild it was by comparison to what had happened since.

"Yes, Master."

"Stand where you stood that day."

Saskia pulled herself up off the floor and dropped the wooden stick in the trash on her way to the desk. She stood in the same spot she'd been. That day she'd felt fear and revulsion. But now? It was hard to put a label on it. It was embarrassing to think how much her inner monologue had changed where he was concerned.

Quill moved behind her and placed his hand in the center of her back, pressing her forward until her cheek rested against the desk. The movement and touch of his hand was so similar, she could close her eyes and mentally project herself back in time. He nudged her legs apart. His hand skimmed up her thigh. Today he went further and cupped her mound. She didn't ask him to stop this time.

"You are so fucking wet."

He rubbed between her legs and picked up a thin black remote with his free hand. She thought he'd fuck her with it, but instead he pressed a button, and a screen across the room came to life with the video feed from earlier in the studio with Marcus. The picture was in shocking sharp color, the sound quality crisp. It was as far from low-end surveillance as one could get without studio lighting and a multi-million dollar production budget.

Quill removed his hand from between her legs and gripped her throat, pulling her back against him so that she had a clear, unobstructed view of the screen. She felt her own wetness from his hand pressed against her skin.

"Look at that filthy slut coming for the camera. I couldn't have gotten shots this good with paid professionals."

He held her still, and made her watch the entire thing from the moment Marcus had knelt between her legs until she'd climaxed for him. When it was over, Quill turned it off and pushed her back against the desk.

Minutes passed. The clock on the mantel ticked. Saskia breathed into the stillness of the room, knowing he observed her as if standing back from a painting, taking it all in. She wondered if he intended to put her on canvas like this, if he might be imagining from which angle to best compose the piece.

In the silence, her gaze drifted to the glass dildo on the desk. The rest of the room faded out of focus as she stared at it. It was as if Quill had been waiting for her to notice it like she had the last time she'd been in this room. His fingers stroked the length of it, the girth of it. For a dildo, it was oversized—not an unrealistic fit, but...

He nudged her legs farther apart and stroked her exposed pussy. "I think you're wet enough to take this, don't you?"

She nodded as she continued to stare at it. Maybe it just seemed so big because it was inches from her face. "Yes, Master."

"You may not be able to swallow my cock...yet. But

you can take this inside that dripping cunt. It's about the same size."

A not-so-subtle brag.

"Master, please..." Saskia squirmed against the desk, and he chuckled.

"You just need a good, deep dicking, even if it's made of glass, don't you?"

She whimpered. "Yes, Master."

Quill picked up the dildo and dragged the tip gently over her back, sending a chill down her spine in its wake. But he didn't press the toy inside her. Instead he laid it back on the desk as if he'd lost all interest. Did he mean for her to beg even for a glass cock?

He left her like that and crossed to a mini-fridge in a corner of the study and took out a large cup of water with ice in it. The look in his eyes made it clear he didn't plan to drink it, or for her to drink it for that matter. He placed the water carefully on the desk beside the glass toy.

He bent to her ear and whispered, "You're getting no lube, so you'd better stay nice and wet for me. Otherwise, this might hurt."

Against all rational expectations, her body responded to his words as if he'd spent months training it to do so.

Quill put the dildo in the cold water. Oh. That. She should have known. It wasn't as if this were her first experience with such a toy. If you'd asked Saskia on any other day but this one, glass sex toys were entirely underrated. They could be sterilized easily. They could be heated or chilled. No amount or type of lube could destroy them. They were simple, they were classic, they were...

Saskia gasped when he took the glass from the iced water and plunged it inside her. She'd braced herself against the desk, tense and waiting for something rough, but he was careful, patient, gentle. Things she never would have expected from this man, and which she drank up as if she were languishing in a desert.

"Too cold?"

"N-no, Master."

It only took moments for her body heat to warm it. Any shock of cold was already too far in the past to worry about. The toy went back into the water, and then it was inside her again.

He kept one hand pressed against her back. A subtle restraint. A message. *Don't struggle. Don't try to get away. Just lie there and take it like a good girl for me.*

She was only too happy to comply.

Quill increased the tempo until she was on the edge of release. She squirmed underneath his hand as if her frantic movement could make him go harder or faster or just a little deeper and maybe to the left.

He slowly pulled the glass out of her and pressed it against her mouth. It was warm, almost hot now.

"Lick it."

She whimpered. "Master, please."

"I said, lick it."

She obediently cleaned the toy with her tongue. Quill set it down and drank down the cup of water in one long gulp.

"You may rise off the desk," he said finally.

He was leaving her like this? Not finishing? What a bastard.

"Please..."

He put the cup back down. "In a little while. First we have business to discuss."

Saskia eased off the desk, the wetness dripping down her thighs. She was frustrated and angry and suddenly very self-conscious over her state of undress. She didn't know if she was more angry at herself for letting him do this to her or at him for not completing the job.

Quill nudged her aside and opened a drawer. He pulled out a large black ledger and laid it on the surface Saskia had just been draped across. The book fell open to reveal her name written carefully in all capital letters on the front page. He really had made a ledger just for her.

"You have a very large debt, my dear. You're going to have to start making a dent in it. I've thought of two ways you can pay me back. Your art and your body."

Hadn't he already more or less expressed this? But the next words out of his mouth made her blood run cold.

As if expecting her misunderstanding, he said, "I don't deal in intangibles, Miss Roth. I can have you any time I want any way I want, but there's no money in that. And Marcus isn't paying me. But others will."

She stiffened and shook her head as tears began to slide down her cheeks. "No, Master, please don't..."

Quill opened a fat lower drawer in the desk and took out a first aid kit. He led her to the sofa and sat, pulling her down with him, cuddling her in his arms as if to soothe her. "Settle down. I won't share you with just anyone. They will pay me, but you will want them. I'll let you choose who—only those who excite you. You can set limits with them. You won't get limits with Marcus or with me, but you will have them with the others. And Marcus will be there to protect you if you need him. Sometimes it won't be sex—just some kinky play. You will learn to trust me."

Trust. That word was mockery when it fell from Quill's mouth.

His hand moved between her legs again. "Just as I suspected. Even wetter. Tell me you'll comply."

She searched his eyes looking for something, anything she could trust like he wanted. But all she saw were his impossible demands and no clear way to escape them.

She couldn't force the words he wanted past her lips. But he didn't punish her. Instead, he opened the first aid kit and arranged her on the couch so he could take care of her knees. Crawling over the terrace and floor hadn't drawn blood, but they were bruised and sore and scraped up pretty badly.

Saskia hissed when he applied the antibiotic. Quill bent and blew on it before taping the gauze in place.

She wanted to stay here with him forever in this brief shining moment where he took care of her and she felt safe.

He closed the box and set it on a side table, then he took both of her hands in his. "Tell me you'll comply."

When she'd fantasized about the Joseph Quill Experience, it wasn't as if she'd fantasized about monogamy and romance novel sex with candles. But the fantasy was safe, while the real man felt anything but.

"Saskia, my patience is wearing thin. I will reward obedience, but what I won't do is negotiate with you. Let's not forget why you're here. After conning me out of millions, this is a better outcome for you than prison. Trust me on this."

But was it?

Quill stood, a look of disappointment on his face that utterly crushed her. "Get dressed. We're going out."

8

He hadn't specified what he wanted her to wear, so she'd put the jeans and black cami top back on. This time, she added a bra.

Quill stepped into the gallery looking GQ in all-black business-casual. The natural light grew weak as the sun began its descent.

He took one look at what she was wearing and shook his head. "No."

"I-I'll change."

He stopped her with a hand on her waist before she could go search for something more appropriate—however he might define that. His hands slid up the back of her top and unhooked the bra. He removed it like a magic trick and tossed the offending article of clothing to the ground.

"No bra. You were happy enough to display those pert nipples earlier in the day, so you'll display them now."

Whatever frenzy had overtaken him, it couldn't be good.

"But... where are we going?"

"Out."

That much had already been made clear.

Quill dug through a box of her things until he found a black skirt. It flared out in a way that was a bit too cute and young for her and ended a couple of inches above her knees.

"Put this on. No panties."

Saskia changed clothes, too nervous to question him. He dug through more of her boxes and found a pair of high-heeled black leather boots that came just over her calves. She hadn't known what she was thinking when she'd bought those. She'd tried them once with this skirt, but the ensemble just looked too slutty. Quill had caught up with her in Venice before she'd had a chance to return them to the store.

"And these," he said, tossing the boots at her.

"Please, can I wear panties, Master?"

"No."

"What about the bandages?" She would be mortified for someone to see them. He had to let her wear pants or something to cover it.

He appraised her with a quick once-over and a dark smile. "Where we're going, I want everyone to know you've been on your knees."

She didn't bother asking again where exactly that was.

He practically dragged her outside to the Bentley.

Marcus waited next to it. He gave her a quick once-over. The desire in his eyes was unmistakable. "Sir, do you want me to..."

Quill held up a hand. "No. I've got it." He opened the passenger door for her and got in on the other side.

The car buzzed with his energy as they pulled onto the main road, leaving Marcus behind.

"Master, am I being punished?"

"No."

"But where...?"

They were only a couple of streets down from the house when he pulled onto the shoulder and turned toward her, his face serious as a eulogy.

"Saskia, do not speak again until you are specifically addressed for the rest of the night."

She shrank back as he started the car again and continued to wherever he was taking them. He could say it wasn't a punishment all he wanted, but it felt like a punishment. He seemed angry, though she wasn't sure if she could differentiate between anger and simple intensity from Quill. It all seemed to jumble and blend together into one living, breathing thing that threatened to pull her under.

They left the city. When they moved onto a long patch of lonely isolated road in the desert, Saskia started to cry. Why was he taking her out here in the middle of nowhere? Was he going to kill her? Leave her on the side of the road like an unwanted mutt? In the middle of the desert, abandonment would be a death sentence.

But surely there was some reason beyond vulnerability and last-minute humiliation that he'd dressed her this way, some purpose he had planned that she still might survive.

His hand moved to her knee in an odd gesture of comfort. "There is no need for you to cry. I just want some peace and quiet for a while."

Saskia nodded and wiped the tears away. His hand resting calmly on her leg, and those few words *did* inexplicably soothe her, but that was only until they reached the warehouse.

It was a couple of hours outside the city, perhaps a little farther. The large boxy building couldn't hide behind trees. There were none. The landscape was utterly barren. A high fence wrapped around the warehouse to obscure the parking lot.

A sign on the outer gate read, "Mr. Fizzy Pop Bottling Company".

Saskia had never heard of any beverage called "Mr. Fizzy Pop". It sounded like a fake product and a fake company.

Quill stopped the car just outside the gate and left it running. He got out and entered a long numbered code into a keypad. The gate opened.

Inside, the parking lot was full. Nice cars. Mostly black. Definitely not bottling company factory workers. Either it was a company that had once existed and the sign had been left, or Mr. Fizzy Pop existed only in someone's fevered imagination.

He parked near the front in a handicapped spot that she guessed he wasn't going to get towed or reprimanded for taking. "Let's go."

The temptation to ask questions or plead with him to take her home was intense. But if she wasn't being punished now, she was very sure she would be if she spoke when he'd specifically told her to be quiet.

Quill came around the car and helped her out. He shut the door and pressed her against the side of the Bentley. He pulled her top up, and sucked first one nipple into his mouth and then the other, until they were fully hardened.

"That's better," he said, pulling her shirt back down.

As if she weren't already self-conscious with the lack of bra and panties. At least there was no easy way to advertise the missing panties, short of ripping her skirt off—which might still happen.

He took her hand and led her to the side entrance, the only place with light—a single bare bulb that creaked and swung lightly on the cool desert breeze.

Sinister clichés abounded tonight.

A bouncer-looking guy stood at the entrance and nodded. "Kane," he said.

What? Who?

Quill nodded back. "Jace."

The bouncer raised a brow at Saskia, his gaze drifting briefly to her bandaged knees, but he refrained from comment. Why the hell had that guy just called her master, Kane? How many aliases did this man have?

They went inside to a small, dimly lit lobby. Quill turned to her. "I go by many names," he said by way of non-explanation. "It's still Master here, to you. So you won't have to keep them straight. You're welcome."

It seemed he spent his entire life creating bubble upon bubble of carefully wrapped identity so that he could be all the variations of himself he wanted without one encroaching upon another, bringing the whole fragile house of cards down. Whoever he was as Kane must also be a threat to Niche Industries.

By now, Saskia was unsure if Lachlan Niche was even his real name. Perhaps there was another layer under that layer that she wasn't privy to. That maybe no one was privy to.

When you thought about it, his real name sounded kind of invented, too. What were the odds someone who created niche computer communications tech would just happen to have the last name Niche? And Lachlan was a Scottish name. He didn't look Scottish to her. Though she wouldn't object if he decided to don a kilt.

The door that led into the main part of the warehouse burst open, sending loud, deep thrumming music pouring into the lobby. A couple of blonde girls squealed: "Kane!!" They ran to him and practically smothered him in hugs.

He raised a brow.

"Sorry," they said together taking a few steps back and bowing their heads. "Sir."

They were about college age and in that Girls Gone Wild phase of life. They wore what amounted to thick black ribbons that wrapped around each of their bodies in criss-crosses, coyly covering them in all the necessary places. Saskia suddenly felt modest by comparison, and let out a relieved breath.

One of the girls glanced at Saskia, sizing her up. Glossy red lips formed into a pout. "I can't believe you collared someone!"

"I wasn't looking," Quill said. "She fell into my lap." An obvious lie, since he'd more-or-less stalked her and had been setting her up for this fall for months.

The blonde batted her eyes at him. "But I fell into your lap that time, and you didn't put a collar on me."

More pouting.

It actually wasn't a huge mystery why he never put a collar on her, but Saskia wisely kept her mouth shut. The last thing she wanted was for Kane... um... Quill... Lachlan... whoever the hell he was... to punish her in front of these women. In some weird, fucked-up way, she wanted him to be proud of her.

"Go on back inside. I'll play with you both in a bit," he said.

"Thank you, sir." They turned and giggled their way back into the main room.

Quill's attention returned to Saskia, as if to survey her reaction. She wiped her face of all expression, not willing for him to know anything she'd just felt.

In the car all she'd been was terrified. Submissive feelings hadn't been at the forefront of her brain. But somehow, in this element, things were different. She'd expected to feel like a sideshow in what she was wearing, but now it felt like camouflage. She never would have blended here in *normal clothes*.

This was obviously a private club, probably not a lot different from the few kinky parties she'd casually attended with friends in the past. She was almost a hundred percent certain that the people here would think she was with Quill of her own free will—that she'd consented to being his collared slave or pet or sub or whatever language was the current trend.

There might be rescue here—if she could get away from him long enough. If she could figure out who might not keep Quill's secrets. But if he went down, she went down. She had no illusions about that.

"Before we go in," Quill said, "let me make my rules

clear. You will do *something* with one of my friends tonight. I don't care what. It doesn't have to be full-blown sex. But there will be a negotiation, and he will pay me. I have friends here who get a thrill out of paying for it. It's their kink, and I'm happy to oblige them. You will be, too. Are we clear?"

Everything inside Saskia felt wound into a tight ball. It was anything but clear.

"Yes, Master."

His lips brushed against her cheek. "Good. Relax, pet. We're just opening a door and walking through it."

Maybe for him that was what they were doing. For her, she was making compromises with her own soul. Did she want him? Yes. Should she? No. Did she want this? This thing that was about to happen? She had no idea, but if she didn't do whatever was asked of her, it wouldn't end well. Of that much she was certain.

But there were so many witnesses. Surely she'd be able to find an ally and escape. But the same ugly question continued to bubble to the surface... escape to where? To what? What kind of life lay beyond his grasp, and did she even want any of the available options?

Quill had no idea of the conflict that churned through her as he opened the door, his hand resting on her lower back, guiding her through. It made her want to move closer for his protection, even though she felt certain he was about to throw her to some wolves.

Saskia turned back and gripped his arms. She must resemble a panicked deer. "W-wait... you said I didn't have to have sex... I didn't think you could do that anyway at these places."

"This is a privately owned space—by invitation only.

It's no different than if I invited everyone to my house. Anyone can have sex with anyone here, but I told you, tonight, you don't have to go that far."

He backed her into the club. Surely someone was going to notice that. But if these were all his friends, there was no way to know if anyone would help her even if she wanted an out. Who was she kidding? She still considered achieving a spot in his bed as some sort of life goal. Being collared by the real life Joseph Quill was like a hot fever dream. Even if she'd had little actual say in the deal.

"If anything happens that you really can't handle and you need it to stop, say *Red*. If they don't stop, I will stop them."

Off her confused expression, he said, "I told you, you'd have limits and boundaries with everyone but myself and Marcus. But you'd better choose those limits carefully. Don't throw that word around just to flex your limited free will."

Translation: it would have to be genuinely traumatic, or she'd be in trouble when they got home.

The first room just past the lobby was a large, wide open space. It looked very much like the warehouse or factory it had been labeled as. The walls were a corrugated metal. Bare rafters were exposed. But the lighting was more like a dance club. At eye level, a mirrored band about two feet tall wrapped itself around the room.

The last thing Saskia wanted to do here was look into her own eyes or a reflection of anyone else's.

A large conveyor belt wound around the room with enough distance between it and the walls for various restraints and bondage equipment at the edges of the room.

The conveyor belt moved at a grindingly slow pace, not fast enough to manufacture or bottle anything. It was easily wide enough for a person to lay spread-eagled on —which was what a few were doing as the machine took them on a tour of the room. Others sat at small tables next to the belt, touching those on the conveyor as they passed.

These weren't casual touches, but lewd groping that everyone on this fun house ride expected from the moment they got on.

Restraints were configured into an upper bar that moved with the belt, allowing people to be bound while standing on the large machine.

A few girls weren't bound, they'd just jumped on and grabbed one of the upper bars, using it to steady themselves as they swayed to the pulsing beats that seemed to cover the entire warehouse in fuzzy unreality.

The lush pounding of the music vibrated through Saskia. It wasn't that it was loud, it was that the bass was cranked high enough that it wasn't so much a sound anymore as a feeling.

This building was so far removed from the world she knew, so cloaked in darkness and drumbeats, that it felt like anything that happened here wouldn't count. And maybe that was what made the space in her mind open up a little to accept Quill's demands.

He guided her to another door. "Let me show you the rest."

From here, there was a hallway with a black-and-white checked parquet floor. The walls were a striking cherry red. On them hung artistic fetish photographs done in black and white with dramatic lighting shining over each image. It was the only illumination in the hallway.

Saskia's heels clicked sharply on the floor as they moved down the hall. The end of the hallway up ahead had another art photo, but it looked as if the hall just stopped in a dead end. Maybe there was a secret panel or something. Anything seemed possible here.

Quill stretched his arm across the front of her body, blocking her. "Careful. I need to lead you down. With those boots, you might get hurt otherwise."

Saskia gripped hold of the concern he seemed to offer. Now that she looked more closely, she could see the hallway didn't end. There was a large square opening in the floor, that turned directly into stairs that spiraled down to another lower level.

He went down a few steps first, then reached up for her. She took his hand and let him guide her until she could grip onto the railing herself. The same music piped in down below. The hallway had buffered and muted it, but in the underground space, it came roaring back to full life.

The lower level appeared smaller than the upper, but the activity was more intense, which surprised her, given the conveyor belt where strangers could grope and finger anyone who moved past.

There was more extreme-looking bondage equipment down here as well as a long row of large, sturdy wrought iron cages. They looked like giant old-fashioned bird cages. A few were empty, but most of them held a nude woman, each wearing a collar of a different style.

Their hands were bound behind them, and they knelt inside their cages, legs spread. They were each blindfolded.

Others, mostly men—but a few women as well— approached and stroked them through the cage bars.

"There's a bit more," Quill said, taking her hand and leading her past the bird cages.

Saskia looked back over her shoulder and saw a man giving money to another man beside one of the cages.

"Come along, Saskia, that's none of our business."

Surely, if they were doing it out in the open, it was everyone's business.

He took her to another door and another hallway. But instead of pictures on red walls, this one was painted solid black and had nothing but doors. "These are the theme rooms."

The first door looked like a school room and had paddles and rulers and spanking furniture. Shackles came out of a desk so one could easily be bent over and fucked. In fact, someone *was* being bent over and fucked. She had dark blonde hair pulled into pigtails with red ribbons tying them in place, a white cropped top, and a short plaid skirt. She wore white socks that climbed to her knees and Mary Jane shoes. A pair of virginal white panties were down around her ankles.

On the blackboard, she'd written lines: "This girl will be a good slut for Sir from now on." They were numbered down the board in two rows, to fifty. There was still chalk dust on her hands.

"Kane," a well-muscled blond man said, not bothering to pause his thrusting. He looked a bit like a Viking. Did no one here have any shame?

"I apologize. This door wasn't locked," Quill said.

The stranger laughed. "It's not locked on purpose. She likes to get caught, don't you, precious?"

"Yes, sir," she said breathlessly.

The man thrust once more hard into her and groaned as he came. Saskia looked away, too uncomfortable with the display to stare openly.

"May we?" Quill asked, when the man pulled out of her and zipped up his pants.

"Be my guest. My slut is your slut."

The man stroked her back, and she mewled in response. He stepped away, and Quill led Saskia to the bound woman.

"Touch her," Quill said.

Saskia glanced up and saw a camera in the corner of the ceiling, angled right down on them, a red light flickering—leaving no doubt that it was on and recording. Everyone knew cameras didn't need to have a red blinking light. This wasn't 1970. There were plenty of modern cameras that worked just fine without any blinking. Yet this camera sought to announce itself—either to warn or to thrill she couldn't be sure.

Saskia pointed at the camera. She didn't have to ask the question that was on her mind.

"There is a screening room. I'll show it to you when we get finished here."

The stranger tossed Quill a key. "Unlock her hands, I want to watch them together. If that's okay with you."

"My slut is your slut," Quill said, as if this were the club motto.

Quill unlocked the woman's wrists from the shackles

and held her steady. "Step out of the panties. We don't need those in our way, do we?"

"No, sir," she agreed, stepping out of them.

The stranger approached, and Saskia took an involuntary step back. She was beginning to privately think of this man as The Viking.

"She's very skittish." He turned to Saskia. "Is this your first time at a place like this, doll?"

"No, sir."

Quill's eyes widened a fraction, and she wasn't sure if it was because she'd called the man *sir* without being prodded or because she'd been to a place like this before. Well, not really like this. This place was more intimidating and impressive. The few parties she'd been to had been amateur hour next to this. High production values was the thought that came to mind as her gaze panned involuntarily up to the camera again.

"I rarely see you here with your own girl," he said.

Quill just shrugged.

The Viking studied her a few minutes longer. She shrank away when he pushed her dark hair behind her ears.

Quill gave her a warning look. "If you can't handle it, safeword out, but don't do this wilting flower routine with me."

"I'm sorry, Master."

"Are you comfortable playing with my girl?" The Viking asked.

Saskia glanced over at the blonde, who now leaned against the desk. The girl looked friendly and happy enough to be there.

"Yes, sir," Saskia said.

He took Saskia's hand and squeezed. "Good girl."

Quill moved to one of the school desks along the back row and sat, his legs splayed in the chair.

The other man sat at a desk in the front row. "Kane? What's your girl's name?"

"Saskia," Quill said from the back, his eyes not leaving hers. She felt as if she were being graded. A school room was appropriate.

"Saskia, are you wearing panties?"

"No, sir."

"That's good. Take off the top for me. I want to see those lovely tits."

She took a breath to still the tremble in her hand and removed the top and laid it across one of the chairs on the front row.

The blonde girl pushed off the desk, and took Saskia's hand. "Don't be nervous," she whispered. She threaded her fingers in Saskia's hair and pulled her in for an open-mouthed kiss.

Saskia sighed against the other woman's lips as the girl's hand reached up to fondle her breasts.

"Put your hand between her legs and stroke her until she comes," Quill said from the back row.

Saskia glanced at the stranger. His expression wasn't lust. It was calculation. He wasn't convinced she was here by choice. How could Quill have thought forcing her into this scenario would warm her up to his grand pimp plans? Or did he just not care if she kicked and screamed the whole way?

She wanted to stop it even if Quill might punish her when they got back to the gallery. But before she could decide to do that, the blonde girl had taken her hand, brought it to her mouth, sucking on Saskia's fingers.

Saskia let out a surprised gasp at the warm tongue moving against her skin.

"Please," the blonde whimpered, "touch me."

She didn't protest as the girl pushed Saskia's hand between her legs. The blonde was excited. Saskia dragged a finger slowly through the trail of wetness between the other woman's legs and then began to stroke her sensitive flesh.

She wasn't sure if this girl liked to be touched the same exact way she did, but the response was encouraging.

The girl moved against Saskia's fingers. "Yes, please... please..."

"Bend her over the desk and spank her," The Viking said. "She knows not to beg like that. It's unseemly. Like a poodle begging scraps."

Saskia pressed gently against the girl's back as she laid over the desk. The girl wriggled her ass in the air, and Saskia took that as an invitation. She smacked her a few times on each cheek until a blush of red burst out over the girl's skin, then she rubbed her heated flesh.

Despite any misgivings he might have about Saskia's presence at the club, The Viking was already becoming aroused again. His erection pushed hard against his pants as if it might burst through the seams. He turned to Quill. "Are you sharing her? I mean, privately?"

"I am. For a price."

Saskia tensed.

The Viking smiled and pulled out a checkbook and pen from his back pocket. Another check-writer. Definitely a friend of Quill's. And yet, the physicality of the moment made a sharp impression on Saskia's psyche.

"How much for an hour with her?" The Viking asked.

Quill glanced at Saskia, who stood frozen beside the blonde girl. "No fucking. She's not ready for that."

"That's fine." His pen was poised over the paper ready to put a dollar value on Saskia's body and time.

Quill smiled. "You want the friends and family discount?"

The Viking didn't respond. He just filled out the check with some mystery amount and got up and gave it to Quill. "Does that work for you?"

"That's extremely generous. Take her."

The Viking smiled and turned toward Saskia and the blonde. He helped the blonde off the desk, and pulled her skirt down to cover her and helped her back into her panties. He kissed her on the cheek. "Go find someone to play with for a while. You will tell me every detail of what you did later."

"Yes, sir."

He playfully swatted her on the ass, then he took Saskia's hand and led her down the hallway as Quill disappeared into the room across the hall.

"Where is he going?"

"The screening room," The Viking said as they moved down the hallway. "You saw the school room. There is also a medieval dungeon, a harem-themed room, a medical room, the mirror room, and this one, which is where we'll be."

He led her into a black boxy room and shut the door. It didn't escape her notice that he didn't lock it. Quill probably wouldn't like it if he did. A camera was aimed down on them from the top of one corner, red light blinking.

The room felt claustrophobic, but maybe that was just the panic moving in. The Viking was in no way repulsive. He took good care of himself. He had beautiful hands and stern, yet kind eyes. His blond hair was sun-streaked and he looked as if he could have just walked off a battlefield.

The idea of doing *something* with him wasn't off-putting. But everything was happening too fast for her.

A single bright spotlight was recessed into the ceiling, illuminating the center of the room. The floor was wood with a very dark, shiny finish—so shiny it was almost a mirror. The color was nearly black, but upon closer inspection—to avoid looking at him—she saw it was a rich deep brown. The walls were black leather with gleaming metal hooks coming out that had various whipping implements and bondage accessories looped over them. On one end was a leather bench built into the wall that expanded to fill the full width of the narrow room.

In the center of the room, under the spotlight, was a single piece of BDSM furniture, a spanking horse with attached restraints. Simple. Classic. In another situation, maybe not too intimidating, but in this one...

"This is the leather room," he said.

Saskia could file that in *unnecessary explanations*. But he didn't seem to be talking to educate her; it was more to calm her nerves.

He took her hands in his and guided her to sit on the bench with him. She stared down at their interlocked fingers. His hands were so big compared to hers.

"Do you want to be here?" he asked.

Saskia glanced up at the camera, then back at him.

"There's no sound," he said. "Only an image. You can speak freely here. I've known Kane for a long time..."

Obviously not if you think that's his real name.

"...but something feels off to me. If you want out of here, I'll help you."

The Viking was at least six-foot-five. And broad. Quill was a big guy as well and might be able to take him. But, then again. maybe not. This guy could possibly get her out.

"If you have nowhere to go, I can arrange something safe for you. Kane is not your only option if that's not what you want."

Saskia was silent, staring down at the shiny reflective floor.

"Look at me."

Her gaze rose to his.

"Are you here of your own free will, doll?"

"It's complicated," she said.

"Well, that's a no." The Viking sighed, disappointed, clearly not wanting to believe his friend would cross the lines and boundaries this man seemed to respect.

He stood and extended a hand to help her up. "Let's go. We aren't doing this."

"But... where are we going?"

"I'm getting you out of this building, and then we'll figure it out from there."

He clearly planned to fight his way out with her or cause a massive scene. It might be the only way he could manage it if Quill was watching from the screening room.

She allowed herself to be dragged down the hall, back toward the big room with all the dungeon equipment and bird cages.

Saskia tugged to try to get her hand out of his grasp, panicking. "Wait, no!"

He stopped in his tracks and turned, concern clouding his face. "I'm not going to hurt you. I don't know what he's done, so I realize that may be hard for you to believe, but I'm trying to help you. If you can just trust me for a short period, you'll see. You will be safe."

The Viking continued to pull her along with him into the main lower level room. Quill was no longer in the screening room. He was in this main room, occupied with the two blondes who'd thrown themselves at him in the lobby.

He hadn't even been watching? What if she'd needed him? But, then again, if he knew The Viking well, Quill knew her boundaries would be respected. Even just looking scared had prompted the stranger to ask all the appropriate questions. He hadn't laid a hand on her in private. Except for the one gripping her hand, trying to drag her out of there.

Saskia wasn't sure where it came from, but the panic rose out of her clear and sharp. She didn't think The Viking would hurt her. She believed he might actually be able to get her out, but seeing Quill against the wall playing with the blondes he'd restrained... Fuck. She had to be crazy, but she didn't want to leave him.

Presented with a real choice, finally, she chose.

"Let me go, I want to stay."

"No, you don't. You're just scared."

"RED!" she shrieked.

He let go of her immediately, and everyone in the room stopped what they were doing and stared in her direction, a few casting disdainful glances his way. The music abruptly cut off.

"Don't tell me what I want!" she shouted. She shook with rage and pent-up adrenaline. She glanced over to see Quill whispering to a man in leather. The man went to work to free the chained blondes, and Quill moved toward Saskia, eating up the path that cleared for him in long powerful strides.

He stood in front of her and faced off with The Viking.

"What the fuck, Ari? You know I wouldn't just leave a girl with anyone else but you like that. What the hell do you think you're doing with her?"

"She looked too scared to me. I was getting her out of here."

"She *is* scared. She's new. I thought that made you a good choice. Did you think I kidnapped her? How would that work exactly?"

Saskia could lay out the process for everyone, but she'd made her choice, and explaining that The Viking was basically right about things wouldn't improve her situation—especially given that she'd decided she wasn't willing to be separated from Quill.

"I'm sorry, I didn't think," Ari said.

"No. You didn't think. Do you see the collar? Should I have had my name put on it?"

Which one?

"Kane, I'm sorry. Really. It was just a reflex."

"Saskia, we're leaving."

"What about my money?" Ari asked.

"You can take a rain check," Quill said.

Saskia glanced at Ari. She may want to stay with Quill, but what Ari had just tried to do for her—yeah, she could play with him later if he wanted.

He studied her a moment, then nodded. "Fine."

She could already see the wheels in his head turning as if he weren't convinced and might try to rescue her again. But she was sure Quill wouldn't be foolish enough to leave her with him unguarded a second time.

The room remained tense and still, all eyes fixed on them as he led her up the spiraling staircase. They moved quickly down the hallway with the nude photographs, through the main warehouse, and out to the car.

They drove for several minutes in silence, Quill's hands gripping the steering wheel. The anger radiated off him.

"Master?" she whispered. "Am I in trouble?"

"Of course not. You did exactly what I told you to do. Safeword out if something is really too much for you. I didn't think he'd try to bust you out of there like a one-man SEAL team."

The lonely desert road stretched out in front of them as if it might go on like this to the end of the earth.

"Tell me, Saskia, are you going to comply with my rules? Are you going to trust that I won't send you with anyone who would hurt you?"

"Yes, Master."

"Good girl."

"Were you giving me an out?" she asked quietly. Maybe leaving her with someone he really trusted and not watching was a way to let her escape if that's what she wanted. Maybe he had a soul in there somewhere, a conscience. She wanted so badly to believe he did. She couldn't handle the idea that the artist she'd idolized was a monster beyond redemption.

Quill stared out at the road, but his hands relaxed their death grip on the steering wheel.

"Even if that's what I did, you're mine now. That was the only chance you had to get away from me. I hope you're happy with the choice you made."

Already she was doubting it. Quill never made anything easy.

askia stood in the gallery fresh from a shower and naked as Quill had requested. Was he finally about to take what he'd laid claim to in Venice?

His gaze panned over her body, but he didn't make a move toward her. "Do you want to know how much Ari paid for you tonight?"

Considering she believed The Viking had planned to bust her out of there and may have been paying for that rather than anything sexual, yeah, she was curious.

"Ten thousand." Off her shocked expression, Quill said, "It's a very private and exclusive club. Lots of money to throw around. And as I said, he gets off on paying bizarre sums of money for women. I think it's because he knows he could get whatever he wanted easily for free. I guess he likes to see how the other side lives."

Saskia tried to process that amount of money for the questionable thrill of spanking and fondling her for an hour.

"I kept the check, so you will be seeing him at a later date. I expect a less dramatic outcome."

"Yes, Master."

He studied her face. "Are you okay with Ari?"

"Yes, Master."

"I want you to be honest. Don't lie just because it's what you think I want to hear."

"I can play with him. I feel safe with him."

"Do you feel safe with me?"

She looked down at the cold floor. "No, Master."

"Then why did you insist on staying with me?"

Saskia shrugged. "I don't know."

"Well, you'll have plenty of time to think about it."

Quill's key creaked in the lock of the cage. The door swung open with a matching cringe of metal as he motioned her inside. Her lip quivered.

"No," he said, his voice flat. "Your tears won't have any affect. I told you this is where you'd be sleeping."

"But..." She'd thought surely if she pleased him enough, if she were obedient enough, he'd forget about keeping her in the cage and let her sleep with him. If he was so set on having her, why would he lock her up in the gallery all the time? Didn't her choice to stay with him rather than flee earn her a place in his bed? She internally cringed even thinking this way. What woman with any self-respect would ever think this way toward someone who obviously didn't value her?

Or maybe she'd thought he was bluffing this whole time. Even with the cage on the plane, she'd just assumed once they were at his house... things would be different.

"In the cage, Saskia. You don't want another punishment just before bed, do you?"

"No, Master." She crawled inside, and he turned the key in the lock.

She reached through the bars. Quill took one of her hands in his and kissed the back of it like some old-fashioned gentleman. Then he retrieved a small remote from his pocket and gave it to her.

"This is for emergencies only. If you need to use the restroom or something of that nature. Do not abuse this. If Marcus tells me you're calling him in for frivolous things, there will be consequences. Press the button now to test it."

Saskia pushed the button, and a few seconds later, Marcus sprinted in as if flames were shooting from the gallery. Even with what had happened between them before, she still felt shy around him. She drew back, covering herself with one of the bedsheets inside the cage.

"She was just testing the remote."

Marcus glanced briefly at her, then nodded and went back to his post outside the door.

"I'll see you in the morning for breakfast," Quill said. He shut out the gallery lights. The switch echoed in the large, hollow room. His footsteps receded, clicking over the marble.

But even with the lights off, it wasn't dark. The moon outside was full, shining almost directly over the skylight, casting a pool of bright illumination over the cage. A surreal sort of feeling swept over her—as if she were about to undergo some monstrous transformation under the light of the moon, and caging her was merely a precaution meant to keep the villagers safe from her evil.

She peered through the bars at the paintings. All these women were inside their own cages, trapped behind glass—desperate eyes looking into her, following her every movement in the cramped quarters she'd been reduced to.

Saskia shifted and fluffed the bedding, pulling the blankets over her. She tried to curl up and sleep, but every time she shut her eyes, she saw the club. She kept seeing that moment... the potential moment of her redemption which she'd squashed like a helpless bug in her frantic bid to stay with a man who simply brought her home and made her sleep in a cage.

She couldn't believe she'd chosen to come back with him. She didn't know where Ari would have taken her or what he would have done with her, but she felt certain that if she'd gone with him, she'd be sleeping in a real bed right now either alone or with him. Both options were better than this.

If she could just find sleep, it wouldn't matter. It would be as if only a few minutes passed, then it would be time to get out. This didn't have to be the end of the world.

But it was.

The footsteps returned. At first she thought Quill had changed his mind about the sleeping arrangements. But the cadence of the steps was different. The length of the stride was different. She knew it wasn't Quill well before Marcus reached the cage.

Even after his head had been between her legs in the studio, she still worried something more might happen between them. And yet...she hadn't had an orgasm since the last one with Marcus. She was sure Quill had intended for it to happen at the club before things had gotten out of control with The Viking.

Marcus sat on the ground, his back pressed against the bars looking in the other direction at some undefined patch of white wall across the gallery.

"Are you going to let me sleep?" she asked.

"I haven't decided yet."

His hand was propped on the floor beside the cage. Without thinking about what she was doing, Saskia reached through the bars, her hand covering his. She didn't want to be by herself in here. Even though she was afraid of what could happen with the whole night stretched before them and Quill asleep in the house, she'd do anything Marcus wanted if he just wouldn't leave her alone.

Their eyes met.

The intensity of his stare held the same frightening edge as Quill's. She tried to pull away, but Marcus threaded his fingers through hers, his grip stopping her retreat. After a while, his thumb began to stroke the back of her hand, and she relaxed into his careful caress.

This was how she found sleep in the cage with her arm stretched out holding her guard's hand in Quill's gallery.

A throat cleared, causing Saskia to jerk awake.

"Sleeping on the job, Marcus?"

"No, sir, I mean yes, I..."

"At least you were with her and not sleeping where she couldn't reach you."

Saskia pulled her hand back through the bars and

watched Marcus get up and wander out of the gallery without even a backward glance in her direction.

She'd thought he'd take advantage of his position of power over her. The last thing she'd expected was for him to sit silently next to the cage until they both fell asleep.

No words had passed between them after their hands had entwined—just a long hollow silence. She hadn't known such large open rooms could be so loud by the sheer force of their existence. She wondered which of them had fallen asleep first. Had Marcus watched her sleep before he'd drifted off himself?

When the outer door clanged shut, Quill turned back to her, his arms crossed over his chest. "Is Marcus your boyfriend now? Are you two going steady? I wonder if he'll carve your initials into a tree."

She stared at the bars. "I fell asleep. I guess he fell asleep, too."

"Thrilling narration. Should I add that to the list of skills I'll be finding a way to monetize?"

She shook her head quickly. Why was he being so weird about this? He was the one who hadn't wanted her sleeping in his bed. He was the one who'd given Marcus free reign with her with few boundaries. Was hand holding on the banned list now? She didn't dare ask. Saskia liked to think she had more sense than that.

If he was going to be so goddamned jealous, he didn't have to let Marcus do anything with her. He could pay him overtime or shift pay or whatever like anybody else. He'd probably add whatever he paid Marcus to guard her to her growing debt, anyway. They both knew he never intended on releasing her. It was all a charade.

He'd probably never stop punishing her for what must in reality be the equivalent of stealing twenty dollars from his pocket.

Quill unlocked the cage. "Go get dressed. I've laid clothes on the bathroom bench for you to wear. Then you will join me in the dining room for breakfast at the main house."

Saskia was surprised he'd allowed her clothing. It was only a short, green sundress, but it was something. Kind of. The dress was the right size, but the straps didn't want to stay up. As usual. At least the bodice would keep the dress mostly in place. He'd left her no panties or bra. Though he'd thoughtfully brought her a pair of strappy gold shoes.

If he'd thought about shoes, the lack of undergarments wasn't an oversight. When the dress was on, she stood in front of the mirror, staring at the black diamonds at her throat. She could never seem to resist pausing in front of any mirror or reflective surface to catch another glimpse of it now.

While she'd never engaged in a long-term BDSM relationship, she wasn't a stranger to the scene. She'd played a few mild games with some friends. She'd dabbled. She knew enough to know that this thing with Quill wasn't a real BDSM relationship. It might have the trappings, but it wasn't the real deal.

He wasn't asking her permission, and the concept of a safeword was nonexistent with him. With his friends? Yes. With him or Marcus? Not on her life. She wasn't foolish enough to think she had such a lofty right with her captor. Still. In that world, collaring someone meant something. Some took it more seriously than a wedding ring. It meant things to them that a ring just couldn't convey.

It signified a kind of belonging to another that came with deeper affection and protection. She knew Quill understood that world. Even without the club the night before, Saskia would have believed he knew. How else could he paint women the way he painted them? How could he seem to understand his subjects like he did and get inside their minds so deeply, otherwise?

Every time she looked at her collar, she knew it didn't really mean the same things it meant to people who lived in this arrangement willingly. But she wanted it to. Couldn't it? Even with the way they'd come to this place? Or was it forever tainted by her theft and his abduction?

A relationship like this had to be built on honesty and communication. Those things weren't possible now with Quill.

Saskia looked away from the mirror before she could catch herself crying like an idiot. There was a deep rift within her. On the one side, she wanted that connection with Quill. And on the other, she didn't want to let herself be taken in by him—or at least not pulled under his charm any further. She wanted to forget who he was and somehow erase the childish fantasy she'd created around his image.

He'd laid out makeup for her on the counter. She might have missed it if not for the embarrassment that had caused her gaze to drop from her reflection.

The makeup wasn't in some large, undifferentiated

pile. He'd chosen specific colors. Not a pallet with forty shades of shadow, but a single pot of lavender. A single light pink blush. Powder, concealer, foundation, mascara. Clear lip gloss.

Quill clearly liked the "natural look". He liked makeup that took just as long to apply as all other makeup but allowed him the illusion that a woman just looked this way rolling out of bed. And of course, he insisted she create and go along with this illusion. Next to the makeup was a bottle of pale pink nail polish—a color so translucent, it seemed somewhat pointless to put it on. More "natural" perfection.

Saskia combed and blow dried her hair, applied the makeup laid out for her, and polished her nails. She would never admit it to Quill, but the polish looked nice. It was so understated and subtle that someone might look at her for fifteen minutes, studying every inch of the facade and still not figure out what it was that made her look so pulled together. It was the kind of secret she wished another woman and pulled her aside and told her about years ago.

She gave herself one last assessing look in the mirror, and then headed for the main house.

For such a big house, there were only a few servants. She'd met Marcus and Lacy—though if not for hearing Quill speak her name, Saskia never would have known it. She'd seen four other servants drifting from place to place blending into the background. Seen and not heard. There could be more, but she somehow doubted it. Did they think she was here voluntarily? She'd certainly walked onto the plane of her own volition. No one had dragged her here in chains.

Saskia wondered if Marcus slept in the house. She wanted to see *where* he slept. She peeked into several doors until she found the one her guard slept in. She pushed the door open, cringing when it creaked. Marcus shifted in the bed. Saskia held her breath, but he didn't wake. A white sheet bunched around his waist, revealing sleek, tan muscle and a tattoo of a black dragon that started on his back and wrapped around his side.

The room was a light blue with white furniture. It looked like something out of some Cape Cod cottage in a beach architecture magazine. It didn't look like how he might choose to decorate on his own.

Had he simply been assigned a guest room? Was this the least offensive of his options? Or had he just been too tired to make it to wherever he normally slept? She watched him for several minutes. Yes, he looked very much like a bodyguard. He felt very much like *her* bodyguard.

She jumped when she realized he was staring at her. She started to back out of the room, but he raised a hand off the pillow and motioned her closer.

"Sit down," he rasped in that husky half-asleep voice some men had.

Saskia sat carefully on the edge of the bed, her thigh inches from the tip of the tattooed dragon's tail. She scooted away from it, as if the ink might somehow pierce her skin. Marcus took her hand in his and squeezed.

"You don't have to be afraid of me. I'm not going to hurt you."

She nodded and used her free hand to wipe the tears that already moved down her cheeks. She believed him. She trusted he wouldn't hurt her or destroy her in any outward or inward way. But Quill's bed was still the one she wanted to be in. Even though he wasn't half as kind.

"He'll be upset if you keep him waiting," Marcus said. "Let me sleep, love. I'll see you tonight. We've got a lot of lost time to make up for."

A phantom chill swept the room, and goosebumps popped out on her arms.

"Y-yes, sir."

Marcus pulled his hand away and closed his eyes, dismissing her for the day.

10

Quill glanced up from his paper. "You're late."

He was dressed in an uncharacteristically casual white T-shirt and faded jeans.

Saskia was just as uncomfortable and nervous this time as she'd been the last time he'd spoken those words to her. Why couldn't he be more approachable?

He hadn't given her a time limit. She'd gotten ready according to his exacting specifications. Surely he didn't think she could just wave a wand, and it would all be done instantly. It took time to look like you'd rolled out of bed perfect.

"I'm sorry, Master. My nails were drying."

That was true. Kind of.

He made a sound halfway between a grunt and a snort and went back to his paper. "Sit."

At the table? Like a real person? To what did she owe that grand honor?

She slid into the chair opposite from him while he

read. Occasionally he brought a white porcelain coffee cup to his mouth. It clinked back against the saucer as he set it down, immersed in the financial news.

A servant brought out a plate of food. "Coffee, ma'am? Or something else?"

Saskia was taken aback by the respect. She'd assumed that if she was crawling around on the floor in Quill's collar, that the rest of the household would treat her like a dog as well.

"Coffee is fine."

The servant disappeared from the room for a moment and returned with the coffee.

"Leave the pot," Quill said not looking up from the paper.

"Yes, sir."

When they were alone, he snapped the pages of the newspaper shut and put it on the table beside him. His plate was already empty. He hadn't bothered waiting for her.

"As soon as you've eaten, we're going to start working in the gallery," he said.

Saskia's heart leapt into her throat. "You're going to paint me again?"

He rolled his eyes. "Of course I'll be painting you again, but that's not what I meant. We're going to work on *your* work. You will paint. I will instruct you and observe."

"Oh."

"Yes. Oh."

Saskia put a bit of butter on her croissant and let it melt into the bread while she ate her eggs.

"And Saskia?"

"Yes, Master?"

"Please do not disturb Marcus like that again in the mornings. He works long hours and needs to be rested to properly care for you at night."

Had one of the servants told him? Maybe she hadn't been as sneaky as she'd thought. Or perhaps he had a tiny screen upon which he watched and tracked her every movement.

She expected some punishment to be announced. But he simply drank his coffee and waited for her to finish the food on her plate.

After breakfast, Quill took her back to the gallery. Unexpectedly, he picked Saskia up and sat her on top of the cage she'd slept in. He unbuckled the straps on the gold shoes and slipped them off her feet.

"You can't paint in these."

Saskia may have fantasized about being in Joseph Quill's bed—of being his muse—but if she were honest, she'd fantasized even more about being taught by him in a studio.

The latter had felt sillier and somehow more embarrassing because of its unlikelihood. She could imagine him fucking her, even painting her. But the idea that he'd take her artistic ambitions seriously enough to waste precious hours of his time teaching her seemed absurd.

He helped her off the cage and led her to the studio. "Stay here. And don't touch anything until I return."

Saskia took a moment to fully appreciate the space. The last times she'd been in this room she'd been too consumed with anxiety to fully absorb it all.

The evergreens outside stood like distant sentinels. The trees were a narrower fir that didn't bush out unnecessarily. Even so, they were far enough away not to cast shadow directly into the studio. Except for a few trailing vines that grew over parts of the glass walls and ceiling, it was full, unobstructed natural light on the southern-most end of the property. Quill must have liked to paint in the mornings. This was the best time to get the cleanest light from this angle.

The wall that connected with the rest of the building had a large stainless steel sink. There were endless rows of brushes and tubes of paint and sticks of charcoal of varying hardness. All of it was kept in containers, coded by color.

She couldn't believe how organized he was. She'd always been a messier painter.

The small room in her apartment she'd used to paint in stayed a disaster as if a powerful storm had just blown through. She probably spent more time hunting for a tube of cadmium red than she did putting the damned pigment on the canvas.

Quill returned with a brush and a hair elastic. "Turn around."

When she turned, he brushed her hair and pulled it back into a low ponytail. He set the brush down on an island counter that was built into the floor near one of the glass walls. He retrieved an artist's smock from a hook in the corner.

It was huge—made for a man. It was already covered in paint, and she found herself wondering if she'd seen any of the paintings that had been brought into the world while leaving all these stains. Despite how organized and clean he kept his studio when not in use, he wasn't nearly so pristine in the act of creation. That made her feel a little better about things.

Quill helped her into the long white shirt and buttoned it up, concealing her sundress beneath it. "Now you're all safe," he said, smoothing the fabric, his hands lingering over her breasts.

If only.

"Where are the turps?" Saskia asked, wondering about the absence of the turpentine. Something had felt off about this room. The distinctive odor she'd come to associate so strongly with oil painting wasn't there. Maybe he used odorless mineral spirits or had exceptionally good ventilation. Now that she thought of it, she hadn't noticed the smell in the gallery while he'd been painting her, either.

Quill began to lay out paints and brushes. "I don't use turpentine or other harsh solvents. I'm going to teach you to paint solvent-free so you can still breathe when you're ninety."

"But you can't paint without solvents," Saskia said, starting to doubt her own knowledge even as she said it. After all, if he painted that way, it was clearly possible. She'd seen his work.

He laughed. "It's true, you do need something to thin your paint and to clean your brushes, but you can do it in a less harmful way. These harsh chemical solvents are a solution looking for a problem if you ask me. We'll use linseed oil, sometimes walnut oil or a little spike lavender oil. Though you won't need very much. I use very high quality paints with high pigment loads. You'll find, the higher quality your paints, the less you have to mess with them to get the desired effect. You can use walnut oil and artist soap to clean your brushes. And we'll use palette paper. I find the mess of palettes completely ridiculous."

Once all the paints and brushes were out, he took a clean canvas from one corner of the room. It wasn't pre-stretched, Saskia could tell by looking at it. He'd stretched and prepared the canvas himself.

"Won't it hurt the brushes to clean them that way?" Saskia asked, still not sure she could wrap her mind around his methods, even if they did make sense, and she *would* like to breathe clean air while she painted. It was the only thing she'd hated about oils.

Quill raised an eyebrow. "Really? You think turpentine is gentle on brushes? And no, it won't hurt them. But even if it would, brushes are cheap in comparison to your health. You can always buy more brushes."

No, *he* could always buy more brushes. But she was in his world of *nothing but the best* now. If he wanted to supply her with ridiculously high quality art supplies, she probably shouldn't try to talk him out of it. Saskia didn't know what compelled her to keep pushing, but now that she was on a roll, she couldn't seem to stop. "I thought you wanted me to suffer for my art."

He was becoming clearly exasperated now, and she wondered if she'd gone too far. Maybe the plan for the day would change to punishment instead of painting if she continued to be so belligerent.

"I don't want you to suffer, Saskia. I want you to have an experience and a feeling deep enough and raw enough so you can translate it to a canvas and make collectors care. Otherwise no one will give a shit about you. There are too many artists, and the world doesn't care that you want to be one, too."

He really wanted to teach her.

She let that thought settle in her mind for a moment. He wanted to paint her. And he wanted to teach her. Maybe he also wanted to punish her, but that motivation seemed a distant third to the other two things. Even the idea that punishing her was little more than background for the art felt like too much to hope for.

"Okay, but won't it take forever to dry, thinning the paint that way?"

Quill laughed again, this time more of a deep rumbling chuckle. At least she amused him. "You certainly do have a deep-running masochism, don't you? It can, yes. There are simple ways around that, but it won't be necessary. We'll be painting wet-on-wet."

"But I can't paint that way."

"You can't paint that way, *yet*," he said.

Quill took a large portfolio from beside the wall where all the art supplies were stacked and organized. Saskia hadn't noticed it leaning there before. Or if she had, she hadn't given it any thought. It had been just more background shrubbery in Quill's artistic landscape. He laid the portfolio on top of the island.

Saskia gasped when he opened it. "Where? How?"

This was *her* work. Work she thought she'd lost in the fire. All that had remained in her cramped bedroom studio had been charred remains.

"I don't understand. Were you following me? Did you set the fire?" Her hands clenched at her sides as tears of rage moved down her face. If she were looking for the

thing that could finally wake her up and make her hate
him, this might be it.

"I didn't set the fire. How could you think that?"

"I honestly don't know what the hell you're capable
of. And it scares the shit out of me." She edged closer.
The paper and canvas were unmarred. There was no
sign any fire had ever happened. In the portfolio were
charcoal sketches, some watercolors, some paintings in
both oil and acrylic on canvas board. It was less expensive than pre-stretched and primed canvas, and she
didn't have the tools or help she needed to stretch her
own. Something on canvas board was unlikely to ever
sell or hang in a gallery, but who was she kidding
anyway?

There were landscapes, portraits, still lifes. She'd
dabbled in a bit of everything except modern abstract,
trying to find her way, figure out who she was and what it
was that she wanted to paint. She'd even done a few
pieces that mimicked Quill's style and subject matter.
And, of course, the fire had spared it to mortify her later.

"I couldn't save everything, but I got what I could
before the fire got out of control."

Saskia gaped at him, certain the confusion had tied
her face into knots. He couldn't have this stuff. He didn't
know her then.

Quill sighed. "After the night you met Derick, I kept
tabs on you."

"You mean stalked me. Just say stalked."

"I mean it's complicated. You thought my assistant
was me. I couldn't tell you the truth. I saw some of your
work and thought you had potential, that I'd like to
mentor you."

Was that what he called all this? Mentoring?

"I was deciding how I wanted to handle things. You were out. Your idiot neighbor on the main level under you had an electrical fire. I knew your place was next. I climbed the trellis, busted the window, and took everything I could save."

Well, that explained some things. Given the origination of the fire, the busted window hadn't made much sense to anyone. The fire department had utilized it for their purposes, but swore up and down they hadn't done the damage themselves. And in all the chaos and destruction, the police had never gotten any clean prints.

"You couldn't have given me my stuff then?"

Quill laughed. "Right. And how would that conversation go down? 'So, I've been stalking you off and on for a while and happened to notice your apartment going up in flames. Here's your art.' The media would have had a field day with that."

So he was admitting to the stalking.

Saskia thumbed through her work again as if she couldn't believe it was all really here. "I *mourned* this stuff. Of all people, as an artist... you should understand what I went through thinking I'd lost everything. I couldn't bring myself to paint anything new after that."

"I know."

"And then, before the fake heist, you had the gall to ask me why I didn't do original work when you knew why!"

"I didn't know. I suspected."

"So, after the fire, you bumped into me on purpose at that party when I was drunk?"

"Guilty."

"Did you set me up to con you so you'd have some-thing to hang over my head? So you could coerce me into your bed... I'm sorry, *cage*, since you won't let me fucking sleep in the bed!"

Quill's eyes narrowed. "Careful, Saskia. I'm being generous with you. You should be lashed for this much disrespect. And you give me far too much credit. I had no idea you were planning to fake the theft and run off with my money. That was just a stroke of luck. But I realized you had before I let you leave my house that night. I chose to wait and consider my next move."

He sure liked to wait and consider things.

At the very least he'd been positioning himself to get close to her for clearly nefarious reasons.

"You could have met me in a sane way and asked me out. You knew how I worshiped you. You knew I'd go for this. I would have gone for anything you suggested if you'd asked like a civilized human."

"I didn't know that. I didn't see you at any clubs or parties. I didn't know you were into the things I'm into."

"But you knew I was into your art. That wasn't enough?"

"Not really." Quill began to close the distance between them. "Either way, let's say I met you in some normal way, asked you out, started some kink thing. We're all painting and happy together and all of that nonsense, and then one day it's too much for you and you leave. Like *she* did."

"Oh, anything to justify your felony."

"Glass houses," he said unperturbed by her accusation.

"Do you know what I think?"

"No, but *I* think you should be careful with that mouth."

Saskia ignored the warning. "I think you don't want something consensual. I think you just wanted what you wanted. Just like you wanted to take that painting from the Raine Estate when they wouldn't sell it. You think everything is for sale. And if it isn't, you'll just take it."

"It's been working for me so far." Quill stood mere inches from her. He dragged his finger across the front edge of her collar. His voice dropped an octave. "Tell me who you belong to."

She just stared at him.

"Tell me, Saskia!"

She shook her head.

"You fought to stay with me last night."

Already everything at that weird isolated club felt like a blur. Or a dream.

"Because I'm a starstruck little idiot!"

"Still. It meant something that you did it. And I told you there was no going back. So you may as well get over this snit. *Who* do you belong to?"

She didn't know why she was upset with him. He'd saved her work. Not all of it, but most of it. She thought she'd never see *any* of it again. Maybe it was that a small piece at a time he kept breaking apart her image of him. He'd been this lofty untouchable artist. She hadn't wanted to learn he was just a man. And not the nicest one sometimes. But at other times...

Beyond that, he'd set up this fucked-up scenario, and a part of her thought all of this was a lie as well. She wasn't his. She'd never really be his—even though some destroyed part of her that she didn't want to think about still kind of wanted it. To be his. The ground under her feet didn't feel solid anymore.

"Do you think this is a game, Saskia?"

"Yes. I very much do. I think you're rich and bored, and playing with people's lives is what gives you a buzz. I think you'll drop me off in a gutter somewhere the moment you grow restless again. And God help me if I ever actually feel something beyond this childish crush for you."

"*She* abandoned *me*. Not the other way around," Quill said.

The mystery woman in those early paintings. The only one with a jeweled collar. She was an enigmatic Mona Lisa, and Saskia was sure he'd never utter her name—as if he'd sworn some blood oath to never allow that word to caress the air around him again.

He pulled Saskia away from her salvaged art and pushed her back on the chaise. He stood straddling her, holding her down against the furniture. "Let me take away your foolish illusions. You know far too much you shouldn't know. You have information that could destroy my company before the next opening stock bell rang. More than that, you could have me behind bars."

"I thought you said you wouldn't go to prison, but I would."

"That fucking mouth," he hissed. "If it's the last thing I do, I will fix that fucking mouth. I said I probably wouldn't go to prison. But that was about the art theft, not keeping you here as my slave. There is no way out with me, and you don't want there to be. You love the fucking cage I've put you in. Admit it."

"Fuck you." She knew she was pushing his buttons,

and a part of her was afraid he'd just haul right off and slap her. She'd seen that look in his eyes. He was already holding back, but she just kept pushing. And she wasn't even sure what she was pushing for. Or why.

But all he did was arch that smug perfect brow. "I said not until you beg. That wasn't nearly sweet enough for begging."

Quill got off her and backed up a few feet, giving her space. "Come with me."

"W-where are we going?"

"We're going to teach you who you motherfucking belong to, and if after this point you ever forget again and refuse me the title I demanded, there will be hell to pay."

"Master, I'm sorry."

Quill laughed in response. "A few seconds too late, I'm afraid."

He dragged her into the large, open gallery. This time they bypassed the columns with the attached shackles. Instead, he led her to a piece of sex furniture at the north end. It was made of dark stained wood and soft black leather. It looked a like a spanking horse, except the angles were all wrong and part of the furniture dipped in a way that wouldn't work lying across it on her stomach.

She eyed it skeptically but didn't say another word as he unbuttoned the artist's smock he'd just put on her and removed her dress. Silent tears slipped down her cheeks.

What if he decided not to teach her? She'd been so close to the dream of one-on-one instruction from Joseph Quill. *That fucking mouth* was right. If not for her smart mouth, they'd be painting right now. After all the drama, who knew if he'd still consider her worth the effort to train her in any art beyond being his slave.

"I'm not punishing you, so you may as well put those tears away."

The only consolation was that he didn't know the real reason she was crying.

"You're not?"

"No. It's been a fast-paced few days, and it occurs to me that you haven't had the opportunity to really understand this. Given the unusual nature of things..."

False imprisonment. Coercion. Threats.

"... I've gone a bit off script."

Was that a good thing or a bad thing? It was hard to know with him.

He stepped back and appraised her. She knew from the way he looked at her that he couldn't escape the desire to have her in the best light, from the best angle— the artist in him constantly setting up the next piece he might paint.

Quill pointed at the furniture. "Sit on it, facing me."

Oh. Now it made sense. The small concave space of leather was meant for her to sit on.

"Spread," he said.

Two short, narrow padded benches protruded from the sides of the concave space, meant for her to straddle in a sense. It was something like gynecological exam stirrups, except without the stirrups. Her feet rested on another piece of padded leather that came out from the bottom of each side.

Metal cuffs were built into the furniture, and Quill wasted no time locking them around her ankles. The design of the furniture made her body spread wider than she'd thought possible.

"Are you in pain?" he asked.

"No, Master. I just feel really stretched." *Like one of your canvases.* Was that the point?

"Good. Stretching is good for you." He took her arms and crossed them directly over her head to bind them with the cuffs coming out from the top.

She wasn't lying flat, but was instead arched at a small angle so she could see him without straining or craning her neck.

Quill dragged his box of terrible wrong things from the other side of the gallery where he'd last used it, making sure to put it behind the furniture she was strapped down to, obstructing her view.

But that wasn't enough for him. He took a strip of black silk from the box and blindfolded her.

She felt more vulnerable than she'd ever felt, exposed and open to him, unable to even know what to flinch from.

"I-I thought you said you weren't going to punish me."

"I'm not. But I still don't want you to see what's coming next. It kills the experience. Just trust me."

She snorted at that, and he smacked her thigh in response.

"Don't make me change my mind about punishment."

They hadn't started this from a place of trust, so how could he possibly think they could end there? Between her con and him taking her as property in retaliation, how could this ever end well? It was hardly a Meet Cute story.

In a warped way, she understood how losing his muse might make him avoid attachment or connection with women. And once he'd decided he wanted Saskia, it was also easy to see how he'd chosen this course to secure it.

He didn't want a repeat of the mystery woman, and he seemed willing to do whatever it took—however extreme and immoral—to prevent that unsavory outcome a second time. Despite how he'd acquired her or how he kept her, when his hands were on her, she wanted them there.

Saskia tensed when something soft began stroking her skin, starting with her neck, then moving slowly downward over her body. She relaxed when she realized it was a dry paint brush. When she concentrated, she could see it in her mind. It was a very large, soft-bristled fan brush. It could be used in landscapes to cover an oversized canvas. She imagined giant, lush green bushes might be painted on an enormous mural with such a brush.

But Quill wasn't a landscape guy. He'd obviously bought this brush only for the purpose he used it for now.

These brushstrokes didn't feel like foreplay meant to arouse her, although it was beginning to. Instead, she felt what it must be like to *be* his canvas. Each stroke was deliberate, focused. Some strokes long, some short, moving over her body the same way he moved over his paintings as he worked.

Saskia jerked in her bonds when he brushed over the top of her foot.

"Ticklish here?"

"Yes, Master."

He didn't comment further, but he didn't stop his meticulous torment either. He avoided her face and the place between her legs. When he'd given her the sensation of being total painted—save for the small details—he put the brush away.

A much smaller fan brush—just as soft—fluttered over the contours of her face around the blindfold. It gently caressed her cheeks, the tip of her nose, her lips. Then that same brush moved southward, in one long stroke down the length of her throat, stopping to tease over each of her nipples.

Then the brush resumed its trail down over her belly and to her mons. She writhed as the brush carefully stroked over each line and curve, each fold of flesh blooming with arousal and need in response.

"Please," she whimpered.

His mouth moved to her ear. "Shhhhh." The smaller brush clattered inside the box.

There was the rumbling sound of things being jumbled around and a plastic bottle of something being squeezed of some of its contents.

When he returned, his finger circled her clit in a careful pattern. She was already wet, but the cold lube from his finger joined her natural moisture as he stroked her. She arched up toward him, and the moment she did, he slipped something hard and lubricated into her ass.

She cried out in shock, not expecting the penetration. She'd thought that entrance safe, but he'd drawn and lured her into raising her ass off the seat, angled toward him, her dripping cunt begging... allowing him to seat the butt plug inside her with little trouble.

"Breathe. You'll adjust to it. It's not very big."

That was a matter of opinion.

"A-are you going to fuck me there, Master?" Why else would he seek to stretch her this way?

"No. Even I'm not that cruel. I am plenty aware of my girth."

Any opportunity to brag.

"Just relax, I'm keeping it there until I'm done with you, so you may as well get used to it."

Quill's focus returned to her clit, rubbing the swollen bud until she arched again and came for him.

He massaged her breasts. Each one fit neatly inside his large hands as if she'd been designed specifically for him to fondle. He sucked each nipple into his mouth until they hardened into points. She arched toward him, pulling against the restraints that held her wrists tight over her head.

He stroked the side of her face. "I love how you respond to me."

She whimpered in reply. He was right. So much had happened in such a short period. And he'd spent more time isolating her or sharing her or punishing her than anything else. She hadn't known what pleasure from his hand would be like.

She could finally empathize with the women who'd been lured into his bed.

She'd thought surely he must be a selfish lover from the way he'd denied her. But now, the careful attention he paid to each inch of her body unsettled everything she'd believed until this point. No truth ever stayed bolted down for long with Quill. There was always a new layer to pull away. Some of them made her hate him, and some of them only made her want him more.

A desperate mewling sound left her mouth when he pulled away from her. Moments later, she heard buzzing. He pressed the vibrator against her nipples as if to give her a sense of it. It had a small rounded tip, meant to stimulate externally only. She found herself disappointed it wasn't something larger—something meant for penetration. She needed a full thick cock so much she was practically salivating for it.

With the blindfold covering her eyes, the only images she could see in her mental field of vision were dicks and phallic-shaped objects. It was like a sexual acid trip. She didn't feel real. Nothing felt real except the need.

He moved the vibrator between her legs, dragging the tip over her labia, circling back each time to her clit, then away, then back. Driving her insane. Which was probably his intent.

She might need regular psychotropic medication just from her interactions with him.

When he allowed her to come again, the sounds emitting from her throat were nothing short of a primal scream.

As soon as her orgasm ran its course, he went back to the box. She tensed when she heard the rumbling of the search, still not convinced pain wasn't coming. Maybe he'd lulled her into a false sense of safety with plans to rip her out of it more violently later.

First a gasp, then a deep moan left her as a hard glass

dildo started moving in and out of her. She was so wet by now that it made an embarrassing sloshing sound.

"Yes, you *should* blush," Quill said. "Such a filthy sexual animal. You may as well be rutting in a cornfield somewhere."

And those words.

Those fucking evil words just made her wetter and hotter for him. And he knew it. There was no mistake as the sound grew more intense. She lifted her hips trying to gain deeper penetration. It was smaller than the toy from his office, which only made her want his cock instead of this lesser substitution. And she was sure he knew that. She was convinced by now that he knew everything.

Slowly in. Out. In. Out. Like yogic breathing or gentle waves beating the shore at low tide. He pulled another orgasm from her this way... a deeper one, one that erupted from inside and flowed outward. When he touched her clit, she wanted penetration. When he penetrated her, she wanted him to touch her clit. He alternated back and forth between the two forcing her body to accept orgasm over and over in whichever way he chose to deliver it.

He never told her how many times he'd make her come. She never asked him to stop because he always switched the stimulation to a less sensitive area long enough for her to recover.

Suddenly something hard and plastic prodded at her mouth.

"It's water. Drink. You're going to fucking dehydrate at this rate." As if this were her fault.

Saskia gratefully drank down the water as he tipped the bottle back for her.

When she was finished, he went back to the vibrator, focusing it in intense circles in exactly the right spot. She was on the edge again when he stopped, and the buzzing stopped.

She squirmed, shamelessly humping the air. "Please..."

He removed the blindfold. Was he done with her? What about his needs? She could now see the impressive erection straining against the fabric of his pants. She couldn't believe how badly she wanted it inside her.

"Please, Quill... please fuck me... I need..."

He froze. "What did you just call me?"

"I'm sorry, Master." Saskia looked away, sure her face must be bright red. She couldn't believe she'd called him that out loud.

He chuckled, an amused sparkle in his eyes. "That's fucking adorable, but it's your last slip-up. You absolutely can never call me that in public."

"Y-yes, Master."

"So that's the version of me you've settled on. That's who you see me as in your head. I suspected it would be. It's the only way any of this can be okay for you isn't it?"

"Yes, Master."

He nodded. "So tell me... Who do you belong to?"

"You, Master. You. Please fuck me... please," she whimpered. It was so pathetic that if she'd had any shame left she surely would have died of it.

Quill crossed his arms over his chest and regarded her seriously. "No. Not yet. I told you. You haven't begged enough yet. But I won't leave you completely frustrated."

He turned the vibrator back on. "I want your eyes on mine this time. I want you with me while this happens, okay?"

"Y-yes, Master."

It was more difficult than she imagined to hold his stern gaze as the vibrator caressed the bundle of nerves between her thighs. The blindfold had been a sort of mercy. Closing her eyes would have been equally kind.

But he refused to let her hide from him. As if she weren't already as open to him as she could possibly be —he wanted her with him mentally and emotionally. Simple eye contact was the most naked of all the things he'd demanded of her.

The instinct to close her eyes to seek some private shelter in which to find her pleasure was strong, but she forced herself to hold his gaze as she came again.

"Good girl," he said as he turned off the vibrator.

Saskia's panting breath slowly resumed its normal cadence. She couldn't stop the words that spilled out next. "I don't understand why you won't fuck me. Do you not want me? Don't you find me attractive?"

God, was she *really* doing this? Was this his plan? Play on her insecurities? If so, it was working. Perhaps too well. She'd been so busy being half afraid he'd rape her that she hadn't been prepared for this utter rejection. She'd thought she'd have to steel herself against the idea of him fucking her because there still existed a hollow echo of the way she'd seen him when he was just a too-rich business man who always got his way.

Instead, she was begging for it. Just like he'd promised she would. Yet somehow she'd believed he was all talk, that she might have to beg in some token way, and then he'd fuck her. She hadn't even believed she'd be safe from his cock if she chose not to beg. She thought he just had that much ego.

He *did* have that much ego, but she kept falling into it and rolling around in it like a wanton whore.

"Yes, Saskia, I find you very attractive. But despite all other evidence, I'm not an animal. And I said I would own you. I didn't mean I would just control you physically and restrain and imprison you. I meant I would *own* you. I said you would beg and worship my cock. And I've decided it's not time to fuck you yet. When I decide it's time, you'll be the first to know."

"But... I don't understand why you don't just take it...how can you...?"

"How can I resist you? My, what a high opinion we have of ourselves. I get all of my needs met. Don't worry."

Somehow it hadn't occurred to her that he was fucking other women. Of course he could hold out indefinitely with her if that were the case. He could torture and tease her forever and never give her the filling penetration she so urgently needed now.

She wasn't his only source of pussy.

But hadn't she seen that was the situation with her own eyes at the club? He hadn't been fucking those two girls, but that didn't mean he hadn't planned to. He'd just been interrupted.

And with her sleeping in the cage in the gallery, anyone might be warming his bed at night.

She felt suddenly more exposed lying as she was, spread open before him, evidence of her pleasure sliding down her thighs. While he rejected her.

"Jealous?" he asked.

She looked away.

Quill moved closer until he stood just over her. The fabric of his pants brushed the insides of her thighs. Her gaze slid involuntarily to the bulge in those pants.

He took her chin in his hand and raised her gaze to his. "It is not your concern who I fuck. You belong to me, not the other way around. Is that understood?"

"Yes, Master."

"Good girl."

She glanced back to his erection. "But don't you at least want...?"

He smiled that dark smile. "Don't I at least want what?"

Saskia licked her lips. "Can I? Um... please can I... help you out there?"

He smirked. "Not right now. We have a lot to accomplish today, and we've wasted far too much time already. Contrary to what young men may have told you to get inside your panties, we really won't die if we don't fuck something."

Quill removed the butt plug. Saskia had somehow forgotten it was there. She'd been too distracted by the endless pleasure to be concerned about a little mild anal penetration.

He unlocked the cuffs around her wrists and ankles and pocketed the key. "Now, pull yourself together, get dressed, and come back to the studio. We have a lot of work ahead of us."

He left her and shut himself in the bathroom. From this end of the gallery, she could hear the shower water running. Saskia was sure he was jerking off in there and found herself strangely jealous of his hand.

11

Saskia's hand was cramping by the time they'd finished painting for the day. She lay back on the chaise while Quill straightened the space. It didn't matter how much they'd worked; he wasn't willing to let the studio turn into her own personal hurricane.

"Stay here," he said when all the tubes of paint were closed and put away and the brushes had been cleaned.

She was only too happy to comply. They'd taken a brief break for lunch and another for dinner, but both had been hurried. No words had passed between them in the dining room as they'd eaten. There had been no time for anything fancy for lunch. Just sandwiches. One of the servants had somehow gotten him to sit still long enough for roasted chicken when dinnertime came but only because it was done and ready to put on the table when he reached the dining room.

There was an intensity about Quill while he was in this art zone. Saskia had never seen anything like it.

Once they'd started sketching and painting, sex wasn't a thing that existed for him.

There was no innuendo, no inappropriate touches. It was as if everything that had happened before in the gallery had been a mere mirage. She was sure if she asked him about it, he'd tell her she was crazy, that it had never happened.

How could he flip a switch and compartmentalize all of that? As much as he liked his kink, art came first. If she wanted to be jealous of something, it should be the art. The art was his first love, and Saskia would never unseat her.

When Saskia stood behind a canvas with a brush in hand, she was just his student. All he cared about were the colors, the brush strokes, and bleeding her soul out with carefully mixed pigments for the consumption of the masses. Or that was the hope, anyway—that the masses would consume.

Nothing could sway his focus from trying to teach her to somehow translate all the things pent up inside her onto canvas.

She'd had no idea what she would paint until she started. Saskia closed her eyes, remembering what Quill had said in the studio.

"You don't decide what to paint. The subject picks you. What's inside you? What are you consumed with?"

"I don't know."

"You know. Put it on the canvas."

She hesitated.

"I need to sketch it first."

"I don't care what you need to do. Do it. Stop holding back. You have so much promise. It's all there in your portfo-

lio, you have to stop painting what you think the world wants to see and start painting what you actually have to say. No one in this world gives a shit about your hollow fakery. Least of all, me."

She'd been so intimidated by his technique. She knew even beginning painters could learn to paint wet-on-wet, and she could do it if someone held her hand step-by-step and gave her something specific to paint and walked her through it. But she just couldn't see a painting that way. She couldn't think that fast. Quill had confirmed that the thinking has to happen first, because when the paint is out, it's too late to think. The luxury of slow-drying paint is necessary in wet-on-wet. But even that can only go so far.

The Italian word for the technique was *alla prima,* which means: at first attempt. The idea of painting something *right* the first time in a single session or a couple of them stretched over two days at most—and that only if the paint dried slowly enough—intimidated the hell out of her. And it didn't help with the artist she worshiped hovering over her. She was sure he would be more impressed with her if he'd let her paint the traditional way she was used to. Many layers... letting each dry in between. Then she could take days, weeks, months, a year or more if she wanted on a single painting. It was so much less pressure.

"No, you're overworking the brush. The colors are going all muddy," he said.

"I can't do it this way!"

"Of course you can. This is a single afternoon. Do you think I learned to paint like I paint in a single afternoon?"

"No, but... I've been to art school. I've been painting for years."

"Not the right way. As far as I'm concerned you're starting from scratch."

"Are you implying alla prima is the only right way to paint?"

"Of course not, but if you have to let every layer dry, you're stretching out the learning curve. You have to paint a lot to become great. You have to practice. The only way to do that with your technique and to actually progress at a reasonable rate is to have ten or more paintings going at once. And you'll see uneven progress that way. If you will just try it my way, in a few weeks it will feel natural. And you'll be able to produce far more work. I'll walk you through it."

Saskia's gaze drifted to her new work drying on the easel. It was a scene from the club they'd been at the previous night—everything she could call forth from memory of the rows of bird cages with women inside.

Yes, he'd held her hand and walked her through each step of blocking things out and what to paint on top of what and when. The hardest part was not muddying the colors because she was used to not having to worry about that much at all. She disagreed with him that they were starting at square one. After all, she'd learned to draw in art school. She'd learned color mixing and canvas prepping and brush strokes. She'd been briefly taught wet-on-wet, but admittedly her instructor in that technique hadn't been very good at teaching it. Not like Quill was. He seemed to anticipate her every question and frustration moments before she reached it.

She hadn't been able to remember the women clearly

enough to paint them right because she'd had a hard time looking at them. The faces she painted instead were generic, invented in her mind. But even then... she'd been away from her own work for too long. Outside of forgeries, she was out of the practice of calling a vision forth from absolutely nothing and turning it into something worth looking at.

"It's a start," Quill said, as he studied the finished piece hours after she'd blocked in the first bird cage. "We have a long road ahead of us, but it's something. No promises, but I think I can work with this."

At least he got to paint a live person in front of him. Creating someone from imagination or re-creating them from a snapshot in one's mind was a whole other skill set. He expected too much from her. He was the one with the track record—proof the world cared about his work. Saskia had no such encouragement beyond his word that it was inside her. But how could he possibly know what was inside her when she wasn't sure herself?

Quill returned with a cloth-covered first-aid wrap with a clay pack inside. He wound the cold pack around her hand. "I realize that was more than you expected to do today. I'll try not to go so hard on you in the future. I know it's been a long time for you." He bent to stroke the side of her face. "It's been a long time for me, too."

He could fuck or play with a hundred women, but painting together was an intimacy he couldn't and wouldn't replace with another. It didn't come close to forgiving the stalking, but a part of her understood the longing he'd felt to connect with someone on that level. To find someone to create with. In a way it was what everyone else did. Only others created babies, while she and Quill made art.

She still couldn't believe the first thing he'd painted after such a long hiatus, had been her. It was right out of her silly daydreams.

"Rest your hand. Marcus is on his way to take care of you for the night."

Quill paused in the door on his way out. "For what it's worth, I think you're on to the right subject matter. I just don't think you're giving me everything. You're playing too safe. You're not *saying* anything. I don't feel anything from you. You're just documenting. Learning a new technique aside, what you gave me today is not the kind of thing that can make your name. You have to be willing to give more. I guess the real question is, how badly do you want it, Saskia?"

He didn't wait for an answer. If someone had asked her five years ago what she wanted, the answer would have been easy: To meet Joseph Quill. To paint like him. To become an artist who could live off her work while she was actually still living.

Like him.

Even if it turned out that most of his money came from running a tech company, it was still clear from the extraordinarily high prices his work fetched that he could have lived easily on just his painting if he'd wanted to. Though perhaps not to the same degree of comfort he enjoyed now as a *dead artist*. Or a living tech tycoon.

He certainly wasn't the only artist who hadn't had to become a pretty corpse before making it, but he was the one whose work excited her the most—who most closely echoed what she wanted to be. With all her still lifes and innocent portraits and landscapes, she'd been dancing around the things she really wanted to paint. She wanted to paint the darkness, not the light... the shadows under the surface of a civilized world barely contained by rule of law.

She was afraid to paint the things she felt, to be that exposed on the canvas. Even with the way Quill painted her, it wasn't the same as extracting her own soul by her own hand and allowing others to see. It felt like a kind of psychic suicide. Far too dangerous to commit to.

She couldn't give him what he wanted on that canvas. The closest she could get was abandoning sunsets and apples in a bowl. She could only look through a dirt-smudged window and bring back the shifting shadows she saw there. Saskia wasn't sure what it would take to open her soul and set the artist free. But she knew Quill would go to any lengths to bring it out. A thought which both terrified and excited her.

She'd felt his frustration as he'd cleaned the artistic debris. But what did he expect? She was surprised she'd let him in this much. If she'd met him in a normal way and he'd wanted to teach her, this wouldn't have been what she painted. It would have been a flower or a water-fall or something nice and sweet and innocent. Something that could hang in a hotel lobby without fear of the slightest offense.

Not a single person would look at it and panic or clutch at pearls.

Even knowing what he painted, she wouldn't have been able to be so bold if he hadn't already stripped her bare in other ways. It was hard to work up much shame for what she wanted to create after that. It wasn't Quill she worried about seeing her work. It was others.

She jumped when she realized Marcus leaned in the

doorway, quietly watching. He pushed off the door frame and joined her.

"Let me look at that." Marcus unwrapped her hand from the ice pack and pressed lightly against her skin in various places.

Saskia winced.

"These muscles are really tight. Do you want to soak it in the tub in the salts? It might help."

"Yes, sir."

Marcus helped her up and led her back to the bathroom. As water filled the tub he said, "I like your painting."

"Thanks. He doesn't."

"He doesn't know everything. Did you do that from memory?"

She nodded.

"Impressive. You're practically a camera." He must have been to the club before to see the original cages.

Somehow Saskia doubted having such a great visual memory meant much to Quill. A machine could create a photo copy. Copies weren't art. Quill was right. He was being generous. The painting was dead. It had no heart or honesty. It was hours and hours of work that showcased technical skill but no true artistry because she didn't have the courage to say what she felt.

She was afraid for Quill to see how conflicted she was by both the beauty and ugliness of his world. And letting others in was out of the question.

Marcus left her to soak in the tub. When the water turned cool, she drained it and put on a robe that was lying on the bench.

She wasn't convinced Quill even wanted her. If he

did, wouldn't she be in the main house with him in his bed?

The marble sent a rippling chill through her as she walked across it, her feet bare. Marcus sat on a bench outside the main gallery lost inside a book. He slid a bookmark between the pages and laid it beside him.

"It's late. You should try to get some sleep."

"Do I have to sleep in the cage?"

Marcus rose from the bench and moved a stray bit of damp hair behind her ear. "I'm afraid so."

"Do you have to lock me in?"

"Yes. Come on. Don't make a fuss." Marcus took her hand and led her back into the gallery. The painting Quill had done of her the other day already hung on the wall in its own glass case. There was still plenty of empty space in the gallery—room for many more paintings—but she wondered where he would put them when he ran out of wall. Assuming he kept painting her. Maybe he'd run out of interest before he ran out of space.

When she and Marcus reached the cage, he opened the robe and slowly slid it off her shoulders. She had the uncontrollable urge to cross her arms over her chest, but he stopped her.

"No. I want to look at you."

She forced her hands to her sides.

Marcus's finger gently grazed her collarbone. He used both hands to cup her breasts. Then he quite unexpectedly hooked one hand behind her neck and pulled her in for a softly consuming kiss.

When he stepped away, he searched her face. Whatever he was looking for, he seemed to find. "I'm going to finish my book. After that, I'm coming back for you. You'll want to rest while you can."

He opened the cage and motioned her in, locking the door behind her. Saskia stretched out on the bedding and fluffed the pillows.

She thought she'd only closed her eyes for a moment when he returned but if he'd finished his book it must have been hours. He'd still been in the first half when he'd put it down to lock her in the cage.

At first, he didn't speak, and neither did she. She didn't want him to know she was awake. He must have watched her for ten minutes or more before he finally lowered himself onto the ground beside the cage. She arched closer when he stroked her leg, first over the blanket, then underneath it.

Saskia drew in a sharp breath.

"I knew you were awake," Marcus said. "Did you think I'd leave you alone if you were asleep?"

"No, sir."

"Liar." But his tone was light.

She opened her eyes and watched him. She remained curled in the blankets, her head cushioned on the pillows.

"Are you going to open the cage?"

"No. I like you in there. Scoot closer. I want you to move the blankets out of the way and flip over so that you're on your hands and knees. Press yourself against the bars so I don't have to reach for you."

A flutter of excitement shot between her legs as she moved into the requested position.

"You'll need to put your legs through the bars so you can get closer to me."

The black metal bars were cold against her thighs as she pressed against them.

"Lie on the pillows. You'll be here a while."

Saskia pulled the pillows under her and lay down, closing her eyes as Marcus began to caress between her thighs.

As he stroked her, she pressed harder against the bars, so hard, she was sure they would leave red impressions against her skin. She couldn't get close enough to him, and she was convinced he was staying just far enough away that she'd keep pressing harder to reach him and the pleasure he teased her with.

It felt as if days passed while Marcus touched her. He took his time, letting her excitement and arousal build until she was sure the lightest feather touch would send her over the edge. Finally, he let her come.

She stole a glance at him as he licked her juices from his fingers. Then she collapsed in the cage, her breath still heavy and her heartbeat thudding against the pillows.

"My turn," he said.

Saskia let out a pathetic whimper, not having the energy to move that far to the other end of the cage. Marcus came around to the other side nearest her. He unzipped his pants and thrust his already hardened cock through the bars closest to her.

Tentatively she reached for him, remembering how Quill had slapped her hand away and not wanting a repeat performance from Marcus.

"No," he said. "Not your hand. I want that warm, wet mouth. I want you to suck me like I'm the last thing you'll consume."

Saskia scooted closer to him. "I-I don't think he would... I'm not sure that's allowed."

"You're not here to think," he said. "You let me worry about him and what's allowed."

She took him into her mouth and began to gently suck.

SUN STREAMED down from the skylight above, making continued sleep impossible. Saskia stretched in the cage. Her arms reached out between the bars, fingers brushing against a thick piece of paper. She opened her eyes and rolled over to find a charcoal sketch of her sleeping. He'd signed it. A small 'J', a giant 'Q', and then a flourish that was supposed to be the rest of his name.

The woman reflected back to her looked blissed out in a post-orgasmic cat nap. Her body was loose and relaxed, extending the full length of the cage. The sheets had fallen away to reveal a bare hip as well as a breast.

Quill must have returned after she was asleep again and drawn her like this. It was the only work of his she'd ever seen where the subject's eyes didn't pull all the focus. But then her eyes were closed.

It was a snapshot of contentment inside a cage. It was how he saw her despite any outward protest she might seek to make. How easily he seemed to capture and transmit what he wanted to say. It wasn't just a drawing. It spoke the truth as he saw it.

She couldn't decide how she felt about the depiction. Everything about it seemed so incongruent, and yet there she was. She couldn't deny what he'd seen clearly enough to sketch on paper.

It was more than a little disturbing that each time she woke in a cage seemed less upsetting than the time before. Was she becoming acclimated to this confinement? People fought and died for freedom and railed on endlessly about it, but in the end, didn't most find a quiet cage to curl up in, accepting, almost craving some level of restriction? As long as it could be comfortable? Almost everyone preferred safety, no matter what lies passed through their lips. If they wanted freedom so badly, the way they reacted to their various forms of enslavement didn't make any sense.

This sketch sure as hell didn't.

But then, Saskia had just had an orgasm before drifting off, and Marcus had been with her. He'd stayed at least until she'd fallen asleep. Had he been there while Quill sketched her, or had he left the artist alone with his unconscious subject?

Precise footsteps clicked across the floor. Quill. Marcus's stride was much different. Quill moved with a kind of smug entitlement that was hard to fake. She found herself both repulsed and pulled under by his demanding confidence.

"You've got thirty seconds to make a case for why I shouldn't whip the hell out of you for what happened with Marcus last night."

What happened with Marcus? She searched through the mental files in her brain trying to come up with what could have pissed him off so much. He'd obviously seen something from the video feed. Had he watched it before or after he'd sketched her? It had to have been after.

There was an almost tender affection in that drawing. The man looming over her now didn't seem capable of tenderness.

Marcus rushed into the gallery, exhausted from the night shift. "You know that's not her fault."

Quill spun on the guard. "No. It's your fault. I said no fucking, and what did you do?"

"I didn't fuck her!"

"So I just imagined your cock in her mouth? My mistake. It must be my advancing age. Things are so confusing now."

"When you said fucking, it seemed clear to me you meant what normal people think fucking is!"

"I meant I didn't want your cock inside any of her orifices. Perhaps I should have spelled that out better."

"Perhaps you should have. I don't see what difference it makes when you plan to whore her out anyway."

Quill opened the cage and dragged Saskia out. She was still too disoriented to struggle or fight him.

"She was locked in a goddamned cage," Marcus said. "How could she have stopped me? What powers did you give her to protect herself from her bodyguard?"

It was a good question. It was bewildering what he was even guarding her from. Maybe it made sense for Marcus to be there if she needed something, since Quill insisted on this cage business and couldn't be bothered to keep her in his own room. But otherwise, it was doubtful someone would break in to steal her. She wasn't a Monet.

A light bulb seemed to appear all at once over Marcus's head. "Oh. I see what this is, what you're doing. You think I'll volunteer to take her place. And Saskia seeing the gory mess unfold will somehow be even worse for her. You just love fucking with people, don't you?"

"You think I'd whip you instead?" Quill asked, amusement threading his voice.

"Hell yes, I do. I think you've been setting me up from the beginning because you want me back in your chains."

Saskia's eyes nearly bugged out of her head as she looked from Quill to Marcus and then back to Quill again. She'd thought the two of them were friends. Surely there had to be something closer than just employer and employee for Quill to share her. It had never seemed like a logical employment perk. But the last thing she'd suspected was that Quill once had something kinky going on with Marcus. Or was she misreading this somehow?

His gaze flicked over the guard in that same proprietary way he so often looked at Saskia. Nope. Not imagining that.

"I've asked, and you've said no. So you won't do it for me, but you'll do it for her?"

"I didn't say I'd do it for her," Marcus said.

Quill sighed, his gaze sliding to Saskia. "It's going to be a brutal day for you, sweetheart. You'll have Marcus to thank for that."

It felt like he had something to prove, and that scared her. She didn't know how bad he might get under those conditions. Quill grabbed her wrist and pushed her against the column. He was about to lock the first shackle when Marcus's voice stopped him.

"You know she didn't do anything wrong. All she has

done since she got here is try to please both of us. She doesn't deserve this."

"I know. Life isn't fair. It's all very sad."

Quill finished locking Saskia into the chains and went for a whip. She jumped when he snapped it in the air for effect.

"Master, please." She'd always had a healthy fear of him, but things had escalated far beyond either healthy or fear. A quiet place inside her head kept whispering he might lose control. She might not get out of these chains. The next box she might occupy might be made of pine rather than black metal bars. "Please," she whimpered.

Saskia couldn't stop the tears or the trembling. He'd whipped her before, but before he'd seemed in control of himself. Right or wrong, he'd had an end game in mind that probably didn't include her death. Now he didn't seem to be thinking beyond the next fifteen seconds or about any consequences which might unfold past that. A lot of permanent damage could occur in just a few seconds with a very strong person wielding a whip and little reason.

"Goddammit!" Marcus said. "Unchain her."

Quill smiled. "So you'll take her punishment?"

"It's intended for me. You just want me to ask for it."

"Good boy," he said, a slow smile spreading across his face. "You still can be taught."

Marcus angrily stripped off his clothes while Quill unchained her and put her back in the cage.

"You will watch, Saskia. You should see firsthand just how kind and patient I've been with you," Quill said.

She scooted back against the far end of the cage and

wrapped herself in the sheets. Marcus seemed resigned to his fate. He wasn't afraid, just pissed off.

He didn't make a sound as the whip came down. Occasionally he flinched, but he wouldn't give Quill the satisfaction of breaking. Not like Saskia had. Quill could turn her into a bundle of trembling nerves and tears with only a few lashes—or even the threat of them. Like today.

Marcus's back muscles clenched. It appeared as if the black dragon would leap off his skin to seek vengeance against Quill. But the large ink reptile kept its fire safely in check.

That awful whip crack echoed off the walls in the gallery without another sound in the world to dampen its thunder. And still, Marcus didn't beg or scream. The only sign he was being hurt at all were a few silent tears that trailed down his cheek and the bright red anger Quill painted across his back.

Saskia counted twenty excruciating lashes. It was obvious Quill held back far less with Marcus than he had with her. He laid the whip down and ran his hands down Marcus's sides, groped his ass, then pressed a possessive kiss against his throat as if he were branding him.

"Tell me how much you miss this," Quill growled against his ear.

Marcus shook his head. "I'm just doing my job. Protecting her."

"How noble. You protect her because I told you to. You need to submit to me like you've always needed it. Even if it's under the guise of *doing your job*."

Quill's hand wrapped around the front of Marcus's

body, and Saskia watched the pumping motion. Even though she couldn't see the erection, it was obvious Marcus was already hard.

"You do miss it. Come for me."

Marcus jerked and let out a groan—the only sound Quill had managed to extract from him the whole time he'd hung in the chains.

"We should get Saskia to lick that up, don't you think?" Quill said.

Marcus just glared.

Quill unlocked the chains and let the other man fall, then he returned to Saskia's cage and opened it.

"He takes care of you. Go take care of him. I'll see you at breakfast."

"M-master, what should I wear?"

He was so particular about everything that she didn't want to risk riling him up even more at the moment.

Quill's gaze panned over her. "I like what you're wearing now."

Nothing.

She swallowed around the hard lump in her throat. "Yes, Master."

Saskia watched his retreat. She didn't dare leave the cage until he was safely outside the building.

Marcus stretched out across the marble, his cheek pressed to the floor as he watched her approach. His breath was still a pant but slowly returning to normal.

"D-do you want me to prepare a bath for you?" Saskia asked.

He nodded, giving no intention he ever planned to move from that spot.

"I can't carry you. Can you make it there on your own?"

"I'm fine, Saskia. It's all surface shit. That bastard hasn't owned me for a long time."

This *surface shit* looked pretty bad to her. Quill had broken skin. Marcus would need to be bandaged up.

"Are you sure you want to soak like this?"

"Put the salts in. It'll help me heal."

She started to cry.

"It's not that bad," he said. "I'm not distraught. There's no reason you should be. You're just playing into his bullshit."

Saskia wiped the tears off her face. "I've played into his bullshit from the moment I knew who he was. He knew I wouldn't be able to resist him if I knew he was Quill."

"This is all a chess game with him. He's always playing six or seven moves ahead. He's patient. God only knows how long he's been jerking off thinking about doing what you just witnessed. You can't let him inside your head."

It might have been nice to have these warnings much earlier—like the day she'd brought the reproduction to the house and first met Marcus. It was far too late for disclaimers. Quill was already deep inside her. And he hadn't even fucked her yet.

12

Marcus let out a pained hiss as he lowered himself into the oversized tub.

"Is the water too hot?"

He shook his head. "It's fine, love." He extended a hand. "You can come join me if you want. There's plenty of room. You don't want to keep him waiting. You clean up while I soak."

She kind of did want to keep him waiting. She was beginning to grow strangely attached to and protective of Marcus, which made it feel like a betrayal to be near Quill. She wasn't sure if she could sit at a table with him and eat breakfast and pretend nothing had happened.

Marcus watched as she got into the tub. "You belong to him. If I ever come between that, it won't be good. For either of us. I can only protect you so far. You have to do the other part by remembering who you prioritize."

Quill was the last person she wanted to prioritize. Of course, that would only remain true until he sucked her into his web again, or painted her or painted *with* her. He made her weak in so many ways.

So much about Marcus made sense now—so much about his reaction to her from day one. She couldn't believe she hadn't picked up the undercurrents between the two men.

Now that Marcus had acclimated to the heat and the sting, he'd closed his eyes, his head resting against the tile. His arms were stretched over the edge of the tub as the steam rose off him. He didn't look like a man who'd just been beaten in her place. Even if physically it might take a bit longer, emotionally he seemed to mend at a speed bordering on supernatural. It may have been a while, but this didn't seem to be an unusual event between them. Quill had just needed an in.

"Sir?"

"Hmmm?"

"Can I ask you a question?"

"You just did." After a long beat of silence, he said, "Go ahead."

"How long did you know what he was planning to do with me?"

He let out a long, resigned sigh as if he'd been waiting for this question. "I didn't know exactly, but I suspected he was planning something early on. I didn't know what, but I knew he was far too obsessed with you." He cracked a grin. "I can't believe you conned him out of all that money. He was mad about it for the first few hours after you left that night, but then I guess his evil plan started forming, which pacified him for a while."

"Were you watching me in Venice?"

"That was my assignment, yes."

"Why didn't you warn me?"

He shrugged. "What attachment did I have to you?"

It felt like a lie, or part of a lie. Had Quill promised him a piece of her that early in the game to gain his enthusiastic surveillance? Marcus had selected that white nightgown so quickly. Had he seen her in it already in the villa? She didn't verbalize any of these questions or thoughts. She didn't want to know. She still wanted to see him as her protector.

She took the bar of soap and a loofah from the tile and began to bathe. If she dragged things on too long, Quill wouldn't be happy. And Marcus was right. That wouldn't end well.

"Why did you let him beat you?" she asked.

Another sigh. This time he opened his eyes and sat up to level a warning look. "This is a lot more than one question."

"I'm sorry."

"If I hadn't, it would have been you. It would have been bad for you, and you didn't deserve it."

"So? What attachment do you have to me?"

His hand dipped under the water to squeeze her thigh. "Let's just say you're growing on me, and I've developed an interest in your welfare."

She tensed, but then relaxed again as he kneaded the muscles in her leg.

"Is Lachlan even his real name?"

Marcus shook his head. "No, but if I told you his real name, what you just witnessed would be mild compared to what he'd do to me. And remember, the great and powerful Oz sees and hears all." He pointed to the camera staring down at them over the tub.

She wasn't sure how, but she'd nearly forgotten the cameras. There was no such thing as a private moment on Quill's property.

"Turn around and let me get your back," Marcus said.

Saskia turned and leaned against the edge of the tub as Marcus's hands moved slowly over her. Her muscles bunched into tight knots as he touched her. She couldn't relax with him again, not after the price he just finished paying for it.

"He's watching this," she whispered.

"Probably," Marcus said. "He likes to watch."

"But aren't you worried...?"

"It was a misunderstanding on the meaning of the word *Fuck*, Saskia. Relax. He's not going to punish me for this. He wants us to bond. He just wants me to remember which one of us is at the top of this food chain. As if I'd ever forget."

Punish. Marcus might not think Quill owned him anymore, but if he thought in those terms—the same terms she thought in—he was already Quill's again. Their master kept them both in a cage with only each other for comfort. And she wasn't convinced he wouldn't make up rules on the fly just so he could take his sadism out on her protector. Marcus seemed much more confident of Quill's inherent sense of fair play than Saskia was.

Marcus rinsed her back. "Okay, you're done."

Saskia got out and grabbed a towel from a shelf.

"Why didn't you just fight him? You could probably take him."

The look Marcus gave her told her everything. He was half in love with Quill, too. And like her, he knew how utterly foolish such feelings were.

"Once he recovered, he would have taken it out on you worse. It was the easiest way to appease him. I'm not that breakable."

No. He wasn't. And underneath the fear for him and the distress, she'd been excited by Marcus's display of strength, as if he could take the whole world on and resurface whole when the debris cleared.

Marcus let the water drain and got out of the tub. Saskia passed him her towel. He wrapped it around his waist and sat on the bench. A brief, cozy domesticity.

"There's a first aid kit in the lower cabinet," he said.

Saskia retrieved the large box of ointment and antiseptic and bandages. Quill's estate was practically its own pharmacy. She opened the container and laid everything on the bench.

Marcus pointed. "The peroxide, then this ointment, and these bandages. They breathe better." Spoken like a man who'd been here before.

He turned away, and Saskia went to work on his back. Marcus was so cavalier about all of it that it was easy to brush off how harsh Quill had been, even now, looking directly at the damage. If it had been her there would have been screaming and endless tears and begging. It would have been impossible to dismiss the weight of it.

Marcus's stoicism made it easy to forget just how raw and broken the skin on his back was—except for the dragon which remained untouched. As out-of-control as Quill had acted, he'd had the presence of mind to avoid the tattoo.

Saskia's fingers trailed over the ink.

"A few years ago he wanted to collar me," Marcus said. "I said *fuck no*. He felt compelled to mark me in some way. We agreed on the ink."

"But that's permanent. You can take a collar off."

"Not while with him, I couldn't. And we see how far I've managed to wander beyond his reach. A collar is too on display for me. Not my thing. This was a compromise I could live with."

It explained why the tattoo had escaped the bite of the whip.

"Why a dragon?"

"It's a subtle reference to a part of his real name. I can probably say that much, at least, without his ire. It's like a *property of* stamp, if we want to be crass about it."

So much more permanent than a collar.

"I thought you said he didn't own you anymore."

Marcus sighed. "In ways he does. In ways he doesn't. Our relationship is complicated, but it's not something you should worry about."

He winced as she dabbed the peroxide on his back.

"I'm sorry."

He squeezed her free hand. "Do what you have to do."

When she'd gotten him bandaged, he returned to the gallery to dress. Saskia followed. Her things were all in a pile of boxes she still hadn't had time to sort through. It wasn't as if the gallery had drawers or closets to stash her stuff. The haphazard way everything was stacked in the gallery made everything feel very temporary. But the heated possessive looks Quill —and sometimes now even Marcus—sent her way, made it feel as if her confinement inside Quill's gallery would stretch the full length of her remaining existence.

Marcus tossed her a robe from one of the boxes. She grabbed the garment out of the air when it reached her and stared at it for a full minute as if it might attack.

"Just wear it to the house. You gotta figure out the loopholes if you're going to make it with him, love."

"Are things going to be weird now?"

He pulled his T-shirt back over his head, careful not to disturb the bandages she'd taped in place. "Weird how?"

"I mean is there going to be jealousy?"

Marcus grinned. "Not from me. I have a feeling you and I are not interchangeable cogs in his machine. But if you get *weird* as you call it, there will be punishment from me. I might not want to hurt you, but you're not going to run over me, either. So don't get any ideas."

"He said you couldn't..."

"He said I couldn't break skin. I can spank you, cane you, and whip you so long as I don't break that rule. And there are many ways to punish a person that don't leave any marks which I'm more than happy to explore with you if necessary."

An electric jolt ran down her spine. "Yes, sir." Getting into a pissing match with him over Quill was the last thing on her mind anyway.

"We better get back to the house."

Inside the large hall of the main house, Marcus

pulled her into an embrace. His lips pressed against the shell of her ear. "Be good. I'll see you tonight."

He drifted off down the hallway toward the room she'd found him sleeping in the day before.

Saskia took a deep breath and dropped the robe before going to meet Quill for breakfast.

He was reading the financial papers again, his breakfast dish already picked clean. The coffee cup moved absently to his lips every few minutes as he scanned the news.

He glanced up. "Come here."

She'd been about to sit, but she abandoned the chair and edged toward him.

"I'm not going to bite you."

His assurance brought little comfort. But when she reached him, he pulled her onto his lap and just held her for several minutes, his fingers trailing through her hair.

"It's important you know that Marcus can be punished as well and that I watch those video feeds."

Lacy came in with an ice pop in hand, gave it to Quill, then left without comment.

Saskia hadn't detected sexual undercurrents between Quill and Lacy—even when she tried looking for them. And she'd tried. But the subtext had always been there with Marcus. It just hadn't occurred to her that Quill liked to play on both sides so she hadn't noticed. Admittedly it was only stereotypes that had prevented her from seeing it. Both of them were so traditionally masculine that it hadn't occurred to her they might have had a sexual past together. She knew there was no universal law that said one or both of them must be stereotypically feminine. That was just her fucked-up lens of things—her own issue to work through.

Whatever was between her master and her guard was something raw and animal and so innately male that it would have been impossible to look away, even if Quill hadn't ordered her to watch it unfold. It wasn't hard to see Marcus's appeal to her master. Someone who could hang in chains and take lash after lash without so much as a peep. No whining or begging or screaming or crying. Sure, Quill might like such desperate displays well enough. But Marcus's ability to take whatever was dished to him without complaint expressed a kind of peaceful strength she both envied and admired.

Quill studied her and stroked her throat as he might stroke a mare he was preparing to ride.

"I noticed in the video that you were able to take Marcus pretty well. He's not unendowed."

Maybe not, but he wasn't as endowed as Quill. Did he think she'd just been pretending he was too much for her to take? Some kind of ego stroke or manipulation on her part?

She wanted to stay furious with him for what had happened in the gallery, but sitting on his lap with his arms around her, his erotically charged energy directed at her... it was hard to maintain those feelings. And if Marcus wasn't upset by any of it... He was right; she had to figure out how to play Quill's game and find all the loopholes if she wanted to survive here.

Quill tore the paper off the ice pop. "Open. You're going to take this. Then you'll take me. If I'm satisfied by both performances, you can have breakfast."

Saskia's lips parted as he slid the ice pop in and out of her mouth, going deeper each time.

"Relax your throat, Miss Roth."

It was perhaps the first time calling her Miss Roth had sent a burst of excitement straight between her legs. She squirmed to try to ease the ache forming within her.

He smacked her thigh. "No. You were very bad. You're going to take care of my terribly fragile bruised artist ego. Or my cock. Whichever. And perhaps you will be allowed pleasure tomorrow or the next day. Everything depends on your progress here."

She allowed the cold treat to cool and then numb the back of her throat until she could take it as far as he wanted without gagging.

"Good girl. Now me."

Saskia slid to the ground under the table between his legs as he undid his pants. She took advantage of the still numb sensation in her throat to take Quill as deeply as she had the ice pop. He let out a pleased groan. His hand pressed against the back of her neck, a gentle intimidation, but he didn't shove her down any harder.

When he came, she swallowed the results of her efforts and he stroked her hair.

"Lacy, Saskia will be having breakfast now," he said loudly enough for her to hear.

Saskia went back to her chair, trying to force the heat from her cheeks.

13

Weeks passed like this, and Saskia forgot the outside world existed. Quill kept her working in the studio nearly every day and long into most nights. He was a man possessed.

They alternated days. One day would be focused on her work. The next, on his. On the days he painted, he chained her up or chained her down—depending upon the apparatus of choice. He'd give her pain then give her pleasure until she was wrung out. Then he would paint the results of what he'd done to her. Each painting he produced seemed to dig deeper and deeper inside her soul, so far that she wasn't sure what she could possibly have left to create her own work with.

Before long, the gallery was filled with her image in oil, somehow more alive than a photograph. Each night, she stared out from between bars in the cage he still made her sleep in at the paintings trapped inside their own cages of glass. Surely they couldn't breathe in there.

But could she out here? Her reality had tilted and turned into a fun house mirror.

Each night, as she was about to drift off, Marcus's strong familiar hands would creep through the bars of the cage to touch her. Her legs would fall open for him; he'd stroke her until she came, and then she'd return the favor. Hand jobs had been deemed acceptable.

After the first few days at the estate, Quill had let her move most of her things into one of the rooms in the main house. She wasn't living in the main house, but at least most of her things were.

A minimal amount of clothing at a time was left for her in the bathroom in what she'd oddly come to think of as *her building* because it certainly wasn't a room or a suite or an apartment. It was just where Quill kept his private collection of art.

It might have taken this full couple of weeks for that reality to sink in—that she existed as part of the collection. And that might be all.

It was her day to paint, which meant nothing but sexual frustration because, to Quill, playing with her was meant only to prepare her to be put on his canvas. It was all work to him—one way or another. With each day he continued to refuse her his bed, she'd grown increasingly convinced he didn't want her that way at all.

Maybe he was just into Marcus. She was sure something was going on between the two of them again. Maybe while she slept. It was hard not to be jealous, no matter what Marcus said about them not being interchangeable cogs. She felt she was nothing *but* interchangeable. Replaceable. Forgettable. Just like everything she painted.

Maybe Quill could close his eyes and imagine her mouth on his cock was Marcus's mouth, but he could never fool himself that way if he fucked her.

Quill looked over her shoulder at the new painting and sighed.

Every time he did that, she deflated a bit more. Somehow, his disapproval each time she painted something new was more humiliating than anything else that had happened between them. At least she was managing the *alla prima* technique admirably. It was just what she painted with it that earned his disdain.

The first week he'd been content with—or at least tolerated—her dark photocopies as she'd begun to think of them. She didn't know why she couldn't let the things inside her out. It was what he wanted, and all she wanted was to please him. She couldn't even fight with that thought anymore. It was too exhausting.

She wanted him to want her. She wanted him to fuck her. She wanted to sleep in his bed. She wanted him to look at her paintings with pride and satisfaction. She wanted him to think her work was brilliant.

Saskia felt as if at some point she'd jumped onto the wrong train, pulled into the wrong station, and then just decided to stay at the new destination, scrapping every other plan she'd made for her life—such that they were.

Quill was the wrong train. But he was the train she so desperately wanted to ride.

She wasn't sure she had the heart to beg him anymore. She couldn't handle more rejection.

He sighed again. "No. Why am I wasting this time on you if you're not going to give me anything?"

He took the canvas off the easel and flung it across

the studio until it hit one of the glass walls, flinging tiny specks of still-wet paint onto both it and the floor.

Saskia slid to the ground and started to cry. "I'm sorry, Master. Maybe it's not in me. I was kidding myself to ever think I could create like you."

In a rare shimmering moment, his expression softened. He sat on the ground beside her, pulling her into his arms. He petted her hair and rested his chin on the top of her head. It was familiar in a way he never allowed himself to be with her.

"If I didn't believe in you, I wouldn't bother. I'm frustrated because I know it *is* in you. But this isn't working."

He got off the ground and picked up the painting to put it with her others. She stayed there, still crying, while he cleaned the mess he'd made as well as the mess she had. He was so particular about his tools and paints that she was almost afraid to ever help him with the clean-up process, afraid he'd snap at her when she put the tube of burnt umber next to the cadmium yellow. He had a system, and even though she'd watched him, she didn't fully understand it or want to do yet another thing wrong to disappoint him.

"I'm sorry this is so hard on you... that I'm so... intense," he said.

Intense. Or abusive. But he was the typical temperamental artist, and no one had ever bothered to rein him in. And it wasn't as if she had the power to. Or the will.

He hadn't mentioned her theft in a while. It had only been a rationalization to do what he would have done anyway. They both knew that. But with her running all over the world throwing around millions of his dollars, he'd been able to more easily pretend this was some sort of justice he was meting out. As if she deserved it. As if stealing a human being and stealing mere money had moral equivalence.

"If I hadn't conned you, would you have still found a way to have me?"

Quill looked up, his head whipping around so quickly, it seemed as if it might pop right off. He'd been standing by the sink, cleaning the brushes.

"Where is this coming from?" he asked, back to practiced indifference.

She shrugged. "I just wondered if this was really all something I brought on myself or if you would have let me go if I'd stolen the painting for you like I promised."

"It makes no difference now, does it? You're here. You picked your course. I picked mine."

But it mattered to her.

He let out a long sigh. "I don't know, Saskia. I'm sure I would have found a way to get what I wanted. You always had a price. I just had to figure out what it was."

He washed his hands with the artist soap and returned to her. He offered a hand, and she took it as he pulled her to her feet.

"I think we need to go out."

"To the club?"

She wasn't sure if she was yet prepared to be back at the club with him. They hadn't returned since that first night. They hadn't even left the house. If she were being honest, she'd developed some cabin fever. And while she was sure Quill had gone out a few times, if he had, he hadn't gone far or been gone very long. He must be as ready to do something else as she was.

"Not the club. Something much better." He took an envelope from his back pocket and gave it to her.

It looked like an invitation to a ball. When Saskia removed the crisp linen card from the envelope, she found her speculation wasn't far off. Another fancy party at a museum in the city.

"It's an opening for a new exhibit. All the top donors will be there, including most of my friends."

It felt as if there was a hidden meaning there, one Saskia thought she knew but decided to pretend she didn't.

Quill continued, "I want you to wear that dark purple gown you wore that night." He meant what she'd worn to Eric Raine's twenty-first birthday party.

"It's been stuffed in a box and hasn't been cleaned..." It was silk. It needed to be dry-cleaned.

"I took care of it earlier today. It's hanging in the bathroom. We all need a night out."

"We all?"

"Marcus is coming."

Of course he was. Why did she have to feel so jealous of and attracted to Marcus at the same time?

SASKIA JUMPED AS champagne flutes clinked and raucous laughter filled the large open space in the museum where the party was being held. The new exhibit was just down the hall.

She was so jumpy. She hadn't been around this many people in a while. But it wasn't as if she'd been isolated from all human contact. There was Marcus and Quill and the servants who drifted in and out at the periphery —most whose names she still didn't know and likely never would at this rate.

They avoided her—probably on direct order from Quill. He might keep secrets from the rest of the world. He might have endless social groups and various aliases within each, but inside his home, there were no secrets. And it was understood no one would cross him there.

Saskia began to wonder if he had horrible secrets on all of those in his employ. Or did he just pay them an astoundingly large sum of money—plenty to keep their mouths shut? Or did he keep them in an orgasmic stupor, falling all over themselves trying to please him like she and Marcus did? Even though Marcus would never fully admit to it.

She took a glass of champagne off a passing tray and glanced around for a sign of Marcus or Quill. One moment they'd been there with her, the next... gone. She knew what they were probably doing, somewhere in some dark corner of the museum. And the jealousy tugged at her again.

She was still surprised he'd brought her out into the open like this among the normals. Didn't he worry she'd say something? Run away? Find a police officer to have him arrested?

But despite Quill's current downplaying of the situation, she knew he could bring out the trump card of her theft at any time. And she was sure he'd meticulously preserved all the evidence. He was smart like that.

And she'd walked on that plane voluntarily. And it wasn't as if she was dirty or had physical signs of damage. She certainly wasn't chained down or locked in a closet. Who would believe her? Wandering around in a fancy dress at a fancy party?

A stranger caught her eye from across the room. He was tall, athletic, blond. He reminded her in a way of Eric Raine, except that his eyes weren't the same guileless blue topaz. They were slate gray, older, wiser, more shrewd. They'd seen things. And she didn't have to use much imagination to figure out what types of things they might have seen—if the way his eyes slid over her curves were any indication.

She looked away, flushed and suddenly very concerned with finding Quill, but this man had long powerful legs and smart but sensible dress shoes, while she was encased in ridiculous heels. They matched the dress perfectly, but good luck escaping any hungry predators. It wasn't as if she could stun them with her impressive color matching and then escape to safety.

"Hello," he said when he reached her. His voice was even more cultured than she expected. Somehow *hello* felt stuffy and formal after the way he'd just visually undressed her. It already seemed they were beyond that. "You belong to Andrew Drake, don't you?"

"I'm sorry?" Unconsciously she touched the black diamond collar at her throat. She'd convinced herself no one could tell or possibly know what the collar meant.

Amusement lit his eyes at her confusion. "He goes by Kane at our club. Has he not even told you his name? And yet he put that collar around your throat? How intriguing."

Oh. Another name of Quill's to file away. He was moving dangerously close to his own basketball team of fake identities. Drake must be the real one. Marcus's words about the dragon tattoo jumped to the front of her mind.

"I-I was just caught off guard. Excuse me, I need to go find him."

The stranger smirked. "I'm sure that you do. And I'm equally sure that you and I will have another encounter later. Perhaps one that involves less fabric." Another glance down the length of her dress. But he didn't dare touch her because, as he'd put it, she belonged to Andrew Drake.

This was news to her.

It was somehow horrifying that she'd *belonged* to a man for so long without knowing his real name. Even so, Quill was the only name she could mentally attach to him. It wasn't as if she would start imagining him as Andrew or Mr. Drake. Or even just Drake.

Saskia couldn't think of anything intelligent to say to the blond man, so she just turned, flustered, and escaped down the long hall away from the party.

As she passed the new exhibit and moved into the echoing silence of the main part of the museum, she chanced a glance behind her. But he hadn't followed.

A rope blocked the rest of the museum, but she knew her two escorts were somewhere behind it. She found herself angriest at Marcus for the abandonment. Wasn't he supposed to guard her? The moment someone appeared that she might like to be guarded from, he was nowhere to be found.

She wandered through darkened exhibit after darkened exhibit. The main lights of each room were off, leaving only a dim recessed light above each piece. It felt spooky, haunted. If she were watching this on a screen, she'd ineffectually shout, "Don't go down that hall!"

Yet down it she went.

Saskia opened door after door after door with nothing but dim spotlights and paintings and sculptures to answer her search. Finally, tucked away toward the back of the museum, she came upon the final door. It opened into a grand gallery which would have been framed in an overwhelming amount of natural light if it were daytime. One entire wall was nothing but floor-to-ceiling windows.

The room was filled with hand blown glass art in all different colors. She imagined many of the colorless pieces prismed into rainbows across the white walls when the sun hit it just right. This room must be lovely in the day. Outside the window, the bustling city below was lit up by street lamps and car headlights and decorative storefront lighting.

She turned, about to give up and go back to the party, when she saw another door at the end of the gallery—almost hidden—tucked away behind a large red glass piece.

Even before she turned the knob, she knew this was the door. Yet she still wasn't prepared for what she found when she walked through it.

It wasn't so much the activity being engaged in, as the fact that both men were entirely naked. Sure, they'd gone off the beaten path, but anybody could wander down that same path—as she had.

Marcus was on his knees in front of Quill, the black dragon on his back seeming to ripple as he moved, sucking Quill's cock with such expert finesse she had no idea why Quill bothered even trying to teach her how to take his full size. It seemed Marcus was fully on top of that task.

She forgot to be jealous, as she took in the electric eroticism in front of her. Quill's fingers were tangled in Marcus's hair while Marcus's hands gripped Quill's ass, pulling him closer and closer as if he couldn't go deep enough for either of their tastes.

Quill looked up, not taking his eyes off Saskia as he came. Marcus's throat continued to work, swallowing until Quill pulled out of him.

When Marcus stood, he sported his own raging erection.

This room was dimly lit like the others, but nothing seemed dark enough to cover the nudity on display. Though, as she glanced around, she realized it wasn't just Marcus and Quill who were unclothed. The walls were covered in nudes. A few of them were Quill's work. The sculptures in the room were nudes as well.

Along one wall was a sofa so fancy and frilly, she wasn't sure if it was art, or if one could sit on it. It wasn't roped off, but still she didn't dare chance it.

"W-what about the cameras?" she blurted. She couldn't tell if they were on or off. Nothing blinked.

"The museum director turned them off for me in this room."

Quill must donate a lot and must know the director well for such a large and dangerous favor. It had to violate insurance agreements and employment contracts. She wondered how many millions it had cost to secure that donor perk. It probably wasn't listed on their yearly membership drive pamphlet. *...And if you* *donate ten million you can fuck in front of the art with the security cameras off.*

"Come here," Quill demanded.

Saskia's heels clicked against the hard floor as she tentatively approached the two men.

"Turn toward Marcus."

When she did, Quill began to unzip the long plum gown.

"Master, please," she whispered.

"Shhhh. You chose to come back here. You chose to interrupt and watch like a naughty little voyeur. Don't you think you should be punished for that?"

She didn't reply because there was no reply that was acceptable. A *no* would earn her more punishment and the word *yes* contained far more masochism than she did.

"W-what if someone comes in?"

"Then they'll get to see a wide variety of lovely nudes in erotic poses. You among them." He pushed the straps of the gown off her shoulders and the dress fell, causing the silk to pool in a pile at her feet. "Step out."

She did, and Marcus led her a few feet away from the dress. Quill ran his hands over her black lace panties and bra. "Very nice." Slowly he removed those as well. "I want you to leave the shoes on."

"Yes, Master."

"Marcus, hold her."

Marcus took one wrist in each of his hands, and held them up to eye level. His grip was strong but not painful. His eyes locked with hers. Quill had no implement to whip her with, but he didn't need one. His hand was plenty strong enough.

She didn't cry out when he started to spank her, but the tears slid down her cheeks all the same. Marcus watched her cry with only mild interest in his eyes.

The sharp, hard smacks against her ass rang out in the room. It felt so loud she was sure it would call the whole party back there, even though the music on the other end of the museum was loud, and most wouldn't venture beyond the ropes even if they heard a disturbance.

When he finished, he rubbed some of the sting out, then dipped a finger between her legs. He chuckled at her wetness.

"Get on your knees and take care of Marcus."

"But I thought you said..."

"You can do it if I'm here and directly order it. I want my fantastic cocksucker serviced. So service him."

Marcus released her wrists, and Saskia dropped to her knees in front of him. As she took Marcus into her mouth, Quill began to kiss him.

Then the door opened. She jerked away from Marcus and looked up, startled to find the blond athletic stranger smirking at her from the doorway.

"I'm sorry, I don't mean to intrude." he said.

Quill laughed. "Of course you do, Phillip." He gestured to the sofa against the wall. "Sit. Enjoy the show."

He nodded and sat on the sofa, his legs spread wide, as if inviting Saskia to crawl over to him and blow him next. She wasn't sure that wasn't on the menu of options at this point.

"Miss Roth?" Quill said. "He can watch you blow

Marcus, or he can watch you get punished again and then watch you blow Marcus. Your choice."

She wasn't sure where the resolve to obey him came from. Maybe it was that no matter how wrong and fucked up it all was, the pulsing need between her thighs only pulsed stronger with each successive minute inside this room and each degree farther they all fell into depravity.

Saskia dragged her tongue along the shaft and took Marcus back into her mouth. She used her hands to help her, but she was getting better at going deeper, longer, relaxing her throat like Quill had taught her even without the aid of something cold. Quill went back to kissing Marcus.

When Marcus came, she didn't even think about not swallowing. It would be too mortifying for Quill's friend to watch her get punished for that. And she knew exactly what her master wanted from her—though the why of the sharing still eluded her.

She scooted away from Marcus as he put his pants back on and zipped up. For now, he didn't bother with the white linen shirt or jacket or shoes.

"May I have a look at her?" Phillip asked.

"Of course," Quill said. He helped Saskia to her feet. "Go to him," he whispered.

She looked at her master, uncertain, her eyes begging. The man on the sofa was not without his charms, even though she'd sought to escape him earlier. She hadn't been repulsed, just uncomfortable and partly afraid that she might get in trouble for appearing to flirt with someone else. Quill giving him some level of approval softened her to the idea.

She moved on shaking legs to Phillip. He held out both hands to her, and she took them when she reached him. He held her steady.

"Spread your legs, petal," he said.

Saskia looked over her shoulder to Quill. He nodded and she widened her stance.

Phillip slid his hand between her legs. He looked past her to Quill. "How much?"

"I'm not ready to share her yet."

Saskia released a breath she hadn't realized she'd been holding.

"Oh?" he said mildly.

"I'd like to fuck her first," Quill said.

Phillip seemed surprised by the admission that her master hadn't taken her yet. He was late to *that* party. She'd been in a perpetual state of surprise about his restraint and increasingly convinced he wasn't into her at all. Maybe not even that into women.

"Saskia?" Quill said.

"Y-yes, Master?"

"I'll fuck you if you agree to let Phillip and Marcus watch."

Marcus had already joined Phillip on the sofa. They both looked expectant, ready to be entertained.

"She's not a virgin, is she?" Phillip asked.

"She's not," Quill confirmed.

"Pity. Watching you deflower that sweet little redhead is one of my fondest memories."

She couldn't believe they were discussing her as if she were livestock ready to be bred. And she couldn't believe how hot it was getting her. She felt that heat rise to her face and was thankful for the low lighting that shielded how deep her blush really went.

"Well, Saskia, how badly do you want my cock?"

Quill had already recovered from Marcus's mouth. He was full and thick and hard again, and the only thing she wanted in the world right now was for that hard thickness to be inside her. She could already imagine how he'd stretch her, just like the large glass toy from his office.

She whimpered. "Please, Master." The tears that slid down her face were equal parts need and fear.

He smirked. "Is that please, Master no, or please, Master yes? I'm feeling strangely benevolent tonight, so think it through before you answer."

Her eyes met his. Her breath rose and fell heavy in her chest. "Please, fuck me."

His brow arched in mock surprise. "Saskia! In front of Phillip and Marcus? You filthy slut. Well, crawl over here. I want you on your hands and knees where you can look into their eyes, and I want them to be able to watch your tits bounce with each thrust."

The breath caught in her throat.

"Is that too much for you?"

"N-no, Master." If she couldn't please him with her art, at the very least she could do it with her body and her obedience. She hoped.

She crawled across the floor to Quill and positioned herself as he'd asked. She shivered as he stroked down her spine. His fingertips started at the base of her neck and grazed all the way to the concave hollow just above her ass. His hands lingered there on her cheeks. Saskia's gaze dropped to the ground.

A hard smack landed, and she gasped.

"Don't look at the ground. I told you where I wanted you to look. Lock eyes with Phillip. He'll tell me if you stray."

Why not Marcus? At least she'd had intimacy with Marcus. She could hold his gaze while Quill fucked her. She wasn't sure if she could hold the gaze of an amused stranger.

Phillip's smile widened. "She's much more timid than any of your other girls. So... refreshingly shy."

"I know," Quill said as if it were a personal accomplishment.

"This is almost as good as the redhead."

Quill's hand dipped between her legs, pressing against her mound, his warmth seeping into her. The moment went on forever during which time she was compelled to hold Phillip's gaze.

Quill pressed one finger, then two into her and stroked her inner walls as she grew wet enough to create a sound Phillip could hear. She knew he heard it from the sofa because of the way his smile grew as if he were calculating all the filthy things he would do with her as soon as he was granted access.

A moment later, Quill moved his hand away, and pushed his cock inside her. She let out a cry at the sudden intrusion. He filled her as completely as she'd always known he would. A perfect tight fit. She was thankful she was so wet; it was the only thing that spared her pain.

As Quill drove into her, Phillip's gaze drifted downward to her breasts, watching the way they jiggled. Then he looked up at Quill. Some silent question and answer passed between them over her head, and then Phillip got up and moved closer. He sat on the ground in front of her while Quill fucked her, wrenching deeper and deeper moans from her mouth.

Phillip stroked her throat, and then her breasts, pinching and tweaking each nipple in turn. When the pain from his pinches and the pleasure between her legs finally grew too strong to handle, her release came, followed quickly by Quill's.

Phillip quietly moved back to the sofa as if he'd never left it.

When it was over, when the excitement and arousal had run their course in the explosion of orgasm, and her brain was fully functional again, Saskia scrambled the few yards to her pile of clothing to seek the refuge of modesty.

She could still feel the pulsing throb between her legs and the ache from the sudden emptiness. She wanted to go again, but Quill needed time to recover, and the way Phillip looked at her... it was doubtful she would be with her master again tonight.

"So, now that you've had her..." Phillip smiled, his gaze panning over Saskia in the same way he had at the main party before he'd seen everything. Yet he still looked at her as if her body remained a mystery to explore. The only mystery left for him would be how wet and warm and willing she'd be for him when he fucked her.

Quill nodded. "Very well. Meet us at the house. We'll discuss the financial terms there. Marcus, you ride with him. I'd like time alone with Saskia."

"Yes, sir."

Marcus finished dressing, and the two men left. Saskia stayed with Quill. He stepped behind her and zipped up her gown and ran his fingers through her hair, pulling it forward to frame her face. Then he got dressed himself.

She stood awkwardly to the side, waiting for him to finish zipping and buttoning everything.

"Saskia?" he said after several minutes of silence.

"Yes, Master?"

"I'm very pleased with you tonight. But I told you, when it comes to the other men, it's lady's choice. If you don't want to do anything with Phillip, I'll send him away."

"D-do *you* want me to be with Phillip?"

"If I didn't, he wouldn't have been invited back here."

Oh. He'd known where Marcus and Quill would be all along. He'd merely hung back and waited for Saskia to find them before joining the party. The entire evening had probably been choreographed down to the last detail. She was such an idiot.

"Come here."

When she reached his side, he pulled her into his arms and kissed the top of her head. He lowered his head so that his lips were at her ear.

"The more men you give yourself to for me, the more deeply you are mine," he whispered. "I ask for it, because I know it's hard for you. I know how vulnerable it makes you. You have to trust me, that I won't share you with someone who would hurt you or shame you in any way. Do you trust me?"

It was the most ridiculous question. If they'd met in a

different way... If he hadn't felt the compulsion to have her by any means necessary... And yet...

"Yes, Master. I trust you."

He searched her face, looking for the truth or the lie. When he found what he sought, he nodded. "Will you let Phillip play with you tonight?"

"Yes, Master."

"Good girl."

His hand slid inside hers, and they walked together like some normal couple out of the museum and into the cool evening.

PHILLIP HAD ALREADY PAID for her by the time she reached the guest room he waited in. She'd been directed by Quill to change clothes as soon as they'd gotten back. He'd selected a pair of black heels from her things as well as a long black satin night gown with thin straps and a slit up the side. It was sexy, but didn't make her feel too naked. It didn't make her feel dirty.

Marcus stood outside the door, his face impossible to read.

"The gloves?" Quill said.

Marcus passed him a pair of long black opera gloves.

"Phillip likes them," Quill said. "You will always wear these whenever you see him." He pressed a kiss to the top of her head and left her alone in the hall with Marcus.

Saskia stared at the gloves. Marcus gripped her hand, and she looked up.

"If he hurts you in any way... If you don't want something and he doesn't listen, scream, and I'll stop it."

"What if he stops me from screaming?" Saskia couldn't imagine Phillip doing such a thing, but there were a lot of things she hadn't been able to imagine that had nevertheless happened in her time here.

"You know he'll be watching the cameras."

Marcus meant Quill. Saskia was sure he thought of him as Drake or Andrew. He didn't know Phillip had let the name slip at the party. It felt dangerous to know Quill's true name when he'd used so much subterfuge to keep it from her. Though maybe he was just used to being secretive about everything, hoping his lives didn't overlap or intersect in the wrong way at the wrong time.

She still wasn't sure why he'd chosen to introduce himself to her as Lachlan Niche. She supposed, in the end, it created fewer questions. As Drake, he'd have to make up a story of where his money came from, which might lead around to Niche anyway. Perhaps he'd thought it better to just give her an alias with a ready-made recognizable fortune and penchant for art collecting behind it.

"Love?"

"Yes, sir. I'll scream."

He nodded.

Although she'd agreed to this back at the museum, she wasn't sure now if she could bring herself to fuck a stranger with Marcus listening right outside the door and Quill watching on a screen in another part of the house. She wondered if her master would be in his room —the mysterious room she still hadn't been granted access to. Would he watch and stroke himself? Would he be jealous like he'd acted toward Marcus? Or was it only because Marcus had held her hand and shown her affection? If Phillip just used her like some *thing*, would he be angry at her treatment or happy that he didn't have anything to compete with?

She put the gloves on and opened the door. When she stepped into the room, she let out an audible gasp.

"I take it, you've never seen this room before?" Phillip said. "So you must be new to this side of your master's demands."

The room was dark red with gold shimmery sheer fabric that billowed and hung from the ceiling. Oriental rugs covered the floor in a patchwork that overlapped so completely that hardly any floor peered through. What little did show was a dark polished wood.

Large cushions were scattered about, and there were several dim lamps lit. In fact, all the light in this room was indirect. Soft. Flattering. Not that Phillip hadn't already seen plenty of her tonight.

"Y-you're my first," she said, her gaze dropping of its own accord. She still wasn't quite sure why she couldn't bring herself to try to escape this place. It wasn't as if there were no ways out. Worst case scenario, she could go to a homeless shelter. She could figure something out, and yet she kept choosing Quill's dark demands and the art between them—pretending any of it meant something.

"Sir," Phillip corrected. His voice was stern, but not unkind.

"Sir." She felt weirdly grateful he'd set a tone for them. She hadn't been sure what she should call him.

"I'm honored to be the first," he said, patting the bed

beside him. It was large and round and covered in pillows.

She went to him, still taking in her surroundings.

"This room is inspired by the harem-themed room at the club," Phillip said. "It's my favorite room, both there and here. I find it comforts newer girls. It's not too harsh."

"How many women has my master shared with you? I thought he only collared one other person besides me."

"Formally, you are his second, but he's had several others on a probationary basis. They never seem to last very long. I'm surprised he put a collar on you before putting you through your paces."

Phillip spoke as if she were a show horse. If he only knew the sordid way she'd come to be Quill's. Like Ari, Phillip seemed to think her being here was fully voluntary—just a bit of kink she was exploring. She wondered how he'd feel if he knew it wasn't, if he knew just how real Quill's ownership of her was.

From the few parties she'd attended and the private club Quill had taken her to, it seemed many of these types tossed around words like *owned* and *belonged to* in an almost flip way. Most would be horrified if they knew how very literal this enslavement was.

"Close your eyes," he said when she joined him on the bed.

Saskia closed her eyes and let out a long shaky breath as Phillip's hand moved under the slit in the gown and up her thigh.

"You are so sweet," he whispered in her ear. He kissed her cheek and along her jawline, down the side of her throat until he reached her collar, and then over her shoulder.

Yes, the sweet girl who conned a man out of millions, Saskia thought.

She heard his weight lift off the bed. "Stay. And keep your eyes closed."

Minutes later, rich, sad cello music poured into the room. Phillip covered her eyes with a strip of soft fabric. "It's not that I don't trust you," he said, "But I wouldn't want you to slip and earn yourself a punishment. Not your first time with me."

When the blindfold was in place, he took her hand and led her to what felt like the center of the room. She stood, waiting for a command as he slid the straps down her shoulders, slipping each arm out in turn. The gown was form fitting and even without the straps holding it up, the top of it bunched at her waist, leaving her partly covered.

She felt his eyes on her breasts, even if she couldn't see it.

"Lift your arms above your head."

She hadn't noticed the shackles that must have hung from the ceiling. Phillip locked one wrist in, and then the other.

"We'll leave the gloves on," he said.

His hands skimmed the sides of her breasts, then down over her ribcage, and finally he shoved the rest of the gown off her hips until the garment pooled at her feet in a soft swish. He helped her out of the pile of fabric and moved it out of the way.

"We'll leave the shoes on as well."

He moved to another part of the room. She heard a

light pop and then liquid pouring into a glass. Phillip returned.

"Open your mouth, petal."

Saskia hesitated, but finally obeyed. He tipped the glass back and a tart sauvignon blanc slid down her throat.

"Are you trying to get me drunk, sir?"

He chuckled. "No, dear. Just pleasantly buzzed to relax you."

He let her drink probably a full glass until the gentle warm wine buzz prickled out over her face.

Then he retreated to refill the glass. When he returned, instead of giving her more, he spilled a bit of it down the front of her body, quickly catching the trail with his tongue. He must have drunk a full glass of his own this way, licking and sucking wine off her breasts, letting some drip between her thighs and kneeling to lap it up there.

"You are so sweet," he said again, his voice drifting up from closer to the ground. This time he meant it in a different way.

"Have you ever been cropped?"

"Uh... riding crop?"

"Yes."

"Yes, sir."

"Good."

She felt him rise from the ground. He went to another part of the room and sorted through some things until he found what he was looking for.

The crop fell across her back in short, hard snaps. "Do you like this?" he asked after the first several strikes.

When she didn't answer, Phillip's hand moved

between her legs. "I know the truth. It's coating my fingers. So say it. Do you like being struck this way?"

"Y-yes, sir."

"Good girl. Will you cry for me?"

"Yes, sir."

"I'll only strike you as hard as I have to for you to cry. Give me what I want easily, and we don't have to make dark marks. We don't want to mar this pretty skin, do we?"

"N-no, sir."

It wasn't hard to cry for him. Maybe it was the cello playing in the background. Maybe it was the fact that she still longed to be invited into Quill's bed as well as not knowing what it said about her that she wasn't horrified by any of what was happening now with Phillip, a stranger who bought time with her from the man who owned her. Maybe it was the whole situation.

"That's it," Phillip said. "Let it all out." He put down the riding crop and stroked her back as she cried harder than she'd intended to. He wiped her tears, then stepped away again.

When he returned, he nudged her thighs apart. "Wider," he coaxed. When her legs were spread to his liking, he began running his hands over her hips and ass, his fingers playing in slow circles and figure eights over the skin between her legs.

Then his fingers traced the length of her spine, much as Quill's had at the museum, only he didn't stop at the hollow space her master had. Instead, his finger edged further down, sliding between her cheeks, pressing inside her ass.

She tensed.

"Relax, and take it. If you'll relax, it can feel very pleasurable. I've yet to have any complaints."

Saskia breathed deep as his finger slid in and out of her. He finally pulled it away, only to replace it with a lubed toy. Gently, he fucked her ass with it while she whimpered and writhed in the chains. After a while, her hips began to move as she pressed her ass harder against his hand as if trying to get him to go deeper.

Phillip chuckled but withdrew the toy and said, "That's enough of that for tonight. I like to leave my girls aching and wanting more."

Saskia strained to hear what he was doing next, but it was impossible to interpret the meaning of the light creaks and clicks until she felt slack in the chains holding her arms and almost pitched forward.

"Kneel down on the ground with your ass raised in the air. You can rest on your forearms."

The chains gave way just enough for her to do as he asked. She still felt the slightest tension on them as she moved into position. She spread her legs wide without him asking.

She heard a zipper and then pants hit the floor, and then he was behind her, fucking her.

"I love how wet you are for me," he said.

Saskia pressed back against him. He didn't fill her in the same absolute way that Quill did. She might have been satisfied by Phillip's cock if she'd been with him first, but Quill had ruined her for any other man. Perhaps it was best her master had told Marcus no fucking. It would only be a point of contention when he couldn't satisfy her in the same way Quill had.

She didn't come again, but Phillip didn't seem to

mind. He'd paid for his pleasure, not hers. When he was finished with her, he pulled out and zipped up. He didn't linger or make small talk, something for which she was grateful. Nothing would be more awkward than post-coital small talk with a practical stranger.

Phillip stroked the side of her face. "Goodbye, petal. You were worth every penny."

He left her chained and sprawled on the floor, the door closing softly behind him while the cello music still played.

She lay on the floor in a sort of floaty space. With the blindfold still over her eyes and her hands bound, it was hard to tell which way was up and which was down. The door clicked open.

"Are you okay, love?" Marcus asked.

"Yes, sir," Saskia said, barely recognizing her own voice.

It didn't surprise her that Quill could make her feel this way. And in a way, it wasn't that shocking that Marcus could do it either. The shock was that a stranger could play her body and mind with the same success. It was just another slide deeper down the rabbit hole.

Marcus unchained her wrists and removed the blind-fold. He looked her over for anything he might need to bandage. When he found nothing, he helped her back into her gown, picked her up, and carried her out to the gallery.

She didn't see Quill again that night.

14

Tears streamed down Saskia's face as Quill berated her. She gasped when he ripped the painting off the easel and threw it across the room. The sad little canvas buckled when it hit the wall with a force that startled her. This was becoming a habit with him.

"No! Why don't I just give you a child's coloring book? It'll be just as much art as this is!"

Did he think his abuse would help anything? All this yelling? If possible, she cried even harder.

"But you said I was good!" If he really believed that, he wouldn't be treating her this way. He just wanted a punching bag. What he needed was a fucking therapist.

"You *are* good. Technically. There is precious little I have left to teach you technically. I am genuinely impressed with how quickly you were able to switch to my methods, but you have to give up more of yourself if you don't want to be forgotten. You have to give the work everything you give me and more. Great art isn't made of stitched together rainbows and kittens. It's born of anger and despair and frustration."

"My life hasn't been a cake walk! You know that!" It wasn't even a cake walk now. Quill was making sure of that. How dare he with all his heaping piles of money tell her about what pain and struggle felt like. As if he could remember any of it.

"Then show me, Saskia! Put it on the motherfucking canvas before I have to bleed it out of you!"

He meant that quite literally. He seemed to itch to take her into the gallery to whip her. Maybe this was just an excuse. Her eyes narrowed as her tears ran their course. She felt she might snap the paintbrush in half; she squeezed it so tightly.

"You're angry," he remarked, his tone empty of inflection.

"No shit, I'm angry! I worked on that for five hours, and you've warped it!"

He picked up a new canvas from the ground and set it on the easel. "Put your anger on the canvas. I won't ask you twice. Paint your anger, or you can paint the pain I'm about to deliver."

"You don't paint *your* anger and despair and frustration," she retorted, knowing how dangerously close she was to the threat he'd just issued. The gallery was filled with paintings of her. They were all brilliant, but it wasn't something he could teach. He had to know that by now.

Quill ripped the brush from her hand and threw it on the ground. He stalked her across the studio until her back met the glass. His eyes bored into hers, drilling down into her soul with the smallest effort.

"No, I don't paint that. That isn't where my art comes from. I paint power and control and all the dark urges that live inside me. And you've been an endless source of inspiration for *that*! But that's *my* material. You're living your material and you can't even get it on the fucking canvas!"

His patience had reached an end. He grabbed her wrist and dragged her from the studio, down the hallway, and into the gallery where all his brilliance stared back at her.

His newest work mocked her from the corner. It was her in the high heels and long black opera gloves, blind-folded and suspended in the harem room with Phillip looming behind her with the crop in his hand. Quill hadn't just been watching that night. He'd been capturing it on canvas. Just how large was the screen he monitored the video feeds on?

"I'm doing the best I can!"

"No, you aren't!"

"Master, please. Don't do this while you're angry." He was really scaring her this time. "Please."

He dragged her to the cage and tossed her in and locked it. "I'll be back for you when I've cooled down. But pain is coming, sweetheart. And then you're going to paint it for me. And it will be fucking glorious."

There was an *or else* in there somewhere. He'd completely lost his mind.

Saskia let out a deep breath and stretched out on the giant plush pillow, relieved he'd listened to her plea. She just wasn't sure how much he'd really cool off before he came back.

Maybe an hour passed before Quill returned. He'd changed out of painting clothes and into all black. Black pants, black shirt, black shoes, black gloves. His anger had dissipated—at least the surface of it had. In its place was a cold darkness that seemed to swirl around him like dramatic fog, cocooning all his emotions. Saskia wasn't sure this was better.

He unlocked the cage without a word and helped her out.

"Just let me try one more time. I know I can paint something that pleases you."

"Speak again and I'll gag you."

She closed her mouth and allowed him to drag her through the gallery. He stopped at each piece of BDSM furniture in turn, sizing it up, then sizing her up. His face was unreadable. Unhappy with his options in the gallery, he dragged her back into the studio, and he sat on one of the chaise lounges meant for his softer nudes. He hadn't managed to paint Saskia even once that way.

With her it was all blood and pain and welts. Harsh, dangerous eroticism. Never anything sweet or languidly seductive. It was all work that screamed for your attention at the top of its lungs then held its breath until you looked for good measure.

Quill pulled her over his lap and shoved the artist smock up over her hips. For the past week or two, he'd insisted she wear nothing but the smock to paint. No pants or shirt or skirt underneath. No panties. No bra.

He wanted her in the right mental zone to create the

work he'd said she was destined to create. If she shied away from the subject matter, he'd determined to turn her into the subject matter. This was another lesson in becoming the art. As if there weren't enough canvases splashed with her image to drive that point home already.

He didn't say anything, and she was afraid to. Instead, his gloved hand struck her bare flesh over and over. It didn't matter how she cried out or begged. He would only stop when his hand was tired, then only to rub her heated skin for a few moments before he started up again.

Quill didn't try to seduce her or fuck her or finger her. This wasn't foreplay. It wasn't even punishment. In his own demented way, he was trying to help her, trying to pull her material to the surface so she could see it, so she could feel it, so she could create something raw and vital enough that strangers could look at it and taste the same acrid fear and darkness. All her work was locked away inside her with no clear channel to communicate those things to others.

Eventually, she surrendered under his hand. The begging stopped. The crying changed from attention-seeking sobs to hushed tears.

He pulled the smock back down and she slid onto the ground. Her head rested on his lap. He ran his fingers through her hair absently, then seemed to catch himself. His hand stilled at the nape of her neck and he leaned close to her ear.

"Now. Paint."

Saskia wiped her face and struggled to stand. Quill didn't help her. He merely sat and waited to be impressed. She began mixing pigment and started to cover the canvas.

Five hours later, she was finished with a piece that was emotional, but that was all it was. It was one extreme or another with her. The painting was a mess of erratic colors and harsh lines. She wasn't even sure what she was painting. It was as if she'd changed her mind multiple times in the creation of the piece but each time just moved to a different part of the canvas and started over, never mind what had come before.

In the hands of a better artist, maybe it would have been brilliant, but this was anything but. It felt chaotic and hurt and angry. All her technical artistry was gone, leeched out by Quill's impatience and anger. She was too upset to focus, too panicked and terrified to displease him. He'd terrorized her to the point that she was afraid to paint—especially while he loomed over her, pacing in the background, watching and judging each brush stroke. It made the hairs of her neck stand at attention every time he walked past.

She'd finished it when she'd run out of space on the canvas. Always a bad sign. It meant she was flailing about with no direction or purpose. Quill sensed it, too. Hell, he didn't have to sense it. A child could see it. A child could do better. Any other aspiring artist on the planet deserved his attention and instruction more than she did.

Saskia put the brush down and tensed, waiting for more rage. Instead she got silence. She chanced a glance at him and wished she hadn't. She'd never seen him look so disappointed, like a boy whose ice cream had fallen in the ditch, and there was no more left.

He stared at the canvas as if he could unmake it with the power of thought. Then he sent that same withering look her way as if she'd done this on purpose. Then back to the canvas. Then he turned and left the studio and gallery without a word.

15

A week passed. No new men were introduced. There were no trips outside the estate. The work had ground to a halt. He didn't paint her, nor did she paint. The studio remained untouched. She remained untouched.

At least by Quill.

Saskia wondered if he'd lost interest in her completely. Only Marcus was there at night to comfort her, to touch her, to bring her pleasure and soothe her. She hadn't seen Quill for days. For all she knew, he'd left the country. Maybe he'd gone back to Venice to the villa she'd bought.

Her meals were brought to her in the gallery. And she'd taken it as a signal not to venture to the main house. Maybe he was in there, and he just didn't want to see her.

On the eighth morning of this, it was Quill, instead of Marcus, who let her out of the cage.

He wore dark jeans and a white polo shirt that made him look even more bronzed than normal.

Was he getting rid of her? There was no reason for her to think that, but he'd been gone a long time.

Awful scenarios popped into her head—after all she had plenty of ways to destroy him if he set her free. Would he sell or give her to someone else? Perhaps Ari or Phillip? She tried to imagine belonging to The Viking or Phillip. It wouldn't be a terrible outcome would it?

She stood outside the cage, tears silently moving down her cheeks. She couldn't look at him.

Quill wiped the tears away and pulled her into his arms. She let out a long breath as her body pressed against his.

"Don't cry."

"A-are you getting rid of me?"

He pulled away and studied her, his face a mask of confusion. "No. Why would you think that?"

Was he kidding? He'd completely ignored her. "We haven't painted... or done any other things."

"I've just been very busy."

She wasn't buying it.

He sighed. "I thought we needed a break from the work. I was getting too frustrated with you. I wasn't in control of myself, and I didn't like it. I've been working on some other things."

"Okay, but what about the rest? Do you not want me anymore?" Before Quill, she'd never considered herself an insecure woman. Now she was every woman she hated. The girl who sat beside the phone waiting. The girl consumed only with some man and whether or not he wanted to fuck her. She hated that girl. She thought that girl was weak and pathetic and should develop some hobbies or something.

"I wanted to give you a rest period and let you bond with Marcus. He's... less intense than I am. Go shower and get ready. I want to take you out."

"Okay." Out sounded good. Her mind had been slowly unraveling, locked away inside the gallery, imagining the worst.

Quill's face was stern. "Okay, what?"

"Okay, Master."

"Good girl. And when we go out, you will call me what?"

"Sir."

He nodded and pointed in the direction of the bathroom.

Saskia quickly showered and put on a lavender sundress he'd laid out for her along with a pair of silver strappy sandals.

He gave her a quick once over when she emerged, nodded his approval, then took her hand in his and led her out to the car. Marcus had already gone to the house to sleep for the day.

Saskia wasn't sure what she'd expected, but it wasn't what she got. Quill took her to an amusement park. It was a local family-owned park, named after the large lake situated in the middle of the property.

He won her a stuffed Dalmatian at one of the carnival games. He made sure she got enough sunscreen on her back and shoulders. He fed her corn dogs and cotton candy and held her hand in the haunted house.

They rode all the rides. He talked and acted like a normal person, not the man who'd intimidated and scared the shit out of her from moment one until this morning. As the sun began to glow orange and set behind the trees, they sat at the top of the oversized Ferris wheel. He looked content high above the tree line and crowd.

The ride malfunctioned, and they were stuck at the top for about twenty minutes while someone from maintenance was called to fix the glitch. Stuck in the bucket suspended over the park, far away from Quill's estate, Saskia managed the bravery to ask the question that had been on her mind since he'd knocked the milk bottles down and won her the toy dog.

"What is all this? Why..."

His face appeared relaxed, but she couldn't see his eyes behind the dark reflective glasses he wore to block the glare of the sun. Even as the sun finished disappearing behind the trees, he hadn't moved to take them off.

"Let's not make a big deal out of it. I just wanted to get out. You needed to get out. I haven't been here in a while. I used to come here a lot when I was a kid."

Saskia waited for some further explanation, some cute anecdote that would make him seem less distant, more approachable. But he didn't say anything more.

She wanted to ask if he'd brought the first girl he'd collared here. But there wasn't enough bravery in the world for her to broach that question. She didn't want to see him shift back into the person who pushed her further and further away. She felt like she'd already messed things up somehow. As if he might have let her in a tiny bit if she'd just been quiet and enjoyed it, without making him examine his motives.

Finally the wheel lurched forward and began its descent. When they reached the bottom, a manager handed Quill two free passes. "We're very sorry for the inconvenience, sir."

"It's no problem. Thanks," he said, slipping the passes into his pants pocket.

As they moved away from the ride, Saskia asked, "Can we come back sometime?"

"We'll see. We should get back."

She didn't react at all when his hand slid into hers, afraid if she acknowledged it, he'd pull further away from her.

"Did you have a nice time today?" he asked, sounding almost normal.

"Yes, sir."

"I'm glad."

It was as close to heartfelt confessions as she'd likely ever get from him.

SASKIA FOLLOWED him back into the gallery, startled by the changes that greeted her arrival. Everything was different. There were paintings on the wall, but none of the Quill pieces. And none of her. It was all other artists he'd collected, as well as a few installations scattered about.

A buffet table stood at one end, laden down with all the fancy party foods one might expect at a gallery opening. The servants were putting the finishing touches on the food. One thing was certain: a lot of people would be in this space very soon.

Her cage was missing, though the sex furniture remained in place. The furniture wouldn't be easy to move, being bolted to the floor. But wasn't he concerned about people seeing that? Then again, if it could be rebranded as art it might pass—depending on the intended audience. But you had to be careful. You didn't want to rattle the birds in their cages.

"I'm having a private party," Quill said as if this were a thing that needed stating. "My work has been moved into the main house and replaced with paintings that were on display there. It would look a bit suspicious if everyone I knew saw how many Joseph Quill pieces I own. Don't you think?" The question was rhetorical. "Come."

He guided Saskia to the far end of the gallery where temporary walls had been erected in her absence.

So the day at the park had just been to get her out of the gallery for whatever this was?

"You're going to be part of an interactive installation tonight. You'll come more times than you can count, though I expect you to count your orgasms for me anyway."

No more frightful words than these could have left his mouth.

Before her stood a large white box, taller than both she and Quill. The fourth side was the actual wall of the gallery. There was a small door next to that wall which led into the box.

On the outer front panel were multiple glass dildos in varying colors—some large enough that Saskia clenched her thighs involuntarily at the sight of them.

They were each shaped a bit differently. Who knew phallic came in so many exciting options?

Some were totally smooth. Some had bumps and ridges. Some had large bulbous heads, while others ended in a slightly more defined point. Each of the penetrative toys was attached to a cord on one end, with the other end of that cord attached to the panel so that they all hung around a largish circular opening which was covered by a white curtain from inside the box.

Near the opening, were shackles. Two small podiums stood next to the installation; one was a glass jar that requested payment, and the other was a substantial container of lubricant.

The placard beside the installation read in big bold letters: "TAB A/SLOT B" The artist was listed as Jacob Hunter.

"Another alias?" Saskia asked.

"Yes. It's an interactive piece about how we objectify and commodify women both in art and in life. The cameras will be on. I want to record reactions. Guilt, excitement, whatever I can capture on film."

"You're making a statement about women's objectification by objectifying me?"

Quill's lips quirked in a grin. "Precisely."

She already knew—more or less—what her role would be. It wasn't as if it wasn't already starkly displayed in front of her like a perverted instruction manual.

"My guests will be arriving soon. Let's get you set up. I'm sure you don't want to be seen from the waist up. You've met several of these people before in less compromising settings."

She stopped him with a hand on his arm. "Master, what exactly is going to happen to me tonight?"

"Relax. No one will know it's you. They've only seen you in evening gowns. No one will see your face. You'll lie on the bench with your lower half through the hole in the front panel. Your legs will be spread and your ankles chained. Throughout the night, you'll be penetrated by those toys. Just the toys. No fingers, no tongues. No one will be allowed to fuck you or cause you pain. Only pleasure. You'll enjoy yourself. And Marcus will be with you in the booth to make sure you're okay."

"So, you can't display your paintings for fear of your stock plummeting, but you can have a party like this?" She'd almost slipped and called it an orgy because she felt quite sure it would soon dwindle to that state.

He sighed. "This isn't in the public's face. How many private events of the wealthy do you know the details of?"

"I..."

"Exactly. None. And anyway, all invited guests have signed non-disclosure agreements."

Of course they had. It was his favorite legal document.

She wanted to object, but the truth was that a part of her was excited by Quill's twisted desires and the slight application of force he introduced into the proceedings —never enough to traumatize her, but always enough to thrill. She didn't want to think too hard about what that said about her.

His fingertips trailed over her collar, then he tugged on it to gain her attention. He captured her gaze in his when she looked up. "Be a good girl on this for me, and we'll watch the video in bed together after the party. And then I'll let you spend the night. You can sleep with me tonight if you're obedient."

Saskia tried to tamp down the eager flutter over what he promised. It was all she'd wanted from the first night spent in the cage. She closed her eyes, imagining his arms wrapped around her, as their bodies entwined beneath the covers—falling asleep together like that.

"Okay?" he prodded.

"Yes, Master."

He pressed a kiss to her cheek. "Good. I'm so pleased with you."

Another excited flutter.

He guided her to the side door on the box and knocked. Marcus opened it, and Quill passed her off to him.

Marcus pulled her inside and locked the door. Then he placed a chair in front of it.

"You could wear the dress and just take off the panties, but I prefer you fully nude."

And of course, if he preferred it, that would be what she gave him. Her submission to Quill had easily spilled over onto Marcus. His demands were only a sliver less important than her master's. And he offered the extra bit of kindness that took the edge off Quill's intensity. No matter how much she craved Quill's approval, she needed Marcus to balance him out.

Saskia sat on the bench and unbuckled the strap of her shoe. Her hands began to shake. Marcus pulled the chair up to her and sat, closing his hands over hers.

Marcus undid her shoes and slid them off. "He'll have someone outside the box, making sure they follow the rules. It's just the toys. They're required to use lube. Imagine it's me or him. Once it starts, if it's truly too much for you, I will stop it and talk to him. Okay?"

Saskia nodded. She pulled the dress over her head, and he helped her scoot down the bench.

She jumped when someone grabbed her ankle. "It's only me," Quill said, from the other side of the panel. He spread her legs and locked her ankles into the cuffs. Then he rubbed her exposed clit until the arousal began. "Good girl," he whispered from the other side of the curtain. "Just relax. Let yourself enjoy this. We all know how filthy you are."

Inside the enclosure, Marcus stood beside her, stroking her hair. He kissed her, prodding her to open to him as his tongue moved inside her mouth. Then he started to fondle her breasts. She became so involved with Marcus's gentle ministrations that Quill's voice on the other side of the panel faded into the background even as she heard a larger buzz of noise growing in the main gallery.

Her eyes widened in shock when a cold, well-lubricated toy was pushed inside her. Whoever it was, hadn't bothered with something small and innocuous. The person on the other end moved the toy with aching slowness in to the hilt and pulled it out at the same maddening tempo. This was repeated multiple times until her hips began to move and arch toward the source of potential pleasure. Each hard bump of the glass dragged against her inner walls, teasing her, making her wetter with each stroke.

Her focus shifted from Marcus to what was happening beneath her waist. Whatever fears she'd had evaporated as she began to move with it, trying to take more inside. But she couldn't control the depth or speed or the strength of the thrust. The stranger was in complete control of every sensation between her legs. And somehow she knew they got off on it.

A frustrated whimper escaped her throat.

The person on the other side chuckled. A decidedly masculine sound. Of course it was a male. What woman would participate in this? But maybe one would. Saskia was sure if a woman decided to join in, that she would know it without the aid of a soundtrack.

"Such a hungry pussy," the man on the other side said.

Saskia recognized that voice. Nolan? She thought that was his name. He was a close friend of her master. She'd met him the night of the fund raising event months before all of this had spiraled out of control. He was the one who'd shown interest in her work making reproductions. She felt her face flame at the recognition and tried to stay quiet, paranoid he'd somehow figure out it was her.

Marcus pulled away to observe her the moment she'd started writhing and whimpering. He lowered his mouth to her ear and whispered, "You know him?"

She nodded, and he smiled. He moved the chair closer and sat, his fingers kneading her breasts, pinching and twisting her nipples. She whimpered again, desperately trying not to beg him for mercy. The only thing that made any of this okay was the anonymity she'd been offered. If a single word passed through her lips, it could be compromised.

On the other side of the panel, Nolan teased her

further. He penetrated her now with lightning quick speed, but he'd taken away the deep full fucking. Instead, he only allowed the fat, bulbous tip a mere inch inside her before swiftly pulling it out and repeating again. Endless teasing stimulation.

She was so close to begging him, even knowing he might recognize her voice and know whose body he commanded. But mercifully, he spared her the indignation, driving the toy fully into her at a tempo that finally offered sweet release.

A deep moan rose from her throat as she came. The toy slipped out, and there was silence on the other side. Cool air played over her bare skin. This was the most exposed Saskia had felt since she'd first been strapped in to the installation.

She heard murmurings nearby but couldn't pull out any specific words. She wondered how many people stood staring at her swollen cunt and whispering. It was almost better to be used than not to be. At least while being penetrated by one of the toys, she didn't have to think about anything but sensation. And no one could simply gawk at her spread-open pussy.

Footsteps approached the installation, and then another lubed dildo plunged into her without warning. The lubricant wasn't needed, but Quill had ordered it. And he was nothing if not a stickler for rules. By the end of the party when she was sore and wrung out, she'd probably be grateful for anything that allowed the glass to slide more easily in and out of her.

This time, the person on the other end used two of the toys. One plunged inside her at a steady rhythm, while the other, smaller toy teased her clit.

She lost track of her orgasms and all the dildos that filled her after a while. Several had been used on her more than once, but she was sure each glass phallus had had its turn at penetration. She doubted there was a single piece that was dry.

Eventually, she came to realize the lubricant was being kept slightly chilled and that perhaps it wasn't just meant to keep her wet. Each time a toy slid inside her, she was grateful for the coolness that soothed the heat she'd built. As the strangers played with her, Marcus gently caressed her skin. He ran his hands over every inch of her flesh that was available to him and followed his stroking with a trail of kisses along the contours of her upper body.

Saskia jumped at a sharp rap on the other side of the door.

"It's me," Quill said.

Marcus unlocked it, and her master slipped in, locking the door behind him.

"How is our little slut doing in here?" he asked.

There was a chuckle on the other side of the panel, as if there could be any question how easily his guests could hear any peep that happened behind it. Saskia was relieved she'd kept her silence.

Marcus stroked her hair. "She's being very responsive."

"Good."

Quill's erection strained against the fabric of his pants, and she wondered just how many other men outside the box had a similar problem.

Someone else began to play with her pussy with

another toy, while Quill unzipped his pants, his cock springing free.

More gently than she expected, he gripped the back of Saskia's head and angled her face toward him.

"Open for me," he ordered.

Her mouth fell open, and he thrust into her. As she sucked, Marcus decided to join in. He stroked her as he had before, but this time with one hand because his other was occupied pumping his own erection.

A pornographer couldn't have choreographed the scene better. As Quill's groans grew louder and more insistent, so did Marcus's jerking, and so did the guest on the other side fucking her with the toy.

Saskia's moan of pleasure was muffled by Quill's cock in her mouth. He came down her throat as Marcus emptied on her stomach.

"Make the little bitch swallow," Nolan said from the other side of the panel.

"Don't worry. I've trained her well," Quill answered. They would probably high-five the second he left the booth.

When he pulled out of her, he bent to kiss her mouth, then zipped up and went back out to the party. The man had no shame.

"I'm jealous," Nolan said from the other side.

Saskia lay on the bench panting, barely able to recover before another cool, greased toy slipped inside her.

16

Q uill kept her in the box until every last guest had left the estate, allowing her the mercy of continued anonymity. She was given the further kindness of a robe as Marcus carried her back to the main house.

Saskia felt emptied of all her psychic contents, both good and bad. The deep pleasant internal ache between her legs matched the sense of calm and stillness inside her brain. She felt like she'd been away for a week on a spa getaway. Or perhaps lobotomized. One of those.

She hadn't expected that. She wasn't sure what she'd expected, but it wasn't that. She was starving, though. While she'd been fed a bit before the party, the event had lasted hours.

Hours of being prodded and stroked. Hours of Marcus with her behind the panel and occasional visits from Quill to satisfy the arousal watching her like that kept creating. She wondered how other men at the party had dealt with that discomfort. Had they wandered off somewhere to masturbate or had they found a willing partner to slip behind a bush in the rose garden with? How would those other women feel knowing they scratched an itch Saskia initiated? Weren't they being used as well?

All of them useful objects in the service of the all-powerful male boner—the all-powerful male boner she'd licked and sucked not that long ago with something close to wild abandon. Both Quill and Marcus had fucked her mouth several times during the party while strangers gave her pleasure from behind the panel. It was as if neither man could quite handle not sampling her charms for longer than a half-hour stretch.

She collapsed, boneless onto the chair pulled out for her in the dining room. Lacy put a couple of plates of food in front of her without comment and went back through the side door to the kitchen.

Marcus wrapped a hand around the back of Saskia's neck and pulled her to him to kiss her forehead. "Good-night, Saskia."

"Enjoy your night off," Quill said.

"Yes, sir" Marcus said on his way out the door.

Quill sat across from her, watching as she devoured a giant plate of party leftovers. Such an odd mix of food. Mini quiches, shrimp and cocktail sauce, tiny sandwiches on croissants, fruit tarts, little savory sausages in a tangy sweet sauce. She didn't care. She was too hungry to care. A second plate was filled with desserts that must have taken hours to craft, which she planned to barrel through in mere minutes.

Lacy brought her a goblet and a pitcher of water. Saskia was grateful it wasn't champagne. The way she shoveled food in, something bubbling and alcoholic was the last thing she wanted.

"Nolan has requested a private session with you," Quill said, still studying her.

Saskia's mindless binge halted. Her gaze darted around the room as if expecting Quill's friend to pop through the door at any moment like a stripper in a birthday cake.

"He went home with the others."

Saskia pushed the plate away, no longer hungry.

"Master, no, please. You said none of them would know it was me. Did you tell him?"

Quill shook his head. "Your secret is still safe. He doesn't know. I realize how much I'm asking of you. But he's a good friend, and it would mean a great deal to me if you consented."

"And if I don't?"

He shrugged. "I promised you anonymity tonight. If that's to be broken, it'll be your call. I'm not going to rip it from you. But think about it. Would it be so bad?"

She *did* find Nolan attractive. His hawkish features undeniably worked on his face. At their first meeting she'd found him both threatening and appealing in that way that seemed to be the official template for her sexual attraction now.

"Are you sure he doesn't know it's me? He showed interest when he met me at that fund raising event. You seemed kind of territorial. I wouldn't think you'd want to share."

"I just wanted to establish clearly who you belonged to."

"I didn't belong to you back then." Saskia was probably inches from a punishment with the casual way her mouth was flying off.

"Oh, yes, you did. You just didn't know it yet. And I'm sure he doesn't know it was you. But at least *you* know he likes you both above and below the waist. Be flattered."

"Can I have time to think about it?"

"I want an answer by tomorrow morning."

"Okay."

He raised a brow. She'd clearly hit the end of his patience.

"Yes, Master," she corrected.

He nodded. "Tell me, how many orgasms did you have tonight? I hope you remembered to keep count as I requested."

Saskia blanched. She'd lost count within the first hour. "I-I don't remember."

Quill sighed and rose from the table. He moved behind her, his hands pressed against her shoulders as if she might run. "You don't remember. Well, then, let's watch the video and count them together. Then you'll get a cane stripe for each one, since you couldn't bother to remember."

"Y-yes, Master."

SASKIA AND QUILL stood in the hallway outside his closed bedroom door. Despite how long she'd been with him, she'd never seen his bedroom. He'd kept it just out of reach—a carrot on a string which was always pulled away from her at the last moment.

"Well? Haven't you been dying to get inside? You've

practically crawled after me, begging to warm my bed. And now you hesitate? I'm offended."

Saskia's hand shook as she turned the knob and pushed the door open, almost afraid of what she might find behind it.

Quill's room looked something like a BDSM pornography set. All it needed was lighting equipment and cameras, and he'd be in business. One entire wall contained hooks with every imaginable whipping implement. A bamboo cane lay across a shelf with a little spotlight on it—as if it were his favorite. Or as if he just wanted to terrify whoever entered the room with the possibilities.

One entire corner was set up for suspension. There were hoods, and gloves, and riding crops. There were duplicates of much of the sex furniture from the gallery. Maybe he'd found a buy one get one free sale.

An enormous bed stood at the far end, far from most of his kink accoutrements—a safe space. The bedding was black.

A somewhat innocuous red leather couch angled out from one corner to create a small sitting area. Though it was the kind of couch one imagined a *Dear Penthouse* letter might be composed from.

There was a cage next to the bed—like the one on the jet and the one inside his gallery. She fought not to start crying. She had been sure he'd meant for her to actually *share* his bed. To sleep in it. What was the point of any of this if she'd only be relegated to another cage?

He caught her staring at it.

"I told you, you could sleep with me in my bed if you were good at the party. You've got a punishment coming for not counting like I told you to, but assuming you accept that without excessive whining, nothing has changed."

She nodded, still not trusting herself not to cry. She couldn't sleep in a cage again.

"Lose the robe and get in bed."

Saskia stripped off the robe and got under the covers on the other side of the room while he pressed a button on a remote. A large panel in the floor slid open and a flat screen, lying horizontal, rose into the room. He pushed a second button, and the screen lifted at an angle until it was fully vertical. It was massive, much larger than the screen he'd made her watch herself on before in his study.

She wasn't sure she was prepared to see her pussy in oversized high definition and wondered if she could get away with keeping her eyes closed for this.

"Would you like to know how much of your debt you paid off tonight?"

Admittedly, she'd been curious about how much money had gone into that glass jar. She hadn't been able to help thinking about it every time someone new took a turn with the toys.

"Yes, Master."

"A little over twenty-five thousand. I've already made a note of it in the ledger. That's not bad. At this rate, you may live to be debt free."

"And then what happens?"

He couldn't release her even if she managed to buy her way out of this slavery. It wasn't as if any of this was legal. She had so much on him, it was amazing he didn't keep her chained down 24/7, lest she somehow escape and make it to the proper authorities with a laundry list of felonies to charge him with.

And anyway, Quill was the one setting the prices. If she got close to paying him back, he could simply lower the amount he charged for access to her body. It was all a game to him. A never ending pit of debt. He would arrange it so she could never climb out and was always reaching up to him from the dark hole he'd tossed her down.

"Of course, interest accrues daily."

Of course.

"But, in the unlikely event you ever paid off your debt, I would allow you your freedom if you still wanted it by that point."

How magnanimous of him.

"You aren't worried I'd report you?"

He chuckled. "No. I know you won't report me for the same reason you were so torn up over stealing from me. Because you know who I am. Because you can't bear the thought of hurting Joseph Quill. Tell me I'm wrong."

Joseph Quill was a lie. The art was real, but everything else around him was carefully crafted artifice, yet she still fell for the illusion.

Saskia wanted him to be wrong. Desperately. There had to be something he could do, some line he could cross that she couldn't forgive. There had to be a level of depravity he could take her to, a place so dark that could erase any feelings of reverence she had toward the artist. But so far, her tolerance for his whims seemed bottomless.

Quill stripped off his clothing and draped it across

the couch then joined Saskia in the bed. He pulled her against him, holding her close.

She barely breathed. She could hardly believe they were wrapped up in his bed, skin pressed against skin in something that almost looked like an affectionate embrace. Marcus was kind to her. Why was it so important to her to have Quill's affection as well?

So he was a great artist. So what? There were a lot of great artists. He was an arrogant rich asshole who wasn't worth the tears she'd shed for him or the admiration she'd felt, but as he held her, Saskia was sure there must be something deeper in this man worth knowing and being connected to.

He pressed the button on the remote, and the screen came to life with footage from the party.

It was jolting to see herself this way—as disconnected pieces rather than a whole. At the same time, not having to watch her own facial expressions allowed her the distance she needed from it. It was like watching porn with decent dialogue. As long as she didn't think too hard about who all of this was being done to, it was as exciting watching it as it had been experiencing it.

"We'll fast-forward to the best parts, but even during the fast forwarding, you will count every orgasm."

"But if we're skimming through part of it, how will I know?"

"Trust me, you'll know."

He was right. She *did* know. Even while moving fast, she started to see a small jerk she always made to the right. Like a poker tell. She hadn't realized she did that. She wondered if she'd done it with all her lovers in the past.

He slowed the footage and pressed play to let her see the part with Nolan.

Quill's hand slipped between her legs. Saskia tried to scoot away, but there was nowhere to go.

"I knew you liked him," he said.

She tensed, waiting for that to turn into an issue, but it didn't.

Quill skimmed through most of the film, stopping for each turn Nolan had taken. He'd drilled her with various toys a total of five times. Each of those times, he'd dropped more money into the glass jar. How much would he pay for a private session with her be? Would he pay more so Quill could maintain a defense of his territory, or would he get the friends and family discount?

The only other part of the film Quill slowed down for was the women. Saskia was surprised three women at the party had actually engaged in this. The women were different, though. They giggled at doing something naughty and forbidden.

She'd heard their laughter at the time, but had thought they were only standing nearby. She'd known it was nervous laughter and had wondered if they just didn't want to piss off the men they were with by objecting. Now she wondered if they'd somehow been coerced to join in. Perhaps they'd thought it better to be the aggressor than the one lying naked and vulnerable in the box. And yet, everyone had watched them do what they'd done.

The women had hesitated. The men hadn't. The men, by contrast, showed no shame. They'd felt entitled. Of course, if a woman was spread-eagled near them,

ready and waiting, it was practically their birthright to
plow that field.

In the film's background, Saskia watched couples slip
behind the large Greek columns together—not quite
brave enough for an orgy, but far too bold for a polite
gathering.

Quill skimmed through the last three sessions and
then shut off the video.

"I plan to watch it at my leisure, later," he said as he
stroked between her legs, giving no doubt as to what he
planned to be doing while watching. "How many,
Saskia?"

She didn't bother playing dumb. "T-twenty-two,
Master."

"That's an insane number of orgasms for four hours,"
he said. "You're insatiable. Unfortunately, that also
means you'll be paying for them with twenty-two cane
stripes. If only you'd kept count like I asked, you could
have had them for free."

"I'm sorry, I just lost track. Please..."

Quill shook his head. "No. You know when I lay
down a law, that's it. You have no excuse. I'll spread them
across your thighs, and ass, perhaps a few over your
breasts. And I won't go harder than you can take. Let's
get this done."

"You don't sound like you want to. If you don't want
to, I sure as shit don't want you to."

His eyes narrowed. "Watch your mouth, little girl. I
never *want* to punish you, but I want your defiance even
less."

He turned off the video and pressed the appropriate
buttons to make the screen slide back down into the

floor. The paneling closed over it. He set the remote on the night table and crossed to the other end of the room. His fingertips skimmed the cane as if it were a dear friend he'd lost touch with.

Of course he wanted to punish her. Just like he'd wanted to entrap her and enslave her, and all the rest of it. He wasn't possessed. No one pulled his strings. Who could possibly pull this man's strings?

"Saskia?"

She reluctantly unfolded her limbs and climbed out of the bed, following him to the corner. Quill secured her arms over her head and then stepped back to look at her, circling her a couple of times as if he were imagining this on a canvas. Abruptly he came back to himself.

He nudged her legs apart with the tip of the cane.

"You will count them out loud."

Saskia jerked in the chains as the cane sliced the air —before it even struck her. When it did, it seemed to send ripples of pain that vibrated across the room. The sharpest sensation was the cry it tore from her throat.

"O-one." Her lip trembled when she spoke. She wasn't sure if she'd ever been this afraid of him before. Even the time he'd been angry. The idea of even surviving twenty-two lashes of the cane, especially a cane wielded by Quill was more than she thought she could cope with. Tears slipped down her cheeks.

"I told you that doesn't affect me," he said.

Of course it didn't. He was heartless and soulless. A fucking sociopath with pretty things.

"I know, Master."

Somehow, despite his lack of anything approaching compassion, the remaining lashes were lighter. They still hurt like hell, but it was a hurt that one could cope with. She counted each one dutifully, each one getting her closer to the end of her punishment.

In between each strike she mentally berated herself. Why couldn't she just remember to keep track of the orgasms? At least she hadn't lied and made up a number. That would have been worse when Quill watched the feed and counted them himself. And she didn't think she was a good enough actress to feign a counting error.

Finally, the word "Twenty-two" fell from her lips. Quill let the cane slip from his hand onto the ground. His special precious cane with its own spotlight rattled against the hardwood like a viper.

He unchained her and led her to the bed. "Lie on your stomach."

He disappeared into the bathroom and returned with a first aid kit. "I didn't break skin, but I'm going to put a cream on the welts to take the sting out."

Saskia barely breathed as he sat beside her and began smoothing the cooling cream over each mark he'd left across her skin. She could hardly believe he was doing this. He never took care of her after. It was always Marcus who'd been tasked with the comfort side of things. It had made everything with Quill feel incomplete, as if Saskia couldn't get herself to fully bond with him because he never directly offered her the comfort she needed.

"Sit up, and let me get the ones on your breasts."

Saskia scooted to a sitting position. She remained silent as he rubbed the cream into the welts on her chest. He screwed the lid back on and dropped the container back into the first aid kit. She watched as he crossed to the other end of the room, opened a drawer, and pulled out a short cotton nightgown. Saskia could tell from across the room that the fabric was soft and cool and breathable. He helped her into it and then pulled back the covers on the bed.

"Get in."

She slid under the covers, and Quill turned out the lights and joined her. Saskia drifted off to sleep in Quill's arms, certain something had changed between them for the better.

17

But nothing changed. It was as if Quill had let his guard down with her for one beautiful moment and then pulled it right back up again. Almost immediately, he'd pushed her away, back into the gallery, isolated from him. As if she'd never spent a night in his bed. Or as if it didn't matter that she had, or maybe he'd found her in some way lacking the same way he seemed to find everything she put on canvas lacking.

Anyone else who didn't meet his expectations, he could have sent packing, but she knew too many things that could ruin him, she hadn't signed an NDA, and well, what were the odds he trusted her not to report him for what was essentially kidnapping?

He'd at least started painting with her again, but that same distance permeated the work between them. The only sign of intimacy was the accumulating stack of finished paintings in her image. It was the only real connection between them, the only sign that he felt something deeper when he looked at her.

Beyond that, he'd grown even more distant than before. The only sex or kink they shared was in preparation for a new painting. He was willing to fuck her to capture her on canvas but not for the experience itself. What did that say about her? What the hell did it say about him?

It was even worse with her work. With his, at least there was a sign of life in the finished piece, but when she painted, Quill maintained his distance. He gave no sign of either pleasure or disappointment. And no longer did he give her any direction. No tirades. No pep talks. Just a gaping void of nothing, a space she couldn't seem to fill with anything to regain his interest in her as an artist.

Quill glanced at her newest painting. A still life. BDSM furniture, but still she was regressing. She kept moving farther from the material instead of closer. She wondered if some part of her did this intentionally, to force his hand, to force any extreme reaction out of him. Anything that felt alive like his paintings. She was baiting him.

But he gave no sign that he cared one way or the other about her creation. Instead, he said, "Nolan will be here in an hour. You should probably get ready."

Saskia flung her brush down, but still he didn't react. "Do you really want me to fuck him?"

Why? For what possible reason could he want this? He'd seemed weirdly jealous of Marcus. How could passing her around more help anything? She was perfectly happy to just be his. To truly deeply be his. Why couldn't she just be his? Why couldn't he just let her in? She'd only agreed to sleep with Nolan because

Quill seemed to want her to. She grasped onto anything he wanted like it would be the last raindrop before an endless drought.

Quill moved closer, the whisper of intensity peeking around the edges of his features. "Yes. I want you to fuck him. And I'm going to watch the whole thing on the cameras. I want you to give yourself to him in any way he demands. I want you to be my whore. It's the only investment that's paid off."

She flinched, unsure which stung more, the words themselves or their icy delivery. Once again, she wanted to hate him. Saskia was sure if he were anyone else in the world, she'd hate him. But no matter how much easier it would be and how much she wished she could flip a switch and be done, Quill continued to loom large in her mind, and the hope of something real with him lingered on.

"He wants you to meet him out on the terrace. You can wear a swimsuit. Lacy left one in the bathroom for you. There will be drinks waiting by the pool."

Quill turned to leave.

"Wait. Does he know who I am yet?"

"I haven't told him."

An hour later, Quill was nowhere to be found. In fact, everyone at the main house had made themselves scarce. A red bikini had been left in the bathroom and a matching sarong.

Nolan was in the pool, a piña colada in one hand, when Saskia arrived. She'd taken advantage of the sarong for as much cover as possible. Which was ludicrous. He'd seen everything in excruciating detail already.

It seemed almost comical for someone with such strong male features to be holding a yellow girlie drink with a pink straw. And yet there he was. He'd already downed one and was working on his second.

"Saskia," he said, his eyes widening in surprise.

She couldn't believe he'd actually remembered her name. When she'd met him at the fund raiser, she'd been sure that if she were to meet him again the very next day he would have scrambled to remember it and likely wouldn't have even gotten the first letter right.

"Nolan," she said in reply.

"Great, we both remember each other's names. We're off to a fabulous start. Join me."

Nolan wasn't wearing swim trunks. They floated forlornly in the deep end of the pool like a tragic accident. His erection was visible even from above the surface of the water. He made no comment on the bikini or the fact that she was getting into the pool with him still wearing it.

He handed her a piña colada when she reached him.

Saskia took a sip. "Wow. That's strong."

"It's a lot of rum, very little mix. I imagine that was for your benefit."

As if drunk drowning in a pool could ever be to her benefit.

"So, how's the honest reproduction business?" he asked. "Or are you done with that now that you've landed a sugar daddy?"

Saskia cringed. He'd seemed genuinely interested in what she did the night of the party, or was he only interested in getting her out of her gown? She gestured to the upper corner of the building at the security camera over the pool. "You know he's watching this, right?"

"Our host is a bit of a freak," Nolan said, already forgetting the topic of reproductions. "But then, you knew that already. How did he ever convince you to get in the box at the party? Or are you a bit of a freak yourself?" He winked.

She felt the heat come into her face and took another long sip from her drink. An alcohol buzz rippled over her face, slipping down over her shoulders, wrapping her in a warm hug of slight inebriation.

Nolan's fingers slid beneath her bikini bottoms, pushing slowly inside her. She let out a gasp, not prepared for things to move so quickly, despite knowing the reason she was there.

"I've dreamed about what it might feel like to touch the inside of this pussy with my fingers instead of a glass toy since that night."

A tear slipped from the corner of her eyes, but Nolan didn't seem to notice. He was too wrapped up in fulfilling the fantasy he'd paid good money for.

"I say we move this party to the hot tub," he said. "Even under our host's watchful eye, I feel safer in shallower water. And I'm sure you'll find you're wearing too much in the heat."

He helped her out of the pool and the few yards over to the bubbling hot tub. If anything, the camera here gave an even better shot of things.

The door to the main house opened and closed with some force. Saskia and Nolan looked up to find Quill striding toward the terrace like he was on a mission.

When he reached them, he pulled up a patio chair and sat beside the hot tub.

"Something wrong?" Nolan asked. He was already submerged under the hot bubbling water. He pulled Saskia onto his lap, spreading her legs so Quill could watch his fingers crawl under the fabric again. The water was lit from below, spotlighting Nolan's every movement.

"I haven't decided yet," Quill said. "Saskia, come here."

She waded over to him. He helped her out and took her out of Nolan's range of hearing.

"You don't want to fuck him, do you?"

Saskia shrugged. "I just don't understand why you want it."

Quill stroked the side of her face and then wrapped a nearby towel around her to stop her shivering. "I enjoy watching you get fucked by other men. I enjoy them paying me for the privilege. It's just one of my many kinks. You've had a taste of my kink, Saskia. Why should this surprise you? All these cameras? You know I like to watch."

More than he liked to do?

"But, you were weird about Marcus."

"Marcus lives with us. Marcus belongs to me. As you do. Marcus was reaching beyond his position to play in ways I didn't authorize. He wanted that whipping. Trust me."

Saskia wondered if Marcus had gotten the memo that he still belonged to Quill. Everyone at this house must know it now except for Marcus.

Quill continued. "I want you to submit to Nolan. Spread your legs for him. Let him lick and touch and fuck you in any hole he desires. I'm going to stay out here and watch. I want a front row seat for a live show. Can you handle that, Miss Roth?"

She nodded. "Y-yes, Master."

It was the most intensity he'd shown her in days, and she found herself drawn into it like a vampire's compulsion.

He pressed an intercom button on the outer wall and ordered a drink, then he escorted Saskia back to the hot tub where Nolan waited.

She got into the water and waded back over to him. She glanced back at Quill as Nolan pulled her back into his arms. Would he have stopped things? He'd come storming out of the house almost as if he'd meant to rescue her, but such a thing seemed impossible after the words that had come out of his mouth when they were alone. Still, he'd asked what she wanted, and he'd seemed willing to deliver whatever it might be.

"Everything all right?" Nolan asked.

"Everything's fine," Quill said. "Saskia, were you aware that Nolan plays the cello? I believe you heard some of his music when you were with Phillip."

Nolan raised a brow. "Phillip, huh? How was that? Did he do the opera glove thing?"

The question was aimed at Saskia, but Quill answered instead. "Of course he did the opera glove thing. I've thought of sending him a case full of opera gloves for Christmas. Sometimes I think he might be more attracted to them than the women wearing them. A store mannequin might please him just as much. So long as she wore the gloves."

Lacy appeared out of nowhere like a phantom and

pressed a glass of scotch into Quill's hand. Then she retreated back into the main house as quietly as she'd come out.

Quill took a sip of his drink. His eyes were dark, focused, and intense as he watched the two of them in the water as if they were animals expected to breed in captivity. Nolan seemed to have no real problem with this, and it struck Saskia that he'd probably done this sort of thing with a girl of Quill's before—one of the ones "on probation" that had never reached any full status with him. There was a certain choreography to the night.

Saskia touched the edge of her collar as if making sure it was still fastened in place. She was only the second woman he'd put a collar on. At least he'd committed to having her in his life, unlike the ones on probation, but if he wouldn't really let her in, what difference did it make?

"So," Quill said. "I've seen you play the cello. Now I want to watch you play Saskia."

Nolan laughed. "You've waited a while to use that line haven't you?"

"Maybe. I wasn't aware of your musical talents the last time we did this."

Nolan shook his head but obliged. He pulled Saskia back against him, stroking her throat as if she were his instrument.

"What kind of sounds do you think I can get out of her?" he asked.

"You're the expert," Quill said. "You tell me."

Nolan stroked every inch of her, while Quill sat there, drinking in both the scotch and the scene before him. Nolan's fingers played across her collar bone, down her arms, lingering for several minutes on her breasts. He removed her bikini top and pinched and twisted her nipples until she writhed on his lap and moaned. With one quick flourish, he ripped the bikini bottoms off her and let them float on the surface of the water.

"That was Lacy's swimsuit you just ruined," Quill commented.

"I'll buy her another one." He gripped Saskia's waist, raised her up, and then pushed her down hard on his cock. She let out something between a whimper and a gasp as she fought to regain her breath.

"Good girl, just ride me," he said, stroking her back as she raised and lowered herself over him.

When she looked up, Quill was riveted. She wasn't sure she'd ever seen him quite like that, and once again the hope renewed in her that he'd somehow open up and let her in, that he wouldn't forever hold her at this distance.

It only took Nolan a few minutes to come with the way she grinded on him. He held her firmly in place as he emptied inside her. Quill rose to his feet, kicked off his shoes, and unbuttoned and dropped his pants on the terrace. He unbuttoned his shirt and laid it across the chair, then he sat on the edge, with his legs in the water.

"Come here, Saskia," he said again.

She waded over to him and found herself standing directly in front of one of the jets. If she moved just a few inches, the water would pulse against her clit. From the look in his eyes, Quill knew this. He nodded at her, and she moved those few inches, then he scooted closer.

Her mound pressed against the pulsating jets. Her mouth was mere inches from his erect cock. She didn't have to ask what he wanted her to do next. Saskia ground against the jets while she licked and sucked him. Nolan came up behind her, kissing and biting the side of her neck. His pressed a finger against her ass and she jumped in surprise at the contact.

He chuckled from behind her.

Saskia clenched around his finger as she came from the jets, having nearly forgotten about the cock in her mouth.

"Miss Roth? Don't disappoint me."

Such a statement from Quill carried with it the promise of the most dire consequences. She turned her attention back to her master's cock and didn't disappoint him.

And yet, she slept in the gallery.

"GET DRESSED, WE'RE GOING OUT," Quill said as he breezed into the gallery dressed in all black. Marcus had left her hours ago to go back to the main house to sleep, but Quill hadn't been in yet.

Saskia searched his face for any sign of weirdness from the previous night with Nolan. Quill's friend had fucked her a few more times before he'd retired to the study with Quill for some brandy and cigars, leaving her sore and wrung out from the demands of the two men. She'd wondered if they'd compare notes. Marcus had come out to the pool for her and taken her back to the gallery. Then he'd had his turn with her, albeit a tamer version, given Quill's parameters and rules.

"Where are we going?" Saskia asked.

"Out."

She didn't know why she bothered asking. His answer was always the same.

"Where's that thing you wore to the club that first time?" Quill asked.

"It's in the house." In the room that had become her storage locker because she'd long given up hope that it could ever be her actual room. Even if she never made it into Quill's bed in a permanent way, she'd held out hope for a time that at least she might earn her way into sharing space with her own things. But no.

"So we're going to the club?" she asked.

Quill sent her a withering look. "Just put it on. Have you eaten?"

"Yes, Master."

Lacy had brought her a plate earlier when Quill hadn't summoned her to the dining room for dinner.

"Good. Be ready to go in twenty minutes."

The main house felt strangely foreign when she stepped inside it—like it had forgotten her already. But she shook the feeling off and went to the room with her things and put on the outfit he wanted.

She heard a low whistle behind her and spun to find Marcus standing in the doorway slouched casually against the frame. He looked as if he'd just gotten out of the shower. His hair was wet and he wore only jeans. The dragon twisting around his torso seemed to be craning to get a look at what had caused Marcus to whistle.

"Are you coming with us?" Saskia asked.

"Coming with you where?"

She shrugged. "I don't know. The club maybe. He

won't say." She wondered now if Quill hadn't come to her because he'd been with Marcus.

"Then it's probably the club. He acts as if acknowledging its existence aloud will break some sacred trust. But no, I'm not going. I've been given the night off."

Saskia let out a long slow breath. If Marcus was being given the night off, it either meant she'd sleep in Quill's bed tonight or whoever he was leasing her to wanted overnight privileges.

She met Quill out by the Bentley twenty minutes later. He glanced at his watch but made no comment. He simply opened her door for her and then got in on the driver's side.

They traveled in silence out of the city and into the desert as before. Saskia felt no less self-conscious in the short skirt and boots than she had the last time she'd worn them.

When they reached the gate of Mr. Fizzy Pop Bottling Company, Quill input his code, and the doors swung open again. He parked in the same handicapped spot as before, as if it were his special reserved parking. Without a word, he got out and came around to Saskia's side.

She started to open her mouth to speak, but Quill pressed a finger against her lips and shook his head. He took a black silk tie from his pocket and blindfolded her. Then he pulled the black cami top off over her head.

"No bra. Good girl," he said. Quill slipped a hand under her skirt between her legs to find that she wasn't wearing underwear. "Very good girl."

He'd wanted her dressed the same as the first visit, and she wasn't about to irritate him with feigned ignorance about underwear.

Saskia felt her nipples harden in the cool night air. "Turn around."

She turned, and a moment later, a piece of tight leather with stiff vertical pieces was being wrapped around her. A corset. There were no hooks, no easy fastenings or buttons or zippers for those who just wanted the "look" without the fuss and muss. No, this was a real lace-up corset.

She drew in a sharp breath as Quill cinched her up like he knew exactly what he was doing. And it struck her as kind of odd that he'd never done this before. He'd painted a few other women in corsets, but he'd always painted Saskia nude.

The corset stopped just under her breasts, leaving them pushed impossibly high and exposed for the viewing pleasure of anybody inside the warehouse. Next, she leather cuffs were placed on her wrists. A metal chain clinked as it was attached to a connecting ring between the cuffs.

Quill tugged on the leash. She tottered in the heeled boots briefly, then got her bearings and followed him. He led her into the building, through the loud, grinding industrial beat, through the secondary doors where the beat faded into a hum, then he held her hands and helped her down the treacherous spiraling stairs to the underground level. Even through the pulsing beat, she heard the staccato rhythm of her heels clicking against the hard floor until Quill halted her with a hand pressed lightly to her stomach.

She waited.

He unlocked one of the cuffs, repositioned her arms behind her back, and recuffed her.

There was a grinding sound as something creaking and metal settled against the ground. When a metal door swung open, Quill helped her inside.

"Kneel and spread your legs."

She obeyed, and the door shut. She felt herself rise in the air as the creaking metal—which she realized was one of the bird cages—rose a few feet in the air.

The volume of the music seemed more muted now as a small crowd gathered around the cage. A din of speech surrounded her—deep male voices—but she couldn't pick out a single strand of conversation. Different men's words bumped up against each other as they seemed to circle and prowl around her cage like a pack of wolves.

Hands stroked her spread thighs, pushing between her legs, massaging and caressing her breasts, stroking the side of her face.

"Give yourself over to it," Quill whispered from just behind her, his voice the only one she could piece together with clarity.

A hand slid into hers, and she knew it was her master's.

Saskia began to move her hips, grinding against the strange hands. Multiple hands stroked her thighs now, as two—possibly from two different men—rubbed between her legs. From behind, hands moved on her ass, one teasing her rear entrance. The hands on her breasts became more insistent and demanding. And one hand demanded she suck its fingers into her mouth. She obliged with a whimper as she writhed against the strangers.

"Come for us", the voices whispered. For one crazy moment, Saskia thought she'd wake up in her own cage in the gallery with her own fingers between her legs, but she didn't wake up. Instead, she let the hands and voices pull her under their wave of pleasure as she came moaning for them.

One by one, the hands pulled away, and she was left kneeling in the bird cage with the evidence of the events of moments before sliding quietly down her legs.

Several minutes of silence passed. Then there was the talking again. The muffled male voices overlapping, lowering discreetly when they didn't want her to hear. Saskia felt her whole body blush inside the cage.

She picked up bits and pieces and little phrases here and there, enough to piece together a narrative inside her head. It was a financial negotiation of some sort. What had just happened inside the cage had been... an audition of sorts? A try out for the men who were now talking about money.

Saskia's anxiety ratcheted higher. She couldn't pick out Quill's voice. His hand was no longer in hers. What the hell was happening?

The cage lowered back to the ground, the door opened, she was helped out, and her hands were uncuffed and recuffed once again in front of her. She was led out of the warehouse on the leash the same way she was led in, never once seeing anyone in the club, not even the bouncer outside.

When they reached the car, the passenger side door was opened for her, and she was buckled into her seat belt. The driver's side door seemed louder closing than hers had been. The car started and backed smoothly out of the parking lot and onto the road.

She was still blindfolded and leashed and cuffed, but

now inside the silence of the car, everything felt sharper and the odd fog she'd been in began to fall away. The seat she sat on felt different than she remembered, the leather softer against the backs of her thighs. The car handled differently. Sounded different. Smelled different. She reached blindly in front of her to feel the dash and glove box—very different contours than the Bentley. Her breath sped perilously down the ramp to hyperventilation, but a voice stopped her.

"Relax, Saskia. I'm here," Quill said from the back seat. But who was driving?

She didn't care. As long as he was there. He hadn't abandoned her to a stranger going to God only knew where in the dark of night. For a crazy moment she'd thought he'd sold her off to someone else. Forever.

The trip was much shorter than the time it took to drive from the warehouse to Quill's house. Saskia didn't ask to remove the blindfold, nor did she attempt to take it off herself. As long as Quill was there, she could handle whatever this was.

The car stopped, and again the doors opened. This time, she realized the magnification of the sound of the door shutting had been the back seat and the driver's side closing in concert. Her door was opened next, and she was helped out, led on the leash as she'd been before. She wasn't sure if it was Quill or the stranger leading her.

Water burbled in a fountain a little way from the car. Suddenly she was scooped up and someone started to carry her.

"Is that really necessary?" Quill asked.

"These cobblestones are too easy to trip over in her boots."

Saskia recognized that voice. The Viking. Ari. She relaxed a fraction.

He climbed a set of stairs with her, and then set her down just inside the front door. Her heels clicked against a hard, echoing floor. Then Ari led her through the house on the leash. She heard Quill's footsteps just behind them.

Another door opened, and Saskia was guided through it. She heard flowing water and the crackling, spitting sound of fire in a grate. Ari unhooked the leash and removed the cuffs from her wrists. He raised each wrist and gently rubbed the irritated skin.

"You can take the blindfold off," he said.

Saskia removed Quill's silk tie from around her eyes and handed it back to her master. The room was large and solid white with vaulted ceilings that made her feel as if she were in a cathedral. There was a waterfall at one end of the room that emptied into a giant hot tub. The jets were unbelievably silent, giving the illusion that all the bubbling came from nothing more than the waterfall.

Several feet up—where the flow of water started— was a nook one might curl up in to read a book. She couldn't see any detail in the space itself. She only knew that a person could fit in there and sit and look out over the rest of the room.

"That's where my pet sleeps," Ari said. Saskia knew he didn't mean a dog or a cat. He meant the girl she'd met the first time in the club who'd been wearing the school girl uniform. On closer inspection, Saskia could see light glimmer off the link of a metal chain. She imagined there was a cuff on the end that might be locked around the girl's ankle at night.

"Where is she?" Saskia asked.

"She's spending the night in one of the guest rooms."

Not a cage isolated in a gallery?

The fireplace against the wall crackled and spit some more, and Ari put another log on the fire.

There was a large white bed opposite from the hot tub with an endless pile of pillows on top of it. Metal chains hung from the ceiling, ending in white leather cuffs at various points over the bed. The bed itself was a four poster, the posts made of a sturdy gleaming steel.

There seemed to be endless ways to tie someone to Ari's bed.

The floor was a blond hardwood, but it was nearly covered in white fur rugs so only a few inches of floor peeked from under them at a time. Small white pillows were clustered in a haphazard pile around the fireplace.

"Undress, please," Ari said. "Boots, too." His words were directed to Saskia, but Quill removed his shoes as well to avoid tracking anything onto all of Ari's fine rugs. Ari also removed his shoes, but Saskia was the only one among them who was to be nude.

She wondered if Ari's hands had been on her at the club when she'd been locked inside the birdcage, or if he'd stayed back and watched. She didn't ask because she doubted either of them would tell her.

Quill looked back and forth between Saskia and Ari as if searching for some clue in a great mystery. He seemed to find whatever it was he was looking for.

"Saskia?"

"Yes, Master?"

"I'm going down the hall to play with Ari's pet. You will stay here and do whatever he asks of you." He didn't frame it as a question, but something in the cadence of the sentences made it play that way despite his best effort.

"You aren't staying to watch?" She felt her skin heat when she caught the smirk on Ari's face at that.

"Not this time," Quill said. "You're in good hands." His gaze shifted to The Viking. "I'm sure we won't have a misunderstanding like last time?"

Ari shook his head. "No, Kane. We're good. Besides, where would I take her? We're already at my house."

"Exactly."

Quill shut the door softly behind him. He left his shoes behind in Ari's room.

The Viking moved closer and began to unbutton his shirt. He tossed it onto a chair near the door. He left the pants on for now, but hooked his thumbs into the front pockets as if it were the only way he could control some wild thing inside him that wanted to devour Saskia whole.

He was so tall. Quill was tall. The two men were close to the same height, in fact, but Ari's long blond hair really did make him look like a warrior off an ancient battlefield. As if to put a finer point on it, a faded angry scar slashed across his chest.

Saskia reached out—unable to help herself—and traced the scar. She drew back immediately as if burnt, remembering Quill's sharp rebuke when she'd touched him without permission.

"I'm sorry, sir."

"It's quite all right," Ari said. His smile was easy. There weren't a million cunning calculations going on behind those eyes. Not like with Quill. It seemed that every man she was with was somehow an easier or better option than Quill, yet in spite of all sound reason, Quill was the one she wanted to be close to, and she felt that every man's bed he sent her to warm was just another way to keep her out of his heart so she could be kept at an emotional distance.

Saskia's attention went back to the scar on Ari's chest. "How did it happen?"

He chuckled. "I got that little souvenir when I didn't listen to a safe word during edge play. As soon as I untied her, well... this is what happened. She had a few issues and was off her meds, but I still deserved it. And I knew she was off her meds, so shame on me for that, too. I took advantage from start to finish."

"Oh. It wasn't your pet?" It could very well be his pet, but the way he spoke made it seem more casual.

"No, just someone I was playing with for a night. Don't worry. I learned my lesson. And I have a harsh reminder every time I look at it. It won't happen again. It's one of the reasons I was so concerned that you were truly there at the club of your own free will. I didn't mean to try to take you away from somewhere you wanted to be or from someone you wanted to be with. I never should have doubted Kane."

Oh, no, those instincts were good. But aloud she only said, "It's okay."

Ari moved closer. One hand cupped the back of her neck drawing her forward. He kissed her forehead. "You say *Red*, if you need it. Just like at the club."

"Yes, sir."

"Good. Are you hungry?"

She looked uncertain.

He laughed. "Food. I'm asking about food, doll."

"A little," Saskia admitted. Dinner felt far in the distant past.

"I'll be right back."

Several minutes later, Ari returned with a large glass tray. He laid it on one of the rugs in front of the fireplace.

"Come, we're going to play a game."

There was a pitcher of water and two water glasses. In the center of the tray was an assortment of catered finger foods. There were mini-quiches, chicken salad tarts with grapes, something that looked like cream cheese mixed with something on crackers, butter mints, and fancy chocolates. Each portion on the glass was maybe a full bite or two at most.

"I had a party the other night. These are the leftovers. Unfortunately, some of the better stuff ran out first. Like the shrimp, and my pet polished off the last of the salmon puffs this afternoon."

Saskia glanced toward the door, suddenly wondering what Quill was doing with Ari's pet. A twinge of jealousy shot through her.

Ari's hand pressed against her cheek, directing her attention back to him. "You must pay attention, or I'll have to punish you. I'll be gentle tonight if you'll let me."

Ari's arctic blue eyes seemed to freeze as if mere verbal warning weren't enough.

"Y-yes, sir."

He nodded, the glaciers melting back into a warmer shade. "All right. How hungry are you?"

Now that she thought of it, and now that the wonderful smells were drifting toward her nose... pretty hungry. The Viking only had to see the look in her eyes for his answer.

He smiled. "Good. This game is better if you're very hungry."

Saskia swallowed around a lump forming in her throat. Quill wouldn't have left her alone with him if he wasn't sure, would he? It was just occurring to her that there had been a comfort in knowing Quill was on the other side of a screen watching, that he'd intervene if anything happened that he didn't like. Or when Marcus had been just outside the door waiting to pounce if anyone crossed any lines. They'd both guarded her in their own ways.

But it was just her and Ari tonight.

"Don't look so terrified. I won't be too horrible with you. The game is simple. I issue an order. You do exactly as I say, and then I let you have a bit of food."

Saskia nodded, looking from the tray to Ari.

He poured water in each of the glasses and took a sip from his, then he leaned back against the pillows. "Whenever I issue a command, you will say, 'It would be my honor, sir', and then do whatever it is I've ordered. Sound simple enough?"

"Yes, sir."

"First, I want you to crawl around the room so I can get a good look at you from every angle."

Saskia dropped to her knees. "It would be my honor, sir." She crawled slowly around the circumference of the room, avoiding the furniture and the hard marble around the hot tub.

When she returned to Ari, he motioned her closer and fed her one of the chicken salad tarts—or half of one, anyway. It was all she could get in one bite.

He pulled the rest of the tart away. "Don't be greedy. If you please me, you won't have to worry about starving in my care."

Ari watched her kneeling on the rug waiting for his next command for several moments, then he said, "Go stand under the waterfall and wash yourself for me. I like my toys freshly cleaned before I use them."

"It would be my honor, sir." Saskia rose and climbed the marble steps, then descended into the hot bubbling water. A bar of peppermint soap rested on a ledge just to the right of the waterfall. The entire suite made her think of winter, from Ari's long blond hair, to the fireplace, to all the white fur rugs, and now the soap that made the air feel colder when she breathed in its scent.

She bathed under the flowing water, its warmth hiding how her nerves were beginning to get the better of her. Saskia found herself captivated in Ari's warm gaze. She didn't know how eyes so pale blue could sometimes be so warm. Why couldn't Quill look at her with just a fraction of that?

How pathetic. Her master was pimping her out to all these other men and rather than be horrified by it, instead of hating him, all she could do was wonder why he couldn't touch her with Phillip's care or caress her with the warmth of Ari's gaze. Or why he couldn't watch over her and stay close like Marcus. He seemed to have Nolan's single-minded fixation with little else attached to it. And yet Nolan had made her the most uncomfortable

—the one who'd seemed most like Quill. Shouldn't that tell her something?

"Saskia?" Ari's voice dropped deeper. A reprimand.

She looked up, startled. "Yes, sir?"

"Where did you go just now?"

"N-nowhere."

He didn't believe her. "Dry off and come back to me. I don't want any water dripping on my furs."

"Yes, sir." Saskia took a towel off the rack next to the hot tub and carefully dried off. She left the towel wrapped around herself, even knowing that Ari probably preferred her to leave it behind. But he made no comment.

Instead, he pushed the tray toward her. "Eat whatever you want."

Something had shifted in him, and the game was over before it had started. While she ate, Ari stripped off his pants and got into the water. He stood under the waterfall and used the peppermint soap. By the time she'd finished the food on the tray, Ari was next to her, a matching towel wrapped around his waist.

He offered her a helping hand up from the ground and led her over to the bed. He lay down and motioned for her to join him. They both wore their towels.

"What was that back there with you in the water? Seriously, where did you go? What's wrong?"

Saskia shook her head. She couldn't tell him. She was sure he'd only go behind her back and tell Quill, and then the two men would have a good laugh about it. No, Ari wasn't like that. And when she really thought about it, Quill wasn't either. Her master was hard and demanding and intense, but he didn't make jokes at the expense of others. At least he never had with her, and she'd never seen any indication that such a thing was part of his character makeup.

Tears began to fall down her cheeks before she could stop or hide them. Ari pulled her against him and petted her hair. "You can talk to me. Whatever you say is just between us."

Did he still think she was some unwilling captive? Was she? Was The Viking still trying to save her? There was nothing that could save her from her own self-destructive need to truly be Quill's.

"What's wrong with me? Why doesn't he love me? He's so distant. It's like he doesn't even want me around."

"Kane?"

That ridiculous name. If Ari didn't know any of Quill's multiple aliases, how could he understand any of this? But then, maybe Kane was just who Ari thought of him as, like Saskia thought of him as Quill. There was nothing to indicate how close Ari truly was to her master or how much he knew or didn't know about him and all his myriad lives which lay parallel to one another, trying desperately not to cross-pollinate.

"Saskia, you are the second person he's ever put a collar on. Trust me, it means something."

But did it? If Ari only knew the truth of how she'd come to belong to Quill, it might not look the same. Whatever Quill had with the last girl he'd collared... surely it had been voluntary and mutual. Saskia was certain that the unnamed mystery woman had held some true place in his heart, that she wasn't just some *thing* he possessed. She hadn't been an impersonal acquisition... an asset. Not like Saskia.

Saskia couldn't imagine him keeping that other woman locked away in the gallery away from him. If he had, how could he be surprised she'd left? If he was so empty inside that he couldn't offer even the barest real connection... why did he care who stayed or went?

"Give him time," Ari said. "Do you remember at the club when you screamed?"

She nodded.

"That look in his eyes when he confronted me about trying to take you out of there... I've only seen him that intense about one other person. Maybe he's afraid you'll walk out like she did."

Saskia almost laughed out loud. As if Quill would ever allow that to happen. She'd lain inside her cage in the gallery at night when it was still and quiet, taking her master apart in her mind and putting him back together, making up all sorts of explanations for his behavior. She was sure he'd taken her and started their relationship with a felony just so she *couldn't* walk out. He'd already set the tone and pace for them with that one criminal act. So what the hell could he be so afraid of now?

She'd swung almost immediately back to the idea that he didn't care. He just wanted to punish her for tricking him out of all that money and wounding his ego.

"Can I ask you something?" Saskia said.

"Ask, doll."

"What happened tonight at the club? I thought he was going to sell me to someone, maybe permanently."

"It was an auction, you're right. But just for the night. I was there to make sure it didn't get out of hand because he would never sell you—even for a night—to someone he didn't know well. I jumped in and outbid them to get you out of there without any bruised feelings."

"But I thought this was your rain check from... from before."

"It is. But the others in the club don't know that."

"You still haven't really done anything with me," she said, beginning to feel guilty that he kept getting screwed over, when she really did want to play with him.

Ari pulled her closer, his lips brushing softly against hers. "Just forget about all those buzzing worries for tonight." He gently pulled her towel away followed by his own. And then he proceeded to make slow careful love to her, the kind of thing people who paid for sex didn't offer. When you paid, you were there to take, but Ari just gave... all the things she'd wanted to come from Quill.

Afterward, he stroked her back until she fell asleep.

Saskia woke with her back pressed tight against a warm, solid chest. But Ari was in front of her, perhaps a foot away. At some point in the night, Quill had slipped into the bed. It wasn't his bed, but it was a bed with him in it, his arms wrapped around her like she was something he didn't want to let go of. She wondered if he'd pulled her to him immediately when he'd climbed into the giant bed, or if he'd instead unconsciously reached for her in his sleep.

Had Ari said something to him?

She remained very still the rest of the night, afraid that if she moved, the spell would break and Quill would release her and roll back over, shutting her out again.

18

Weeks passed. Or maybe it was months. It was so hard to tell with how the world all blurred together. Fucking and sucking and painting and being painted and being passed around.

Each time she felt there was some turning point between her and her master, it turned out to be nothing more than the same smoke and mirrors. He always pulled away again as if he'd catch on fire if he allowed even the slightest intimate ember to burn between them.

She had stopped lying to herself, stopped pretending that her master must share her out of fear of intimacy. That would mean he cared. And it was just another fantasy to keep her warm at night. Perhaps he just shared her because he got off on sharing her, on proving how deep her submission to him had grown, how lost she was, how enslaved.

And it had never been about what she'd stolen. She'd abandoned that theory early on. He'd only made the smallest pretense with the ledger. She wasn't even sure he was still keeping a record of what she'd "paid off". Quill got off on prostituting her, on being paid ridiculous sums of money to allow all of his wealthy perverted friends to part her thighs over and over.

So few men had the patience he had... to turn a mind and body and soul so that they craved the chains locked around them, so that they squirmed and mewled and begged shamelessly for more. He was an artist far beyond mere painting.

When Saskia had first been inspired by his work enough to attend art school, she'd imagined that somehow while there she would discover some artistry hidden deep within her. She'd credit Joseph Quill with inspiring her, but secretly she would know that all along she'd had *it*, whatever that meant. His work would have just unlocked it. There would be parties and acclaim. And her work would be talked about in hushed, reverent tones.

But over time with him, she began to realize that maybe she didn't have *it* after all. Maybe she'd only ever been kidding herself. He must have believed in her at one point. Why else would he have become so frustrated when she couldn't deliver what he wanted on the canvas? If he didn't think she could do it, he never would have invested so much of his own hopes and expectations on what she might become.

It had crushed both of them to see it just wasn't in there. Nothing more than hollow technique.

Saskia stood in front of a canvas, painting another scene from the club with the bird cages. This one was a self-portrait. She was the focal point of the piece, locked inside the bird cage, blindfolded, a lost expression on her face like a lamb on an altar. Hands seemed to crawl up out of the cage itself to touch her. In the background were men who all wanted a piece of her, waving money. But she didn't seem able to see or hear any of it. The only reality was that cage closed in around her, and the endless parade of hands poking and prodding her thighs apart.

It didn't really matter anymore if Saskia painted the truth about herself. It wasn't going to ever see the light of day. No one would care. No one would buy it.

She wasn't sure why she painted now. There was no real reason to. She knew she'd never be good enough. She'd never please Quill on any artistic level. Perhaps with her body she could please him—until he finally grew bored with that. But they were not colleagues. He was not her teacher. She was not his prized pupil.

The work wasn't about him anymore. It wasn't about the imagined outcome. It wasn't about money or fame or acclaim or respect. It wasn't about gallery openings and parties. It was just this thing inside her that pushed its way out onto the canvas in spite of all the ways it had been beaten down along the way. When she'd run out of places to hide behind polite landscapes and had run the gauntlet of trying to force the work through a filter of the imagined expectations of others, what was left was an undiluted, raw work that may never hang in any gallery —even this one—but it felt honest, at least.

Saskia stood back from the still-wet painting to take it in, trying to experience it as a stranger seeing it for the first time. She didn't hear Quill come in. She jumped when his hand rested on her shoulder.

"Yes," he whispered.

THAT *YES* FROM HIM... It was everything she'd thought she wanted to hear. And yet, it was the beginning of the end for her. Soon after, more work came, flowing out of her in a great rush like Ari's waterfall in the white room.

When enough had accumulated that pleased him, there was a party in the private gallery. The walls were covered with all her work. Quill invited enough people to fill the gallery, and she never knew which of his aliases all the attendees knew him by because she didn't recognize any of the faces of the guests.

But it couldn't just be his art crowd.

It was a specific gathering of others like him—art married with kink. Not just in the subject matter of the work itself... but a comfort with the real thing. Saskia imagined that most of the people in attendance had been at the party when she'd been in the box. Sure, she'd seen those who'd touched her that night later on the video feed, but it was on a screen and in such brief snippets as Quill had fast forwarded through all but the most interesting interactions.

So if anyone at this party had been at that party, she didn't remember them. There was a price on every painting of hers in the gallery. Not insane prices, but definitely respectable.

If Saskia had expected she would have some grand artist's introduction in good taste in an evening gown, she'd been kidding herself.

The reason she knew this crowd had to be comfortable with the real thing was because she'd been put on display as an art installation once again. Only this time,

Quill didn't grant her the anonymity she'd so craved at that first party, the anonymity she'd reluctantly relinquished, even if only for Nolan. The installation was another "Jacob Hunter" piece. It was called "The Artist, Exposed". Quill didn't go much for subtlety.

For this piece, she'd been stripped bare except for her collar and chained down, straddling a large shiny black round piece of marble. It was a ball just small enough that she could manage to straddle it without too much difficulty. Once she'd been chained in place, a switch was flipped and the ball began to roll gently on top of a sort of platform it was situated on, engineered for such movement. Water gushed forth from small openings in the piece creating an effect of sheets of water flowing over this moving ball.

And as if that weren't enough, the ball itself sort of pulsed and vibrated underneath her. The pulsing and movement and warm water caressing between her legs sent her cresting over the edge of orgasm repeatedly. If it weren't for the intense sensations, Saskia might have been able to appreciate the artistry and engineering of such a contraption. Only from the mind of Quill could such a bizarrely erotic piece have been realized.

But tonight there was no box to protect her, nor any blindfold to keep her in the dark where she could pretend whatever she wanted to pretend. Tonight it was real exposure, and she wasn't entirely sure which thing was worse, the installation she was a part of, or her art on the walls being judged by those with the money to buy it.

Mercifully, at this party, no one was allowed to touch her. It wasn't part of the piece. They were only allowed to observe her. The oddest thing about all of it was that she must have had a good twenty orgasms in the length of time she was kept on the installation, and yet, they acted as if this were some serious piece of art that actually said something instead of Quill just looking for another way to display and humiliate his property.

They spent an equal amount of time studying her as they did studying her art hanging on the walls. There were a lot of "Hmmms" bandied about, and the sharp ripping of checks from checkbooks that had endless check-writing potential. She'd never seen so much check writing. The members of Quill's circle must never have heard of the magic of the wire transfer. Or maybe writing a check was more convenient when one didn't want to be bothered with technology and account numbers.

One by one most of the pieces were bought, except of course, for her.

Eventually the champagne ran dry, and the waiters carrying trays of tiny food seemed to fade into the background and disappear as the guests filtered out, some carrying bits and pieces of Saskia with them in frames.

Quill, being a good host, joined his guests outside to see them off. Marcus remained behind. He unchained Saskia from the installation and caught her as the water propelled her forward without the chains to hold her in place.

She clung to him, her soul eviscerated. She felt that only shattered ribbons of her being remained behind, barely enough to reconstruct a full person even if she wanted to.

Quill had forged her in the fire of chains and whips and sex and slavery and prostitution and violation. And what had risen from that contorted dark wreckage had been a real artist who'd been made to feel so much it had to go somewhere. That somewhere was a canvas for the consumption of the masses.

And Quill was pleased.

And she was barely holding onto the last slip of her identity.

She hadn't known what it would cost her to create like Quill. The things it had cost him were different. It had cost his humanity and any soul which once might have existed within him. It cost her an identity and freedom. And whatever dignity she might have once possessed in some distantly faded past.

Everyone paid a price to speak something worth saying.

Saskia struggled to stand on her own and ran clumsily for the door, not caring about her state of undress. But Marcus stopped her and held her against him.

"Shhhh. Everything will be okay," he said, petting her hair.

She struggled in his arms. He released her but moved to block her exit, leaving no doubt as to whose side he fell on.

Women only came first on lifeboats and elevators.

"How can you defend him? Don't you at least care about me? I thought..." *Oh God, don't say it, Saskia. Don't be even more stupid and pathetic than you already are. Have an ounce of dignity.*

"We both care in our way," he said.

Saskia dropped to her knees, the tears coming full force now. "Please, sir, take me out of here. I'll be yours. Just yours. We can go anywhere you want. Why can't you just report him? Why can't you just leave him? Pick me."

As she said it she cringed at even the idea of leaving Quill. She only found the courage to say the words because she knew Marcus would never leave him either. It just felt right to say them, to make some halfhearted attempt at ending this insanity.

Marcus pressed a finger to her lips. "My place is with him. And so is yours. You need to accept that. We can be comfortable here."

Comfortable. What bullshit. Marcus could be comfortable. She would be destroyed.

The echo of the outer door made her jump. Moments later, Quill was in the gallery, watching her clinging to her guard. Her master's face was inscrutable.

"Marcus. I want to be alone with her."

"Yes, sir."

Quill watched her for several moments after Marcus had gone. Finally, he spoke. "What was that I just walked in on? An escape attempt?"

Was her face that emotionally transparent?

"Master, please just let me go. I can't... it's all..." The words came out among half-strangled cries. If she didn't get them out now, she might never gain the courage again.

Despite the ongoing foolishness of her desire to be his... it was... too much. He was too intense, too frighten-ing, too large for any world to contain. Surely he'd devel-oped some attachment to Saskia in all this time, some echo of love. Surely he would show her mercy and release her from her debt. Hadn't she yet paid for the terrible crime of taking money he'd never needed?

Quill's expression turned dark. "I knew you were just like her. Just waiting to abandon me."

"What do you care? You keep me at arm's length. You won't let yourself get close. You're scared, aren't you? If you're too scared to really have me, why can't you just let me go?"

His hands clenched and unclenched at his sides. "I will *never* let you go."

"I won't tell anyone anything. You know that. I'll keep all your secrets. Please, I'll die like this."

His face was a stone wall; his lip curled in a sneer. "Don't be so dramatic, Saskia. You won't die."

"Please. You know how I feel about you. I love you. I respect you. I would die for you if I could do it in some faster way. But I can't do it like this. You have to release me before I'm too broken to exist outside of you."

He closed the distance between them and stroked the side of her face. In spite of herself, she pressed closer against the warmth of his hand.

"You can relax. We passed that point a long time ago. I felt it the day you broke in my hands."

He was probably right, but knowing that window had already slammed shut didn't bring her any solace.

Saskia glanced around the gallery at what remained of her paintings adorning the walls. She'd created her best work with him—her only work that counted as anything more than mimicry. They were each their best when they were together... artistically at least. Outside the art, they were a tangled mess destroying each other. And it only grew more perverse the longer it went on. Couldn't he see that?

Quill turned and strode out of the gallery, the doors

clanging behind him in a deafening finality that echoed along the walls. Saskia went after him, reaching for the handle to follow him out, but the lock turned before she could pull it open.

"No!" She pounded on the door. "You let me out, you fucking monster! I fucking hate you!"

She slid to the ground, her ear pressed against the wood, listening for the outer door that would signal he'd left her. But there was no clanging outer door—just a silence that was everything but empty.

She felt pressure push back against the wood, and heard a sliding sound and a soft thump, and she realized Quill sat on the ground on the other side, wrinkling his nice suit.

She pressed her cheek against the door. This locked door was always between them, even when it wasn't. He wouldn't let her in, yet he wouldn't let her go. Would she always be in the gallery, frozen in this limbo?

"Saskia..." There was a long pause while he seemed to gather his thoughts. When he continued, the words were broken, filled with more emotion than she'd ever heard from him, more emotion than he ever would have let her witness without the door as a buffer between them. "I know I've destroyed you... I know... I'm fucked up. And I'm not going to stop. You can't rehabilitate me. Your love can't change me. I'm going to just keep pushing you and pushing you until there's nothing left. I know you hate me... and I don't blame you."

"I don't hate you."

"You said it. You said you loved me. And you said you hated me. Which is it?"

"Both."

"You want me to let you go. What will you do if I let you go?"

Die.

"Just let me *in*," Saskia said instead. "I can't stand it out here in the gallery at night anymore. Please. If you aren't letting me go, why can't I really be with you? In the main house. In your room. Please, just let me stay with you."

How had she gone from wanting to escape him to just wanting to be closer to him? Like a child that announces he's running away from home because his wishes aren't being fulfilled only to return in time for dinner.

Quill was so right. She'd already broken apart. There was nothing left to run from or to. Nothing to try to save or salvage. The only thing left was the relief of surrender.

There was a long silence, and she wondered if he was still out there or if he'd abandoned her yet again.

"You will sleep in the cage," he said, his voice back to the cold indifference she'd grown uncomfortably used to.

"I-in your room?"

"Yes."

"Okay." At least it was *with* him. "Will I be able to stay in there with you permanently?"

There was a long pause, and she was afraid she'd pushed him too far, that he might take back what he'd just promised.

"Unless you're being punished for something, yes."

"C-can we go now? To your room now?" She looked

back at the paintings on the gallery walls, convinced she saw some sign of hostile jealousy in them.

"Yes," he said.

The door opened abruptly, and Saskia tumbled backward. Quill towered over her in the doorway, that hard look back in his eyes. He held out a hand, and she took it and allowed him to help her up off the ground. He pulled her against him, closing his arms around her. It was a clawing clinging vise, not an embrace, not a give and take. There was no trust in the movement. Only fear and possession.

Saskia felt his self-loathing in the way he held her. He believed he deserved to be abandoned, and the only way forward was to capture and imprison what he wanted to hold onto. Even if he'd never admit he wanted to hold onto her.

But at least he would imprison her in his room with him. He might never truly let her into his heart, but for now at least, his room was enough.

Quill pulled back and looked hard into her eyes. Time, as Saskia knew it, stopped. She waited for something from him. Anything that would give her some hope that he could let himself care for her, that he could risk some piece of his heart for her soul's survival.

Instead, he said, "Miss Roth, in a just world, we'd both be in prison right now. And in a sense, we both are."

EPILOGUE
QUILL

T *he Past*

"SASKIA ROTH."

Her soft, lilting voice reaches my ears as she says her name to my assistant. He pretends to be interested in her artistic ambitions and the fact that he is the reason she went to art school. Correction: *I'm* the reason she went to art school. She just doesn't know it. Derick has been pretending to be Joseph Quill while I lurk in the shadows, observing the room. I get to be close to my collectors—my admirers—without ever letting them in, without ever letting them really see me.

My excuse has always been that the kind of kinky nudes I paint could hurt the stock price of my more financially successful tech company, and I make a really convincing argument to those who ask or balk at my web of non-disclosure agreements. The truth is I guard my privacy. It's difficult enough to be naked with your art, to put your soul out there for the consumption of the ignorant masses—those who think they know you, but don't have a clue.

Those who would psychoanalyze you and pick you apart as though they had the right.

I didn't want to be consumed as my art is consumed. And so I hide. I create a complex web of anonymity to lurk behind. At a certain point of art world notoriety I had to show my face, or "a" face, and that face was Derick. He approaches me now, the pretty brunette having wandered back into the crowd.

"I'm getting laid," he announces with more glee than I like. Ordinarily it doesn't bother me that he uses my name and my art to build a harem of groupies he can take to bed. After all, there should be some perks to pretending to be me, but this time it's different.

"No," I say.

He reels back as though I've slapped him. "What do you mean, *No*?"

"I mean what it sounds like. No. You are not fucking her. She's mine."

He puts up less fight than I expected he would, and before long he's on to the next groupie. Miss Roth is certainly not the first beautiful woman inspired by my art to pursue her own ambitions, but there is something about this one—something that calls forth the desire to try again.

While she was talking to who she thought was the artist, our eyes met. I held her gaze for several seconds until she pulled away from my intensity and went back to talking to my assistant.

I learn her hotel and room number from Derick. But what would I say to her if I knocked on the door instead of him?

I can't tell her I'm the artist that she so admires. What am I going to say? "Our eyes locked across a crowded room, and I thought I'd follow you to your hotel?" It sounds too much like a creepy stalker. I'm at least a decade her senior, but definitely not more than fifteen years. Still, it's too much of a gap. Though I am very fit, I'd still probably come off like a pervert to her.

And let's be honest, I am a pervert. I have dark and twisted desires that few women can cope with long term. Okay, no woman can cope with long term.

Between my sadism, my exhibitionism, my desire to share my toys, it's just... too much for them. I use my physical sadism more with Marcus. I can't fully unleash that part of myself on a woman. It's too dangerous. But the mental sadism?

I'm fucked up. And I have no excuses for the way I am, for my twisted combination of coldness and cruelty. I don't have a tragic childhood to blame. I've just always been this way. Fundamentally selfish.

I've been trying to track down one of my earliest paintings. Her. The one that got away. My muse. The only one I ever really loved. The one that left me because I was too much. Too dark. Too demanding. Too frightening. A storm she knew would consume her, and so she evacuated to safer ground. Smart girl.

How do I make one stay?

I don't know, but I am magnetized to Saskia Roth. I

don't know why she feels like the one I could keep when I don't even know her. As I lurk in the lobby of the hotel, I have fantasies of training her—both in the bedroom and in art. Of being her mentor. Which is ridiculous. I don't even know if she has any talent. Attending art school doesn't make one an artist.

I don't go to her room. I don't knock on the door.

But I also don't let her blend back into an anonymous life. I follow her. I am that creepy stalker. I am that dangerous man who probably shouldn't walk the streets free.

I'm sitting outside her apartment, watching it. I'm not sure why. What do I hope to glean or learn? I'm trying to manufacture a way to meet her, to interact with her, to lure her into my decadent world of art and kink. And it galls me that she thinks Derick is me. I want her to look at me with the worshipful gaze she gave him. And that look is reserved only for Joseph Quill.

I sigh.

She leaves her building, and I don't follow her this time. I just sit and watch the apartment. Half an hour passes when I hear smoke alarms from across the street, and I see the unit just beneath hers is on fire.

Fuck.

Without thinking, I leap out of my car. I open the trunk and retrieve a mallet which I often use when stretching a canvas. It's a real mallet—instead of rubber—so I have to use a light touch. I'm glad I have it now.

I race across the street, climb the trellis, and smash the window. It shouldn't be this easy to get into her apartment. I want to punish her for making it this easy for me or just any other predator to get into her home.

She should have stronger glass. She should have bars on her windows. She should have an alarm. In this neighborhood?

I feel betrayed that she would leave herself so vulnerable, even if it benefits me. What is she thinking?

Probably that she can barely afford rent and that the structural integrity of her window glass is her landlord's responsibility, not hers. If I were less of a bastard, I'd slip her some anonymous money, but no, I want to find a way to use that weakness to my advantage—to pull her into my world.

I feel the heat rising from the first floor as I hurriedly scan the rooms until I find her art. She has everything in one big portfolio. I double check the rest of the apartment to make sure this is it. I think I've gotten it all when I spot a smaller portfolio on a portable art table. I grab it. A few sketches slip out and feather out across the floor, face down.

I start to go for them, but the smoke and heat are rising, and my one escape route could close to me very soon. I'm not foolish enough to die in here for art that probably isn't even very good. I look one last time at the scattered drawings, my curiosity and greed for them warring with my common sense, but there is no time.

I shove the smaller portfolio inside the larger and go back the way I came in. I drop the art out the window, climb down the trellis, and rush across the street holding it clasped to my chest as though it were a kitten I'd rescued from a tree.

As soon as I get in the car I start the engine and drive a few blocks away. I pass the firetruck. When I stop, I turn on the interior light and finally look at her art for the first time. It's stunning. She does have talent. And now I know I have to find some way to insert myself into her life.

I have to put a collar around that slim throat. I need to be her teacher, her mentor, her master, her everything. I want to pull her into my darkness and share my spotlight with her.

I shake the thoughts away. It's completely insane. I can't just kidnap her. Surely I'm not that big of a monster. But I will find a way to make our interests and needs align so that she will walk willingly right into my cage.

The Present.

I sit in the gallery on the other side of the door. I can feel her, her sadness and desperation—the way she begs me to let her in. I want to, but holding her at arm's length is so much safer. But who am I kidding? I've never held her at arm's length. Even if she doesn't know it. I've always been obsessed, and I can't pretend anymore.

I hear her muffled sobbing on the other side of the door, and I just want to hold her. I don't know why I'm such a monster. I have clipped Saskia's wings so that she can't fly away from me. And I still don't feel any safer because I know she's a phoenix who can rise from the ashes and fly away.

Even if her body is here, she could withdraw her heart from me. She could truly see me. She should have already. It would be safer for her, healthier. I don't want to be the thing that snuffs out her light. I've built an artist who can go out into the world where I can't anymore, and I have taken her to the limits of her own sanity because I'm still locked inside my past.

I'm so selfish I'd rather risk destroying her than let her destroy me.

Finally, I open the door and she tumbles back. I extend my hand to her to help her off the ground. When she's standing, I pull her into me and grip her as though she could somehow evaporate into mist and slip through my fingers at any moment. My desperation is at least as great as her own.

Except that I'm just desperate not to lose her. My new muse. The woman I have so completely destroyed and don't deserve. If I had any decency I would set her free, but I am far too greedy and selfish for such a noble act. She was mine the very first time I saw her, though she didn't know it yet.

I pull back from her and look into her eyes, searching for the hatred and resentment that I know have to be there somewhere after everything that has transpired between us. Finally, I speak.

"Miss Roth, in a just world, we'd both be in prison right now. And in a sense, we both are."

She doesn't say anything to this. What can she say? She is my prisoner—my art kept behind glass—while my cage is my own creation of stitched together cowardice. The fear of being seen and known by another soul in a way where they have the power to hurt me.

Without another word, I pick her up and carry her back to the house. She buries her face against my neck. I feel the wetness from her tears against my skin, and I hate myself for causing them.

When we reach my room, I set her down on her feet and undress her, carefully unwrapping her like a gift, running my hands over the smooth satin of her skin, compelled by the urge to paint her again.

Soon.

I pull back the silk sheets and put her in my bed.

"Master, I thought you said... the cage?" Her gaze drifts to the hated cage on the floor beside my bed.

"Do I have to gag you?"

She shakes her head and just watches me as I remove my own clothing and get into the bed with her. I turn off the lamp and pull her flush against me, her warm skin pressed against mine. I feel the flutter of her heartbeat like a bird flapping in a too-small cage, seeking freedom, and I grip her tighter.

Don't fly away from me. Please don't fly away from me.

It's a silent prayer.

Finally her heartbeat calms into a normal steady cadence, and I loosen my grip enough that she can relax. I press a kiss above her collar and I can feel her tension, the way she holds her breath, like she can't believe a real tender moment is passing between us.

This is how I've starved her.

I stroke my fingertips slowly down her arm and over her hip. She cries quietly beside me.

"Shhh, just go to sleep, Saskia."

I can practically read the thoughts out of her mind. They are so loud. She wonders if this is a brief reprieve in my cold distance, if tomorrow night she'll be sleeping in a cage like a captive wild animal again. But I can never go back now. I'm far too lost. I'm far too greedy to let her out of my bed.

BOOK 2 TEASER SCENE:
THE ESCAPE ARTIST

Ari didn't remember falling asleep. The drug had worked fast. When he woke, he was shirtless and shackled to the wall. There was just enough give in the chains for him to stand, but he remained on the ground, facing the door.

Waiting.

Soon enough the steel door slid open, and she walked in. His breath hitched in his throat, an involuntary reaction tightening his pants. She had long, wavy golden blonde hair and the most striking green eyes he'd ever seen. She wasn't wearing any makeup, but the healthy flush of color in her lips and cheeks made it hard to tell at first.

She was delicate, almost breakable by the look of her. Willowy limbs—like a dancer. And she moved that way, too. She wore jeans and a T-shirt—not one of those scoop-necked tops that let a man have a peek at cleavage. This shirt was modest. She wore no shoes and had a light pink polish on her toes.

She appeared sweet in a way that was almost painful to look at, and Ari couldn't stop the image of her on her knees from flitting through his mind. The phrase *Don't stick your dick in crazy* came to him suddenly as a sharp warning. But he didn't recognize this girl. Whatever offense she may have taken at something he'd said or done, he didn't remember it.

Which seemed impossible. Because if there was one thing he would remember, it was this girl.

She carried in a few plastic bottles of water which she left underneath the metal table beside the food slot. She went out again and came back in with a large bucket of water that she had to drag across the room because it was too heavy for her to carry. Some of the water sloshed over the sides. Then she brought a bar of soap and a sponge that she left with the bucket beside the drain in the corner. Each time she went out, she pressed her thumb to the keypad on the wall. There was no code to punch in, only biometrics.

The last time she entered the cell, she carried only a bottle of beer. She took a bottle opener from her pocket, flicked the cap off and took a long drink. He couldn't decide if she was drinking to taunt him with something he couldn't have but could definitely use right now, or to calm her own nerves for whatever she had planned next.

She had to know there was no coming back from this. She had to know she was going to prison for a long time.

She shoved the bottle opener and the cap back into her pocket.

"The water will be cold by the time you bathe, but if

you don't use it, I will punish you," she said matter-of-factly as if she were speaking to a small child.

"More death metal?" Ari asked nonchalantly. If he had to hear that music for more than a few minutes at that volume it *would* be a kind of torture, but he wasn't going to let her know he felt that way.

"If you don't like the playlist, I can change it. I have an entire two hours of harsh metal gears grinding. I could play that for you at the same volume if you prefer," she said.

"Don't put yourself out."

Her eyes narrowed as she took another long drag of the beer. "Do you think this is a fucking game?"

"No, I think you're ill. I think you need help. Now unchain me, and I will see to it that you get the help you need."

She moved swiftly toward him and slapped him hard across the face. Some of the beer escaped the bottle to hit the floor.

"Don't you *dare!*" she said, her expression morphing so dark and deadly in that moment it was hard to remember he'd found her cute and disarming only minutes before. "Don't you *dare* pretend like I'm the crazy one. You psychopathic piece of shit."

"I've never seen you before in my life," Ari said, keeping his tone calm and even. Reasonable.

"No! You will NOT get inside my head. You know what you did. You *know*. You don't get to play the innocent victim. You know why we're here."

"Refresh my memory."

He jerked back when she bent and ran her fingertips over the scar that slashed across his chest.

But she ignored his question. Instead she rose back to stand and paced the floor, staring at the scar like it would leap off his skin and attack her.

"Why me? Why did you take me?" she asked, still pacing. Her voice trembled, and he couldn't tell if it was from fury or fear. Or a deadly cocktail of both.

When he finally decided what to say, he spoke in a soothing voice. "I don't know what you're talking about. I think you're confused. I didn't take you. You took me. I'm the one in the chains, remember?" He rattled them as if to remind her.

"I mean BEFORE!" she shrieked. "Three fucking years ago? What you don't remember? How many women did you keep in that basement? How many did you kill? And you can't remember the one who got away? Bullshit!" She spoke so fast he could barely keep up with her words.

She raised an arm and slammed the beer bottle against the wall, sending alcohol and glass flying. She advanced on him in a blazing rush, holding the jagged broken bottle under his chin.

"I could slit your throat right now, so you better fucking start admitting to your crimes. Your amnesia act isn't amusing me."

Ari's eyes widened. Things were escalating far too quickly, and he didn't know what to say to keep breathing. Anything could set her off. He sure as shit wasn't going to admit to any crimes he hadn't committed. For all he knew she had recording devices. Such an admission could land him in prison.

She backed off him and tossed the broken bottle on the floor. Then she went over to the door and put her thumb to the keypad and calmly walked out as if nothing had happened.

CLAIRE LEANED against the cell door. She couldn't make her hands stop shaking. She'd actually confronted him. Actually spoken to him when she had the power. But she didn't feel like she had it. She'd had to fight past every instinct not to run from the room the second his eyes had been on her—as if he could somehow attack her in those heavy chains. She'd tested everything. She knew the chains would hold him. Still.

His act was so convincing. She almost believed him, but it *was* him. It was definitely him. That scar across his chest. What kind of an idiot did he think she was? She sank into a large leather recliner and closed her eyes, trying not to return to that basement but knowing her mind was already halfway inside the memory.

He'd been drunk that night. He was going to kill her. Something had set him off and he was tired of her. He was antsy, ready to start the whole cycle again with someone new. Claire wasn't sure how she'd known this, but she'd known.

Maybe it was the knife. He'd threatened her with the knife before, but the way he'd held it... with such purpose, his grip on it so tight. She knew. She'd spent the last three hours struggling in ropes he hadn't tied quite right. It was just enough so she could struggle and have stupid hope but not enough to get free. She wondered if he'd done it on purpose to play with her, to make her think she had a chance against him. Or to make killing her more interesting.

Her wrists bled and burned from the struggle against the ropes, but she'd managed to stretch them. She was almost free.

He paced back and forth in the cell rambling again about the government and the *elites*. And rich bitches like her who had it too good. Too easy. In his drunken haze he waved the large kitchen knife around erratically.

Claire continued to fight with the ropes, biting back the pain as they kept cutting into her in her struggle, feeling the blood as it dripped down her hands. Her own warm life flowing down her skin. She was nearly free. He laid the knife down on the table beside her and turned his back for just a moment. It was enough for her to slip out of the ropes and grab it. She stood and backed away. She was so hungry and weak. She felt dizzy, but she knew if she gave in to it and fainted, she'd die.

He turned and advanced on her. She stabbed at him, cutting him several times but not able to get a good solid jab. The knife was big enough that as long as she kept wildly swinging it around, he couldn't get too close. She slashed out and felt the blade slice through his chest. She didn't know how deep it was. She just turned and ran.

He was right behind her. She fell and the knife flew from her hand as he gripped her ankle and pulled her down.

"NO!" she shrieked, kicking at him, hitting him hard in the face with her foot. He released her and she half-crawled, half-ran up the stairs and out the door into the fresh open air.

Claire pushed the memories away, gripping the leather arm rests, willing her heartbeat and breathing to calm. That was him. She had him in a cell. That was the guy. He had a scar where she'd cut him. How could he lie to her with such a straight face when they both knew he had that scar and how he'd gotten it?

Because he's a sociopath, Claire. He isn't like normal people.

She couldn't let herself forget that—what he was. She couldn't let herself be tricked by the beautiful monster into setting him free and losing her own life. She got up and went to the kitchen, taking another bottle of beer from the fridge. This one she drank all the way down until a light pleasant buzz of calm skated across her skin. She took a long, steadying breath and grabbed the broom and dustbin.

When she returned to the cell at least the arrogance had left his face. Maybe he was starting to understand his situation, that the tables had turned and he was now at *her* mercy. Let him lie about things, as long as she could wipe the smug smile off his face.

She silently swept up the shards of the beer bottle. The last thing she needed was for him to have a weapon. That had been his mistake with her after all.

"You can still let me go," he said. His voice was so gentle and soothing. Calm and reasonable.

He'd never spoken to her like that in the basement. Of course not, he'd had the power then. *He has to placate you now.*

Claire just laughed. "Right. I'm going to let you go so you can hurt me again. Am I supposed to believe you're reformed? After me, you stopped torturing and killing women? You realized the error of your ways?"

"What's your name?" he asked, changing tactics. "My name..."

"Shut UP! If you speak your name I'll kill you. I swear to fuck I will. I NEVER want to hear your fucking name. EVER. Don't you try to humanize yourself. You're a fucking monster, and you know it!"

"I'm sorry," he said quickly, holding his hands up in surrender.

No he wasn't. He was placating her.

"What's *your* name, then?" he said, trying again.

"You know my fucking name. You used to hiss it in my ear while you were..." she trailed off, unable to say the words. She turned away from him and took a deep breath, quickly wiping the tears that threatened to spill over. She was not going to cry in front of him anymore. She'd cried all the tears for him she would cry.

She had the power now. Not him. NOT him. But she was shaking. She could feel the light tremors in her arms. He must be able to see them. He was the one chained up, and he was going to break her again.

Never.

"It's okay if you don't have it in you to hurt me. I don't think you're that kind of person," he said gently.

"Just shut the fuck up!" she screamed. "I should just starve you, like you starved me for the tiniest act of defiance." She turned back to finish sweeping the stray shards into the dustpan.

"Look at me," he said.

It was a fucking *command*. He thought he could order

her around when he was the prisoner? But she turned and looked at him.

"I would never starve you. *Ever*," he said, holding her gaze in his.

He'd already starved her, and they both knew it. These head games... she had to regroup her strategy or he was going to get inside her head and mess with it. If she lost her nerve... if he got free again, she knew he'd kill her this time. She was already in too deep. She had to get her shit together and finish this. It was the only choice.

THE ESCAPE ARTIST is available at all major online retailers in ebook, paperback, hardcover, and audiobook.

ACKNOWLEDGMENTS

Thank you to the following people for their help with The Con Artist:

Robin Ludwig @ gobookcoverdesign.com for the fabulous cover art!

Thank you to Cathy for copyedits!

Thank you to Michelle for great beta read suggestions and for holding my hand while I was freaking out over a new writing process.

And thank you to M for digital formatting! Love you!